Bed, Breakfast,

& Blackmail

Debi Graham-Leard

Riverhaven Books

Bed, Breakfast, & Blackmail is a work of fiction. Any similarity regarding names, characters, or incidents is entirely coincidental.

Published in the United States by Riverhaven Books, Massachusetts.

ISBN: 978-1-937588-94-6

Printed in the United States of America by Country Press, Lakeville, Massachusetts

Edited by Riverhaven Books
Designed by Stephanie Lynn Blackman
Whitman, MA

Previous stories in the Gwen Andrews series:

The Uninvited Guest

2015

Where There's Smoke, There's Trouble

2017

Acknowledgements

My sincere gratitude to the following people who shared their expertise and experience as I penned
Bed, Breakfast, & Blackmail

Pam Loewy
Plymouth Writers Group

Det. Lt. Tom Petersen
Norton Police Department

Deb Ahearn, Investigator
RISEUP Paranormal, Massachusetts

Christine Cook, Genealogist
General Society of Mayflower Descendants

Dr. Walter L. Powell
Author, historian, and consultant

Libby Fox, Reference Librarian
Middleboro Public Library

My sister Jerri Graham Burket, who inspires me daily

Cover Photo: Colonel Blackinton Inn, Attleboro, MA

Cover Designer & Publisher:
Stephanie Blackman, Riverhaven Books

And last, but never least, my husband Vinnie for his
unflagging support of my writer's life

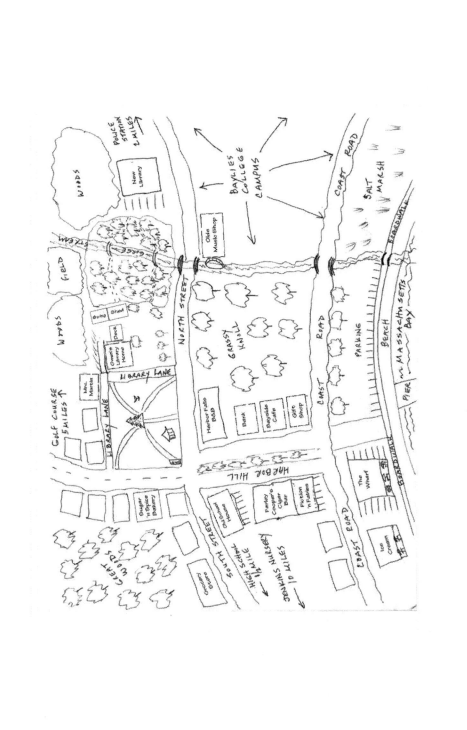

The Christmas season should be joyous.
Blackmail is not the way to celebrate.

… early evening, Wednesday, mid-December

Retired music professor Gwen Andrews loved everything about Christmas. The sights. The sounds. The smells.

On this December evening, a week or so before Christmas Day, light snow tumbled from the sky, dancing in an ever-increasing wind as Gwen crossed the village green. She dodged the slow-moving cars on North Street and ascended the steps to the deep porch of the Harbor Falls Bed & Breakfast. A brass plaque on the shingles proclaimed *The Carswell House 1874*.

An oversized holiday wreath of evergreens and bittersweet adorned the inn's cranberry-red door. Ribbons of silver and gold drifted in curls down the raised panels. Gwen leaned close to inhale the intoxicating scent of New England pine, cedar, and spruce. As she reached for the brass knocker, the door flew inward with a whoosh.

B&B co-owner Betty Owens, wisps of grey hair outlining her round face, tapped a finger to her lips and pulled Gwen into the front parlor. "I was worried you weren't coming, Gwen." Betty slid the pocket door closed, muffling the Christmas music and raucous female laughter reverberating from the living room on the other side of the entrance hall.

Gwen placed her carrier of deviled eggs and Yankee Swap gift on a side table. "I wouldn't dream of missing the garden club Christmas party."

"I'm glad to hear it. Did you walk over?"

Puzzled by Betty's strange reception, Gwen shrugged out of her hooded wool coat. "Yes, I walked. There was no sense in driving such a short distance. Besides, the snow is very light. Why did you shoo me in here, Betty?"

Her eyes darting to the closed door, Betty whispered, "Robert and I have a problem and we need your advice."

"What sort of advice?"

Betty's half smile held little amusement. "Did you know the Carswell House is haunted?"

Gwen's interest spiked as she was no stranger to the spirit world. After her husband Parker's unexpected death four years earlier, his spirit had appeared to her more than once. "I thought the rumors and stories about this wonderful old house were invented. The elderly lady who lived here never mentioned a haunting, not that I bumped into her all that often. Were you aware of the ghost when you bought the Carswell House?"

Betty's emphatic nod left no doubt. "At our first meeting, Clara Carswell told me and Robert that her eldest sister, Theo, died on the servant steps the morning of her wedding day and her spirit has roamed this house ever since."

2

"Interesting name."

"The sister's full name is Theodosia Charity Carswell, but Clara called her simply Theo."

"Did you believe her?"

Betty paced the oriental parlor rug. "We didn't doubt her for a second, so we proceeded with the sale."

"You weren't concerned about a ghost?"

"Not in the least. When I was a youngster, my grandmother convinced me that spirits roam among us, so Theo was an unexpected bonus. Besides, with all the interest in the paranormal these days, Robert and I couldn't wait to advertise our B&B as haunted."

"Did you delay until you saw Theo?"

Betty tapped Gwen's arm in a playful manner. "Of course we did. And it didn't take long. The first morning of the conversion activities, she appeared next to me as if to understand what we were doing. Since that first encounter, she's followed us upstairs and down. She hasn't caused any real trouble, until now..." Betty's voice trailed off.

"What makes you say it that way?"

"For the past few days, we've found candles broken, vases of flowers knocked over, and rug runners bunched up, all on the second floor. Our cleaning lady Gracie swears she's innocent, and I believe her. Accusing our guests is not an option."

"So you suspect Theo is the source of this mischief?"

"Robert and I hate to think so, but it's more than possible. In addition to those minor tricks, there was an incident."

"What sort of incident?"

"Let me fill in a few blanks before I answer that question." Lowering her generous proportions to the upholstered loveseat,

Betty patted the next cushion for Gwen to join her. "The conversion of the Carswell House took longer than we expected. Two weeks ago, we finally welcomed our first group of guests. This past Sunday, our second batch checked in. Four of the six rooms on the second floor are occupied. A family in the two connecting rooms, an older couple in the third, and a single woman in the fourth. Three students from Harvard specifically requested the original maids' rooms on the third floor. Every one of our guests said our ghost is the reason they chose us over the other lodging in Harbor Falls."

"You and Robert must be ecstatic."

"We are." Betty hesitated. "The Harvard boys had a bet. The first one visited by Theo would win a hundred dollars."

"Is this bet connected to the incident?"

Betty struggled to her feet, her hands flitting about like the winter winds outside. "Good guess. This morning at breakfast, Charlie didn't say a word, unlike his usual non-stop chatter. Dylan and Shawn hounded him until he admitted he was shoved from his bed last night."

Gwen straightened at this news, recalling the limited physical ability of Parker's spirit. Could Theo be strong enough to move the weight of a young man? She asked Betty, "Do you believe Theo pushed Charlie?"

"If she's our prankster, maybe. Although Charlie weighs more than a candlestick or a vase. He could have had a bad dream and fallen out on his own."

Gwen stifled a grin. "Do you think he fibbed?"

"If he did encounter Theo, he would've bragged."

Gwen sobered. "You're probably right. I'm guessing Charlie got more than he bargained for."

4

"Very possible. Robert and I assumed from the start that our visitors would hope to *see* a ghost, not have a confrontation with one."

"If Theo is behind these shenanigans, any idea why she chose now?"

"Not really. During my encounters with her, she seemed only curious about our activities."

"Maybe she's upset about strangers in the Carswell House."

"Maybe, Gwen. I just don't know. Robert and I are very concerned."

Gwen's love of mysteries kicked in. "Do you know the date Theo died?"

"Let me think." Betty plumped a pillow and then squeezed it tight against her bosom. "December 20, 1924."

"That's a few days away. Maybe that's why she's restless."

"Maybe," Betty repeated. "Theo's father found her body at the bottom of the servant steps. Her death was suspicious, but there was insufficient evidence to arrest anyone."

"How do you know all these details, Betty?"

"Clara adds a piece of the puzzle whenever I visit her."

Gwen sat up straight. "Wait a minute. Clara's still alive?"

"Oh, my yes." A wistful expression softened Betty's face. "Gosh, she must be approaching a hundred years old. She never married and now lives in a senior complex south of Plymouth."

Gwen's brain clicked into action. "We should visit her, Betty. Clara lived here since 1924. She can tell you how the family dealt with Theo's tricks."

Betty's eyes lit up. "That's a splendid idea. Besides, Clara would love the company, especially during the holidays."

Gwen shifted. "What's the advice you need from me?"

"Well, Robert and I heard that your husband's ghost appeared at your April séance. Maybe your experience with Parker will help us with Theo."

Gwen took a breath. The séance attendees had obviously spread the word about Parker's manifestation. Now, even without knowing that Parker's other-worldly appearance at the séance hadn't been his first – nor his last – Betty and Robert assumed Gwen cornered the inside scoop on ghosts.

Thinking back, Gwen realized Parker's spirit had been kind and gentle, the same essence he possessed as a living being. Gwen compared his visits to the late '60s TV show, *The Ghost and Mrs. Muir.* If Theo's ghost was becoming destructive, Gwen had no basis for advice.

Rather than discourage Betty, Gwen tossed out a new question. "Are you worried Theo will cause mischief during our party this evening?"

Betty shrugged. "There's no way I can know. If Theo is no longer friendly, she might devastate our future bookings."

"Or maybe even more people will want to stay here. Like you said earlier, Betty, lots of people are fascinated with ghosts these days." Gwen included herself in that group.

Betty stared out the front window into the village green where old-fashioned lampposts cast circles of light onto the snowy pathways. "I just don't know what will happen."

Someone knocked on the closed pocket door and called, "Betty, are you in there? The girls want you to start the party."

Betty smoothed her gray wisps. "I'll be right out."

Chapter Two

...early evening, Wednesday

Sliding the door into its wall pocket, Betty revealed Holly Nichols, the current – and most likely the youngest ever – garden club president. Holly towered above them all, but somehow pulled off a colorful elf costume, complete with red-and-white striped leggings plus a tasseled hat with dangling bells. Turned away to speak to the member behind her, Holly raised her knuckles to knock again. If Betty hadn't reached out, the club president would've rapped on Betty's face.

Holly jumped. "Sorry, Betty. How soon are you coming out?" Holly lowered her hand, glancing over Betty's shoulder. "There you are, Gwen! Myrtle Mueller thought she saw our vice president come up the front walk. Let me carry your food to the buffet table." Without waiting for permission, she picked up Gwen's deviled eggs, calling over her shoulder as she exited, "So glad you brought these. They'll be gone in a flash."

Betty lowered her voice and leaned close to Gwen's ear. "Is there any chance you can stay after the party so we can continue our discussion?"

Gwen whispered back, "I don't see why not. Only my cat is waiting for me at home."

"Thanks, Gwen. Cross your fingers that Theo doesn't pull any tricks this evening."

Betty pasted on a smile and waded into the group of women mingling in the entrance hall. "Let's eat, everyone!"

***

7

Moving forward in the buffet line, Gwen greeted club members as they passed with loaded plates. Roasted chicken legs, bacon-wrapped wieners, pasta with meatballs, and sausage kabobs interlaced with red peppers and onions teased her nose. Myrtle Mueller, wearing her old-fashioned brown polyester suit, stopped abruptly, giving Gwen her usual evil eye. "How's your little flute player doing at Baylies College?"

Inwardly, Gwen cringed. After more than a year, Myrtle still held fast to her anger that her grandson Herbert hadn't won the music competition. The winner of the scholarship was Jenna Jenkins, Gwen's most talented private music student.

There was nothing to do but answer the question. "I just saw her grandfather Hal Jenkins last week, and he mentioned that Jenna is loving her classes. How's your Herbert?"

As expected, Myrtle's nose tilted a bit higher, the move not disturbing her shellacked hairdo. "He made the dean's list. I suppose his superior achievement justifies the incredible financial burden on our family."

The woman's dig was hurtful. Jenna's musical talent had won the scholarship fair and square. If Gwen researched student loans and grants, then shared that information with Myrtle, perhaps the woman would let go of her crusty attitude.

Before Gwen had a chance to offer, Myrtle huffed and stomped away. A self-proclaimed master gardener, she was the most crotchety woman in the club.

At last, Gwen arrived at the dining room table overflowing with a vast array of food, mostly contributed by the club members. Desserts were clustered on a sideboard. A woman scurried through the swinging door along the back wall and placed a second tray of roasted chicken legs next to a crock of baked beans. The cold offerings included several salads and deli meats for finger sandwiches. Gwen scooped tiny portions onto her plate and snagged the last deviled egg from her own carrier. The younger woman next in line tapped Gwen's arm. "You should bring two batches. Those always disappear right away."

Gwen chuckled because she'd made an extra half dozen for herself, now safely stored in her fridge at home. "I'm sorry, Alicia. Do you want this one?"

The club secretary waved off Gwen's offer. "No, no, you eat it. There are enough yummy goodies here to keep my belly from growling."

"Okay, if you're sure." Gwen sliced a thin piece of veggie quiche. "The last time we talked, Alicia, you said your husband interviewed for a new job. Did he get it?"

Alicia sprinkled raspberry vinaigrette onto her garden salad. "I'm relieved to say yes. Travis was out of work for a year before he found this position that matches his sales experience. The pay is good, but the kids and I hardly ever see him. He's always out of town at a meeting."

Lifting a plastic glass from the stack, Gwen added ice and poured root beer from a bottle. "Oh, that's a shame. I hope his bosses give him a break during the holidays."

Alicia held up crossed fingers. "From your lips to God's ear. Fortunately for me, Travis caught a cold and came home early today. He's watching our kids so I could come to this party." In the next second, Alicia turned away to answer a question from the woman behind her.

Her plate filled, Gwen headed into the living room and spied an empty chair in the far corner. A roaring blaze filled the massive stone fireplace. At the front windows, a magnificent

Douglas fir with twinkling white lights, silver and gold ornaments, plus clumps of red berries, matched the door wreath. Gwen made a mental note to compliment Betty's decorating skills.

As she savored her selections, Gwen vowed she wouldn't return to the buffet table for seconds. Not that everything wasn't delicious. But she could already feel her stomach straining against the waistband of her slacks. The last thing she needed was another few extra pounds.

Despite the nearly deafening volume of conversations bouncing off the walls of the living room, Gwen joined the banter with the ladies on either side. Someone asked if their treasurer was coming to the party. From the other side of the room, Holly answered that Veronica was out of town at a tradeshow and wouldn't return until Friday.

Gwen wasn't surprised that Holly knew Veronica's comings and goings as the two young women were best friends. In fact, to the relief of the older members, they'd convinced each other to take the positions of president and treasurer.

When the eating subsided, Holly stood and held her glass aloft. "A big thank you to Betty for hosting our Christmas party in her impressive bed & breakfast."

Other voices chimed in:

Kudos to you, Betty.

Here, here.

Love your B&B.

Betty lifted her own glass high. "Glad to have you all. I'm pleased you younger women have joined the club. Nothing like fresh ideas to inspire us old biddies."

As the laughter subsided, the front door opened, admitting

an influx of snow-cooled air. Chatter and stomping feet echoed until four people came to a halt in the archway between the entrance hall and the living room.

"Welcome back," Betty called. "How were your outings?"

Murmurs of *terrific, fun,* and *great* overlapped until the man held up his hand to quiet his brood. "Thanks for suggesting a visit to the Daniel Webster Estate, Mrs. Owens. That's a fascinating piece of New England history. We ate dinner at The Lucky Lobster. Another excellent suggestion."

"Glad you enjoyed yourselves." Betty waved around the living room. "Allow me to introduce the Harbor Falls Garden Club. Ladies, this is the Schuster family from Delaware. This handsome man is Fritz, his lovely wife Isabella, their son Waldo, and daughter Julie."

Fritz waited for the hellos to dwindle. "Nice to meet everyone. We've always wanted to visit New England in December, so here we are."

Isabella pointed out the front window. "Your garden club must have decorated that quaint village green. Very festive."

Betty smiled and nodded. "Thank you."

Spreading his arms, Fritz gathered his family. "Sorry, Mrs. Owens, but we're beat. Enjoy the rest of your evening." The family headed up the front staircase, their son Waldo racing up despite instructions not to run.

Again, the front door opened. Three young men appeared and bowed in exaggerated fashion, their wide grins implying they were feeling no pain.

"We're back!"

"I see that, Charlie." Betty smiled broadly at the lanky blonde. "Did you boys enjoy yourselves at The Wharf?"

11

"Sure did. I can't carry a tune, but Shawn and Dylan made me proud during the karaoke contest." Charlie patted their shoulders. "Hey, Mrs. Owens, any breakfast muffins left?"

Holly stood up, the bells on her elf hat jangling. "There's plenty of our party food left over. I can't speak for the others, but I'd rather take home an empty plate."

Some of the other women agreed:

Me, too!

Help yourselves!

Growing boys need to eat!

Heaving to her feet, Myrtle Mueller called over, "Charlie? Charlie Brewster? Is that you?"

Charlie searched for the source of the voice, his focus landing on Myrtle. He seemed to shrink. "Aunt Myrtle? Gosh, I haven't seen you since I was ten."

Myrtle marched up to Charlie and wrapped herself around his thin frame, laying her cheek against his chest. "Why didn't you tell me you were coming to town?"

Lifting his arms in the air, Charlie glanced down at her curly black hair and wrinkled his nose.

Though smirks appeared on the faces of the club members, no one snickered out loud. Myrtle's unexpected display of fondness was the opposite of her usual superior attitude. Her affection for a nephew she hadn't seen for close to a decade was more than a little curious.

Holding Charlie at arm's length, Myrtle didn't wait for his answer. "How long will you be in Harbor Falls, dear? We must get together before you return to Harvard." She vocally underscored the name of the Ivy League school.

Charlie gave off the vibe of a cornered animal. "Sure, Aunt

Myrtle." He yanked himself from her grasp and linked arms with Shawn and Dylan. "Let's go eat, guys."

They nearly climbed over each other in their rush to the buffet table.

No one said a word as Myrtle returned to her seat with her head lowered.

The door knocker clanged, redirecting everyone's attention. Betty surged to her feet. "That must be my surprise."

Moments later, she reappeared with four women dressed in red glittery tops and black slacks. "This is a female barbershop quartet named Happenstance. They're going to entertain us with some Christmas songs."

The quartet serenaded with holiday hymns and Christmas carols, intertwining their notes, switching from individual solos to four-part harmonies, their tone remarkable. A particular song touched Gwen's heart. Though not a religious woman, she had always loved the musical phrasing of "Mary Did You Know."

The quartet launched into a robust arrangement of "We Wish You a Merry Christmas," reviving Gwen's bittersweet memory of Parker singing along with this tune, not caring that he bungled most of the words and sang off-key.

The entertainment ended with a sing-along of "Jingle Bells." Despite requests for an encore, Happenstance begged off. They needed to hurry for another performance in Marshfield.

Gwen approached the singers as they donned their coats. "Ladies, I'm a retired music professor, and want to compliment your blending. Quite impressive."

The tallest of the group reached into her pocket and pressed a business card into Gwen's hand. "Thank you for saying that. Maybe you'll hire us for another event." The quartet sailed out into the night air and disappeared.

Returning to the living room, Gwen did a quick head count and prepared numbered slips for the gift exchange.

Holly took up a position under the archway and clapped her hands. "Our Yankee Swap is next. If you need to put your plates in the trash or use the bathroom, do it now and we'll begin as soon as everyone is resettled."

Gwen held up her red cup filled with the numbered slips and called out, "Be sure you pick a number to see who goes first, second, etc."

Chapter Three

...mid-evening, Wednesday

Gwen plucked the last slip of paper for herself, then carried her paper plate and plastic utensils to the trash bag in the dining room. Remembering that her Yankee Swap gift sat on the side table in the front parlor, she detoured in that direction. The pocket door was pulled across the opening, but not quite closed. Angry whispers traveled through the slim gap. Gwen came to a halt and couldn't help but listen.

"You didn't bring the money? I told you first payment."
"I heard you. You can go pound sand."
"Aren't you worried I'll let the cat out of the bag?"
"I don't think you have the guts to ruin two marriages."
"Don't push me."
"How did you find out, anyway?"
"Ha! You should be more careful what you say in public."
"Don't you know eavesdropping is rude?"
"That may be so, but I heard what I heard."
"I'm not paying you one red cent. I ended it yesterday."
"That makes no difference. I still know what you did."

The whispery voices were impossible for Gwen to identify. Women? Men? Club members? B&B Guests? The quiet lady who cleared dishes during the party? Betty? Robert?

Gwen normally wouldn't insert herself into the middle of a dispute, but during a holiday party was neither the time nor place for this confrontation. She tapped on the door. "Excuse me. I need to get my swap gift."

The whispering stopped, followed by muffled movement, then deafening silence.

Gwen slid the door into the wall and found the parlor empty. During her few minutes in that room with Betty earlier, Gwen hadn't noticed the second door on the adjacent wall. Although she moved quickly between the loveseat and stuffed chair to peek into the dining room, Gwen couldn't spot the whisperers.

Too many people milling about made it impossible to identify the two who had just rushed in from the parlor.

Having no idea what she'd have done if she'd identified the combatants, Gwen retraced her steps, retrieved her swap gift, and rejoined the party goers.

***

"Who has number ten?" Gwen called out. As V.P., she was in charge of the Yankee Swap.

Starchy Myrtle Mueller raised her hand and chose a beautifully wrapped package from beneath Betty's holiday tree. From the tissue, Myrtle lifted a bright red thong, her face quickly flushing the same color. Hoots of laughter filled the room. Myrtle jammed the garment back in the box and sat in silence, not even requesting a different item from the previous gift options.

For the next hour, each member opened a gift. No one suggested a swap with Myrtle's red thong, sticking her with the most inappropriate item any of them could have dreamed up.

Hearing a man clear his throat at the archway, they all swiveled in that direction. An aristocratic gentleman with his arm draped across the shoulder of a refined woman spoke in a charming British accent. "Excuse us. Lillian and I are curious about your celebration."

Betty hurried toward them. "So sorry, Mr. and Mrs. Pettigrew. My garden club is not known for quiet voices. I'm hosting our annual Christmas party."

"Don't apologize," Lillian admonished in her equally British accent. "Cyril and I love to hear people enjoying themselves." She gestured toward the front windows. "I assume you are the ladies who decorated the village green for the holidays?"

Holly called over, "Yes, that was us. Every year, we assemble evergreen swags with red bows and attach them to each of the posts."

"Charming, absolutely charming," Lillian gushed. "And you call this a Yankee Swap, yes? What a quaint American custom. Why don't you show us your gifts?"

A few women held up their swap item.

If not for the influx of cool air, none of them would have realized that yet another person had entered the B&B. A young woman tried to sneak past the archway toward the staircase.

Betty noticed her and called over, "Miss Hammond, I was beginning to worry about you driving on our snowy roads."

Miss Hammond waved her hand in dismissal. "Please call me Brooke, Mrs. Owens. And thanks for your concern, but driving in the snow is like riding a bike. You never forget how. If you'll excuse me, I feel a headache coming on."

***

After the final gift was unwrapped, Holly again stood before the group. "Betty, how about a tour of the Carswell House?"

Gwen didn't miss Betty's panicked expression. Was she

afraid Theo would create a scene?

Reluctance in her voice, Betty answered, "Well, okay, I can show you around. But I must give you a word of warning."

Choruses of *What warning?* bounced off the walls.

Waiting until the women stopped asking, Betty provided the answer. "This house is haunted."

Gasps erupted around the room before more questions flew.

Who's your ghost?

Is it a man or a woman?

Is it a little kid?

What's the history behind the haunting?

Betty held up her hand to quiet them. When their bombardment ceased, she answered, "Her name is Theodosia Charity Carswell, the eldest daughter of this house in the early 1900s. She wanders the halls and stairways wearing a white dressing gown."

"So why the warning?" Holly asked, her arms crossed.

Betty drew in a breath, exhaling before she explained. "For the past few days, Theo's been unusually active. Robert and I aren't sure of the reason for her unrest. If she makes any mischief, she may frighten some of you."

Holly once more took charge. "In that case, why don't we each decide for ourselves? I can't speak for the rest of you, but I'd love a tour of this historic home, ghost or no ghost."

Most of the members voiced their agreement and pushed up from their seats. Three women didn't budge from the sofa.

Betty made a follow-me motion. "This way, brave souls."

As they moved into the entrance hall, a bearded man strolled toward them from the dining room. His tall stature matched his booming voice. "I heard you ladies would like a tour. Betty, why don't we each take half? I'll take my group to the third floor. You can begin in the kitchen."

Betty laid her hand on his arm and glanced up at him, her gaze adoring. "Wonderful idea." She turned to the group. "Ladies, this is my husband Robert. Choose your guide."

Gwen sidled toward Betty. Next in line was last year's club president Wanda Webb, plant sale queen Dolores Greensmith, snobbish Eunice Flint, outspoken Frankie Peterson, timid Nadine Alexander, and meeting snack provider Loretta Baker.

Robert signaled to the remaining seven women; President Holly Nichols, twins Zoe and Zelda Hobart, cantankerous Myrtle Mueller, secretary Alicia Reed, and red-headed Ruby Cox, followed by Evelyn Woodley and her trusty cane. "Follow me, ladies. We'll begin on the third floor."

As Robert led his half up the front staircase, Betty motioned her troop around the dining room table toward the swinging door to the kitchen. A middle-aged woman barreled through from the other side, nearly crashing into Betty.

Betty gripped the door frame to keep from stumbling. "Goodness, Gracie, we nearly collided. Thanks for your help this evening. I'll see you in the morning. Goodnight."

Gracie nodded as she shoved her arms into her coat, giving Betty a slight smile before moving toward the rear hallway. Two seconds later, the slamming of a door echoed.

Gwen had noticed Gracie delivering chicken legs and later removing soiled serving dishes from the dining room table but hadn't seen her speak to anyone. Maybe the woman was shy.

Seemingly used to their non-verbal exchange, Betty led her charges through the swinging door and into the B&B kitchen, explaining the upgraded equipment. From the kitchen, they

19

circled the dining room, the entrance hall, the front parlor, and living room. All the while, Betty pointed out the architectural elements, the Carswell family furnishings, and the original oil paintings that graced the walls. Leading them up the front staircase, she paused at the final portrait. "This is an artist's rendering of Theodosia on her twentieth birthday." Betty caught Gwen's eye and nodded ever so slightly.

Gwen lagged behind the others and stopped in front of Theo's likeness. Looking back at Gwen through lifelike eyes was a young woman with a long narrow face, chestnut hair artfully arranged, and a demure smile. Hoping for a glimmer of understanding, Gwen lowered her voice to a near-whisper. "We'll untangle your story, Theo."

Nearing the top of the staircase, Betty turned to the members coming up. "The wide upper hallway doubles as a sitting room. Newspaper articles, personal letters, and photographs are displayed on each of the four walls, providing a glimpse into the lives of the family who resided in this home."

Gwen perked up, eager to gain more insight into the other members of the Carswell family.

An ear-piercing scream flew across the open sitting room, followed by the sound of thumping. At the center of the back wall, where a balustrade indicated a flight of steps, Robert stared down. His group surrounded him, each suddenly silent.

Betty grabbed Gwen's hand and walked quickly across the sitting room, marching through the huddle of bodies until they stood beside Robert.

Gwen glanced down to see bare wooden steps. A body sprawled on the lower landing, the head slanted, the angle awkward. Blood oozed from a cut on the forehead. Recognizing the brown polyester suit, Gwen said, "It's Myrtle Mueller."

Robert turned to Betty. "Call 911 and keep everyone up here. Gwen, you come with me." At the bottom landing, Robert leaned close, but didn't touch Myrtle. "I think she'd dead."

Betty called down the stairwell. "An ambulance is on its way, Robert."

The clock ticked in slow motion. Subdued chatter floated down from those huddled at the top of the steps. Finally, the wail of approaching sirens snuck into the Carswell House.

Robert looked over at Gwen, "Would you mind bringing the EMT's back here?"

"Of course not, Robert." Gwen pushed up from her crouched position, hurried along the back hallway, through the dining room, and into the entrance hall.

Chapter Four

...mid evening, Wednesday

Gwen pulled the front door inward as two EMT's hopped onto the porch, stretcher in tow. Behind them, a uniformed patrolman tipped his hat and followed them inside.

The first paramedic stopped beside her. "Where's the injured woman?"

As Gwen led the three men to Myrtle, the wheels of the stretcher rattled along the wooden floorboards.

Robert Owens moved aside, deep concern etching his features. The paramedics dropped to their knees and searched for vital signs.

The patrolman reached out to prevent Gwen from moving any closer. "I'm Officer Ed Bells. Let's the three of us return to the entrance hall. I need information from both of you."

Gwen and Robert followed the officer in silence.

Officer Bells pulled out a notebook and pencil. "Your name, ma'am?"

"Gwen Andrews," she answered.

"And you, sir?"

"Robert Owens. My wife and I own this B&B."

"The name of the woman at the bottom of the steps?"

His tone calm and professional, the officer asked questions and scribbled the answers. "Did you call 911?"

Gwen shook her head. "No, that was Betty Owens."

"Your wife, sir?" At Robert's nod, Officer Bells asked the next logical question. "Where is Mrs. Owens now?"

Robert replied without hesitation. "She's at the top of the back steps with the others who were taking the house tour."

"Tell me what happened to..." Ed Bells glanced at his notes, "...Mrs. Mueller."

Gwen and Robert took turns detailing the request for a tour after the garden club holiday party, dividing the interested members into two groups, then Myrtle Mueller falling while everyone was engrossed in the family history on the walls.

"Are there any others in the house beside the tour group on the second floor?"

"Yes," Robert answered. "Our B&B guests."

The officer pointed his pencil through the archway into the living room, indicating the three women sitting on the couch. "Who are they?"

Gwen answered, "Club members who didn't join the tour."

The front door opened, and a white-haired man entered. Gwen instantly recognized Detective Benjamin Snowcrest. She'd met him the previous April during a murder investigation that involved her best friend Liz. The detective had reluctantly accepted Gwen's amateur sleuthing assistance, and they'd eventually arrived at a first-name friendship of sorts. She hadn't bumped into Ben between then and now. Despite the dire circumstances of Myrtle's accident, Gwen was relieved to see Ben would be taking charge.

The detective approached Officer Bells. "Evening, Ed. I was around the corner when I heard the dispatcher. Give me an abbreviated version of the situation."

After listening, Ben paused. "You bring everyone down here, Ed, including the guests who might still be in their rooms. I'll go check on this Mrs. Mueller."

As Officer Bells headed up the front staircase, Ben turned to Robert. "If I could ask you, Mr. Owens, to stay here and help Office Bells keep the crowd under control."

After Robert nodded his consent, Ben focused his pale gray eyes on Gwen. "Good to see you, Gwen, but we'll have to catch up later. Can you take me to the injured woman?"

***

Ben nearly tripped over his own feet as he followed Gwen from the entrance hall, through the dining room, and along the back hallway. Intelligent, clever, and easy on the eye, she was everything Ben appreciated in a woman, and the first female who'd interested him since his divorce nearly a decade before. He wondered if she'd sensed his interest last April. If she hadn't been seeing that fellow from Jenkins Nursery, Ben would have asked Gwen out to dinner. Was she still seeing that guy?

He shook his head to concentrate on his detective duties. Being distracted by Gwen's presence would not bode well for whatever investigation lay ahead of him.

At the end of the back hallway, they came upon an older woman sprawled on the lower landing. Her legs and feet stretched up the steps, her eyes closed beneath a bloody gash on her forehead. A small pool of blood surrounded her head.

He turned to Gwen. "You go back and wait with the others."

After Gwen was out of earshot, Ben addressed the paramedics. "What's her status, guys?"

"Not good, Ben. Couldn't find a pulse. We tried CPR and the paddles with no result. I'm afraid there's nothing we can do for her. I contacted the dispatcher to request a detective and the medical examiner. How'd you get here so fast?"

Ben flipped his hand. "I was down the street when my

scanner squawked. Can you stick around until someone from the ME's office gets here?"

"Sure, Ben." The paramedics pulled their equipment away from Mrs. Mueller's body and began packing.

As Ben headed back toward the entrance hall, Mrs. Mueller's condition niggled at his detective instincts.

Officer Bells had herded more than a dozen people down the staircase when a patrolman entered the B&B. Ben instructed the young officer to stand guard and not let anyone leave.

Making his way to the edge of the crowd, Ben raised his voice. "Can I have everyone's attention?"

The hushed chatter ceased as the group turned his way.

"My name is Detective Benjamin Snowcrest. I know you're all concerned about Mrs. Mueller's accident." He wasn't about to tell these people she'd died until the medical examiner registered the facts on his official document. Ben's gaze drifted from one anxious face to the next until he found Gwen, her presence providing a modicum of comfort.

Another blast of chilly air swirled into the B&B with a tall man in a topcoat.

Ben addressed the anxious group. "Make yourselves comfortable, but don't leave. I'll be with you as soon as I have an update."

As Ben approached the medical examiner, he lowered his voice. "Evening, Otis. Didn't expect you personally."

"I was having dinner with my wife at The Wharf. Too close not to come. What happened?"

While escorting Otis to the scene, Ben brought the medical examiner up to speed with the sparse information gathered.

The closer of the two paramedics lifted his head. "Hey, Otis.

We couldn't revive this poor woman. She's all yours."

Squatting beside Mrs. Mueller, Otis pressed his fingertips against her neck and then her wrist. He pulled a small mirror from his pocket, held it in front of her mouth, and shook his head. Glancing at his watch, he noted the time of death on the official paperwork before rising to his feet. "Must have been a nasty fall. Appreciate your efforts, guys. I'll take it from here."

Placing their cases atop the stretcher, the paramedics wheeled their empty gurney away from the scene.

Otis pulled out his phone and punched a button, speaking sideways to Ben. "I'm in my personal car, so I'm requesting a wagon to transport this lady to my autopsy suite." With the phone to his ear, Otis surveyed the upward stretch of the steps, then the position of Mrs. Mueller's head and body. "Did you notice that clump of hair on that midway tread?"

Ben followed Otis's line of vision. "I hadn't, but it looks like hers. The crime lab will have to confirm a match. There's also a dent in the wood that looks fresh."

Otis squinted. "Could be where her head made first impact. I can't be certain yet, Ben, but I suspect there's more to this woman's fall than we could possibly know at this point."

"I agree," Ben concurred. "I'm going to grab a roll of crime scene tape from my SUV."

"Go ahead, Ben. I'm not going anywhere."

Minutes later, Ben had cordoned off the area surrounding the top of the steps down to the lower landing.

"Who's going to notify next of kin?" Otis asked.

Ben hesitated. "I need to stay here and take statements. I think the officer out front is trained for death notification."

Otis nodded as he studied Mrs. Mueller's lifeless form.

"Good, I'd rather not be the one to devastate this woman's family just before Christmas."

Ben shifted his weight. "Unfortunately, I'm the one who has to inform those people out there that Mrs. Mueller has gone to the big garden in the sky."

***

Gwen waited with the others. Red, white, and blue slivers of light shot through the windows, marking the walls in a repeating pattern, casting an eerie foreboding.

She glanced around to see how everyone was reacting. Robert Owens stood with Betty beneath the dining room arch, his arm slung across her shoulders in a protective manner. Charlie Brewster slouched at the bottom of the front staircase, Shawn and Dylan on either side. The Pettigrews in their robes, the Schuster family in their pajamas, plus Brooke Hammond – who didn't appear well – all hovered near the parlor door.

The garden club members huddled in small clusters in the living room. The three who didn't join either tour hadn't moved from their places on the couch. The area buzzed with mumbling as everyone speculated what was happening with Myrtle.

When the paramedics wheeled their gurney across the entrance hall toward the front door, a collective gasp filled the air. The flat sheet covered no body.

Ben appeared. The talking ceased. All eyes focused on him.

"I'm sorry to bring you bad news, but the medical examiner has pronounced Mrs. Mueller deceased."

Gwen had suspected Myrtle didn't survive the fall. But to have her death confirmed was unsettling. The parallel to Theo's demise on those same steps sent shivers up Gwen's spine. She glanced over at Charlie to see how he had taken the news of his

27

aunt's demise. Surprisingly, he didn't seem upset.

Ben's voice boomed above the clamor. "I need statements from the people who participated in Mr. Owens' half of the house tour. B&B guests, please return to your rooms. I'll be back tomorrow to interview each of you. The rest leave your name, address, and phone number with the patrolman before you leave. I'll be in touch if necessary. Until we've determined what happened here this evening, don't anyone leave town."

Betty made her way to Gwen's side. "This is terrible, just terrible. I can't believe Myrtle fell down those steps and died."

Robert joined them. "I'm just relieved that Theo didn't make an appearance. Can you imagine the havoc she would have caused on top of Myrtle's accident?"

Lowering her voice, Betty added, "All the chatter and activity might have kept her away." Worry clouded Betty's eyes. "Gwen, I know I asked you to stay after the party, but that's not going to happen now. Can you come over tomorrow?"

"Of course. Call me after the detective has come and gone." Gwen worried about Betty and Robert. Theo's recent antics, the possibility that she'd pushed Charlie from his bed, and now a death on the servant steps could be nothing short of terrifying for the B&B owners.

Gathering her coat and swap gift, Gwen provided her contact info before joining the others on the B&B's deep front porch. The women spoke in hushed voices before scattering in every direction toward their cars.

Chapter Five

...mid evening, Wednesday

Gwen's walk home wasn't nearly as pleasant as her earlier stroll. Chilled not only by the windy weather but also by Myrtle's unexpected death, she pulled her coat tighter.

With the exception of a solitary dog-walker, the village green was deserted. The snow had ceased to fall. Stars appeared and disappeared as lingering dark clouds drifted eastward toward Massachusetts Bay. The half-moon had set at mid-day, so cast no light onto the white blanket covering the ground.

Every few days since Thanksgiving, Mother Nature had gifted Harbor Falls with another few inches of snow. The dreaded nor'easter had yet to make an appearance.

In defiance of her somber mood, Gwen hesitated beside the towering blue spruce that marked the center of the village green. The tree glittered with colored lights, a festive reminder of the approaching holiday.

But Christmas this year would be anything but festive for Myrtle's family.

Myrtle's ear-piercing scream and the memory of her body sprawled on the landing assaulted Gwen's sensibilities. Had the woman simply lost her footing? Or had something more sinister taken place? Were those whisperers in the front parlor related to Myrtle's tumble? Or was there no connection?

She needed to share that conversation with Ben and let him decide if the threats might be linked to the accident. If only she had recognized the voices.

Gwen forced her mystery-loving brain to focus. Who besides Robert stood at the top of those steps as Betty's group hurried across the sitting room? Try as she might, Gwen couldn't recall. She simply hadn't noticed.

Frustrated by her lack of attention, Gwen placed one foot in front of the other, conscious of the icy threat beneath the purity of the freshly fallen snow.

Finally, her beloved library home came into view. The brick and brownstone structure dominated the northwest corner of the village green, exuding strength. The security it offered washed over her, calming Gwen's troubled heart.

The white lights of her Christmas tree twinkled through the glass panes, casting a pale glow onto the snow-covered evergreens tucked into the outdoor window boxes. Battery candles flickered, bathing her home in a touch of nostalgia.

More than a decade had passed since Parker's architectural cleverness had converted the abandoned library into their unique dwelling. Gwen treasured her good fortune to live in such a magical place. But no matter how often Parker's spirit appeared, Gwen sorely missed that marvelous flesh-and-blood man. His warmth, his humor, and his kisses.

Before stepping across the snowy cobblestones of Library Lane, Gwen turned around and located the B&B through the bare branches of the oak and maple trees sprinkled throughout the village green. Even from this distance, she could sense Betty and Robert's concern about Myrtle's death on their property.

Ascending her granite steps, Gwen pushed through the library's heavy oak doors. In the foyer, she paused at the narrow table and lifted the final photograph she'd taken of Parker on their 37th anniversary. He waved back at her as he walked along

Duxbury Beach. She drank in his image. Would she ever connect with his spirit again? Her recent attempts had failed.

She kissed her fingers and touched the image of his smiling face. "Will you ever hear me call you again, Parker?" Her next words caught in her throat. "Myrtle Mueller died tonight."

A meow reached Gwen's ears. She glanced up the staircase that swept to the second-floor mezzanine to see her golden tabby strolling down. "Good evening, Amber. Did I wake you?"

The cat blinked.

Gwen returned Parker's photo to its place of honor and stepped toward her pet. Because Amber had little tolerance for extended snuggles, Gwen merely stroked the animal from ears to tail before continuing to the kitchen. A soothing cup of hot tea with honey was what she needed.

***

Over at the B&B, Ben moved to stand beside Officer Bells. "Have you delivered death notifications, Ed?"

"Unfortunately, I have," Ed answered. "Do you need me to handle this one?"

"I do. Hang on a second. I'll find Mrs. Mueller's handbag for her address." In the living room, B&B owner Robert Owens busied himself with spreading the dying embers in the massive stone fireplace. Ben glanced around at the group waiting to provide their statements. Six women and three young men. Surely those boys weren't members of the garden club. "Excuse me, folks, but I need to locate Mrs. Mueller's purse. Did any of you notice where she was sitting?"

A tall young woman in an elf outfit walked to the end of the couch. She leaned over, the bells on her hat jangling, and lifted a plain brown handbag. "I think this is Myrtle's."

31

Reaching for it, Ben muttered, "Thank you," and retreated to the entrance hall. Opening the flap, he pulled out the wallet and located the driver's license. "Here's her home address, Ed." Officer Bells jotted the house number and street name on a page of his wire-bound notebook.

"You want me to return this purse to her family?" Ed asked.

"No. I'll keep it for now."

As Officer Bells disappeared into the night, two other men arrived. The first in plain clothes carried a satchel with the logo of the Massachusetts State Crime Lab.

Ben crossed the entrance hall, extending his hand. "Evening, Peter. Sorry to bring you out on such a blustery night."

"It's my job, Ben."

The second man, a state trooper wearing a padded winter coat labeled 'Police' brandished a large camera. "Good to see you again, Ben. The D.A.'s office sent me over to take photos. Where's the body?"

Ben closed the door against the chilly night air. "Give me a sec and I'll take you both back there."

To the young patrolman standing nearby, Ben said, "I don't expect any of the witnesses in the living room will try to leave, but I need you to stick around and make sure."

"Not a problem, Ben. I can stay as long as you need me."

Ben moved into the living room. "Sorry for the delay, folks. Mr. Owens, is this everyone in your tour?"

Robert re-hung the poker before studying each face. "Yes."

Addressing the group, Ben said, "I'll return shortly to take your statements."

Ben brought Peter and the state trooper to the lower landing. Otis pointed up the run of steps. "Not that I'm trying to tell you how to do your job, Peter, but there's a clump of hair and a fresh dent in the wood on that midway tread."

"Don't worry that you're stepping on my toes, Otis. Better not to miss anything." Peter slipped blue booties over his galoshes before reaching into his pocket and handing a second pair to the photographer. "Here you go."

"No need," the trooper said, pulling a similar pair from his own pocket, only his were white. "I know better than to contaminate a scene."

Ben surveyed their activity. "You men seem to have this under control. I have to take statements. Peter, I'll need your report of the evidence as soon as possible."

"Sure, Ben. I have to tell you I've worked a few of these step tumbles over the years. Based on what I'm seeing, this one looks suspicious."

"That's what I think," Otis agreed, turning to Ben. "My guys are on their way. But they won't move this woman's body until Peter and the photographer are finished."

The state trooper had moved up the steps ahead of Peter and was busy snapping away. He lifted his head and looked at Ben. "I can email these photos if you want, detective."

"That would be appreciated. Thanks." Ben looked at Otis. "When will you be doing the autopsy?"

"Eight o'clock tomorrow morning. Do you want to attend?"

At Ben's nod, Otis continued. "Don't come until at least nine. I'll get the preliminaries out of the way so we can concentrate on anything that appears out of the ordinary."

"Sounds good. I'll see you there."

Ben left the medical examiner, the crime lab tech, and the D.A.'s photographer to do their jobs and once again headed for the living room. Hurrying through the archway, he searched for the B&B owner. "Mr. Owens, do you have a secluded area where can I take statements?"

"The front parlor," Robert offered, then added, "Both doors close for privacy,"

"That should work. I'll speak with you first. Lead the way."

Following the B&B owner into the front parlor, Ben glanced around the well-appointed room. "This will do just fine." He slid the pocket door across the opening and waved Robert to the loveseat before sitting in the upholstered chair. "First of all, tell me if those three young men are members of the garden club."

"No, they're not, detective. They're Harvard students who are B&B guests. I was explaining the history of the third-floor maids' rooms when they asked if they could join the tour."

Ben made a note. "Where were you standing when you heard the scream?"

"I think I was discussing a framed photograph with one of the garden club ladies."

"What did you do next?"

"When I turned toward the scream, I realized someone had fallen down the steps, so I rushed over to see who it was."

"Who was nearest to the steps?"

"I really can't say, detective. They all surged around me at the same time."

"How long before you recognized the person who'd fallen?"

"Actually," Robert said, "Gwen Andrews noticed the brown polyester suit and realized it was Myrtle Mueller."

"What was your next move?"

"I told my wife to call 911 and keep everyone upstairs. I asked Gwen Andrews to go with me to the bottom because she knew who it was. I have to tell you, Detective, I wasn't holding out much hope that the woman was still alive. There was a pool of blood around her head, she wasn't moving, and she didn't appear to be breathing."

"Did you touch her?"

"I was afraid to touch her, so no."

Mr. Owens looked directly into Ben's eyes, a sign that the man wasn't hiding anything. Ben held out a business card. "Thank you, sir. Call me if you remember any other details."

After walking Mr. Owens back to the living room, Ben signaled the young woman in a red-and-green elf costume who'd retrieved Mrs. Mueller's handbag.

Resettled in the front parlor, Ben held his pen above his wire-bound notebook. "Your name?"

"Holly Nichols."

"What is your position in the garden club?"

Her chin lifted. "This year's president."

Ben scribbled. "Was a tour planned for your party?"

"No. I suggested it because I've never been inside the Carswell House and I thought the others would enjoy it, too."

"Why were only seven of you with Robert Owens?"

Holly paused. "Another half dozen or so chose Betty. A few of our members were scared they'd bump into the B&B's ghost and wouldn't leave the living room."

Ben did his best not to react. He'd never believed in ghosts and wasn't about to change at this late stage of his life. "And you weren't afraid of the ghost, Miss Nichols?"

"That's *Mrs.* Nichols, and no, I'm not a timid person."

Ben flipped to the next page. "Tell me the sequence of events from your point of view."

Holly leaned against the cushions of the loveseat and pulled a red-and-white-stockinged leg beneath her. "I don't recall exactly. I was studying a photograph of a holiday party hosted by the Carswells when Myrtle screamed."

"What did you do then?" Ben was beginning to feel like a recorder on a never-ending loop.

Holly lifted both shoulders. "Everyone rushed to the top of those steps where Robert was standing. I was swept along. I don't recall details. It happened really fast."

Ben reviewed his notes "That's all for now, Mrs. Nichols." He snatched a business card from the pile he'd tossed on the side table. "Here's my contact information. Call or text if you remember anything else."

"I will, Detective."

"Please send in another member."

Holly extracted her leg from beneath her body and stood up. "Of course."

Chapter Six

...late evening, Wednesday

One by one, Ben interviewed the remaining club members.

The secretary Alicia Reed answered all his questions in a trembling voice. As for where she was standing when Mrs. Mueller took her tumble, Alicia had been reading a newspaper article with no idea of who was standing beside her.

And then there came the elderly Hobart twins. Ben barred Zelda from the front parlor while attempting to interview Zoe. But the elder twin kept peeking in through the door from the dining room and interrupting her sister's responses. He finally gave up and questioned them together, though Zelda did most of the talking. She provided lots of details, none very helpful.

The next garden club member was a voluptuous lady named Ruby Cox. Her flaming red hair matched her personality. Ben couldn't help but wonder if she'd been a stripper at some point in her past. Ruby seemed primed to wink at Ben but never did.

Evelyn Woodley was the last member to be interviewed. She hobbled in on a cane topped by a carved duck handle, giving her the appearance of fragility. Ben knew from decades of detective work that looks were usually deceiving, so he wasn't going to jump to any conclusions. Evelyn provided answers, her voice even and ladylike.

Ben escorted Evelyn to rejoin the other ladies in the living room. "Thank you for your patience. I'll be in touch if necessary. You can go home now. Add your full name, address, and contact details to the patrolman's list."

As the six women exited by the front door, Ben turned to the three young men, each sitting sheepishly near the Christmas tree. "You boys are the B&B guests who joined the tour?"

The tall, skinny blonde jumped to his feet. "Yes, sir. The garden club ladies didn't mind, and neither did Mr. Owens."

"I don't need an explanation. I just need to know what happened. What's your name, son?"

"Charlie Brewster, sir."

Ben placed his hand on Charlie's shoulder. "Come with me. I have a few questions."

Settling on the front parlor loveseat, the young man sat up straight, his face set.

"Can you tell me why you joined the tour?"

Charlie's youthful face turned bright red. "Well, here's the thing, Detective. I wanted to spend as little time as possible in my room. Me and Shawn and Dylan are staying in the maids' rooms on the third floor, and it's a little creepy up there."

Ben was almost afraid to ask. "Why do you say that?"

"You're going to think we're strange, but we made a bet."

"And what was the bet?"

"The first one visited by Theo the Ghost would win a hundred dollars."

Ben groaned. The ghost again. Did everyone believe it existed? He had no choice but to continue the interview.

"I don't understand, Charlie. If you were waiting for the ghost, why do you call your room creepy?"

"Because I never expected she would actually appear."

"Are you telling me this ghost Theo came into your room?"

"She must have, because she pushed me out of my bed a few nights ago."

As a non-believer, Ben assumed Charlie's episode was a dream, let the subject drop, and repeated the questions he'd asked all the others. The young man's answers were the same; no idea where he'd been standing or who was near him.

"Anything else I need to know, Charlie?"

Again, the young man's face reddened. "I may as well tell you, because you're gonna find out. Myrtle Mueller is…was… my aunt on my father's side. I haven't seen her for years, and to be honest, she was never my favorite relative. Like I said, I came here with my buddies because of the ghost."

"Is that so?" Ben challenged.

"Hold on, Detective. If you think I was involved in Aunt Myrtle's accident, you couldn't be more wrong."

"You can go now. Send in either of your friends."

Shawn and Dylan provided nothing new.

The witness interviews completed, Ben stood up and stretched before he approached the young patrolman guarding the front door. "Sorry to keep you so late."

"Part of the job, sir. Here's the list of names and addresses. Do you need me to stay?"

Ben tucked the list in the back of his notebook. "Actually, I do. I've cordoned off the back hallway, the landing, and a section of the second-floor sitting room. Use the front staircase and stand guard along that rear wall. Make sure none of the B&B guests trespass until the lab tech and the photographer are finished. Remove the crime scene tape before you leave. "

"I can handle that." The young patrolman bounded up the front staircase.

Ben made his way to the kitchen where he found Mr. and Mrs. Owens drinking hot tea.

Betty Owens jumped to her feet. "Can I get you anything, Detective?"

"Thank you, no. Let's finish up so we can all get to bed. I need a brief chat with you, Mrs. Owens. Follow me."

In the front parlor, Betty's hands fluttered as she answered his questions. Who were the club members in her tour? What did she think had happened when she heard the scream? Who was first to arrive near her husband's group?

With each nervous answer, Betty appeared to be hiding something. On the other hand, having someone die at a hosted party had to be upsetting and justification for her nervousness. Or was she afraid that her so-called ghost had somehow been involved in the mishap?

"That's all for now. I'll walk you to the kitchen."

Waiting until Mrs. Owens sat beside her husband, Ben brought them up to date. "The top of the servant steps to the lower landing are cordoned off with crime scene tape. I've stationed a patrolman to guard the area until the state police photographer has finished snapping pictures and the crime lab tech has collected whatever evidence he can find. The medical examiner has called his office to remove Mrs. Mueller's body."

Robert slid to the edge of his chair. "Was it necessary to treat this accident like a crime scene?"

"I know it's disturbing," Ben responded. "This is standard procedure for a death without the presence of a doctor. We usually find nothing suspicious and close the case with no fuss. I'll return in the morning to interview the other guests. Good night. I'll see myself out."

Ben made his way to the front door. He found it interesting that no one seemed upset about Mrs. Mueller's demise.

As Ben drove back to the station, he mentally reviewed the initial statements from the witnesses. None of the club members or the Harvard students had noticed any unusual movement. It was certainly possible Mrs. Mueller had fallen of her own accord, but too many details pointed to something more than a casual tumble from one tread to the next.

Like Peter and Otis, Ben suspected the woman's death had been anything but an accident. But rather than making assumptions, Ben would wait for Otis' official autopsy findings.

Chapter Seven

...late evening, Wednesday

"Did you call me, Sweetheart?"

The tea kettle dropped from Gwen's hand with a loud clang as she whirled around. "Parker! Where are you?"

"Admiring your tree," came his reply.

She rushed into the living room and moved toward his ethereal self taking shape. He wore the same red golf shirt and black slacks – both now faded – that he'd worn the day a freak thunderstorm took his life. His smile broadened, his pale hazel eyes twinkled with his usual mischief. "You certainly have a way with ornaments."

Each year, she fastidiously decorated her holiday tree with ornaments of silver and gold; glass balls of dusty rose and burgundy; plus cascading ribbons.

Because a physical embrace was an exercise in futility, Gwen merely stretched out her hand. As before, his butterfly-soft touch was barely discernible. "You always say the nicest things, Parker. How did you know I needed to see you? I only said your name in passing."

His wide shoulders lifted and fell in an age-old shrug. "Not sure. Maybe my sensitivity to your voice is getting sharper."

Amber appeared from parts unknown and purred as she circled her master, looking up at his pale likeness with adoring eyes, seemingly frustrated that she couldn't rub against his leg.

When he reached down, the cat stretched her head toward his see-through hand before scampering away. Parker turned his attention to Gwen. "How are you doing, Sweetheart? Are you able to keep up with the maintenance here?"

"I'm managing. Handymen handle the bigger repairs."

"That's good. I'd hate to see you move away."

"I have no plans to go anywhere, Parker. This is the only place you've appeared to me."

He gave her a lop-sided grin. "So far anyway. You still seeing that fellow from the nursery?"

Gwen would never get used to discussing Hal Jenkins with the spirit of her deceased husband. How much weirder could it get? "Hal's just a good friend. I invited him and his granddaughter to Tess's for Christmas."

"The Berkshires for the holidays? What a great idea."

"Tess has rounded up some long-lost cousins to join in the festivities, along with Aunt Nellie."

"I'm glad to hear that. Having lots of people around will help your sister through her first Christmas without Nathan." After a few beats, Parker cocked his pale head. "Did I hear you right earlier? Myrtle Mueller died?"

A lump filled Gwen's throat as she retold Myrtle's tragic death during the annual Christmas party.

"I remember you weren't a big fan of hers, but her death has obviously upset you."

"It's more than my reaction, Parker. The B&B owners are worried."

His pale eyebrows shot upward. "What B&B?"

For a second, Gwen didn't understand why he was asking, and then the reason dawned on her. "Betty and Robert Owens bought the Carswell House and converted it into a B&B. They opened a few weeks ago."

"That explains it. I haven't seen you recently. But why are they worried? Surely Myrtle's death was an accident."

"It's not that. They're worried their ghost was involved."

"The B&B has a ghost?"

"They do. Betty told me about Theo's recent pranks." Gwen concentrated on Parker's transparent face as she decided her next words. "Do you think you can appear somewhere besides here?" She waved her hand to include the entire library.

Parker again shrugged. "I've never tried. Why do you ask?"

"Betty asked me to help her search through the Carswell family history for an explanation of Theo's recent unrest. That's where I'm thinking you could help."

Again, Parker's eyebrows lifted. "Me? What do you have up your sleeve, Gwen?"

She hesitated, searching for the right angle. "Well, the binders probably don't include everyday gossip. I thought you could locate Theo and ask her a few questions."

A mischievous expression appeared on his animated face. "One ghost talking to another? Have you ever heard of such a thing, Gwen?"

"Well, no, but wouldn't it be cool if you could do it?"

"I suppose so. What questions would you want me to ask this Theo?"

"First, what happened just before her death in 1924."

Parker's spirit sobered. "No details were recorded?"

"No arrest was made, but the police labeled it suspicious."

"That is a mystery. What else?"

Gwen loved that Parker's spirit was interested in connecting with Theo. "Was she in the second-floor sitting room tonight? Did she see anyone near Myrtle before she fell?"

"Are you thinking this Theo might have pushed Myrtle?"

Studying Parker's pale green eyes, Gwen answered, "For Betty and Robert's sakes, I hope not, but I suppose it's a possibility. Do you think ghosts are capable of murder, Parker?"

Before Parker had a chance to answer, his form faded and he was gone. Gwen could only hope that he'd one day gain the ability to warn her of his impending departure.

She stared at the spot where Parker had wavered a second ago. Until earlier this evening, only Madame Eudora had truly believed in the existence of his spirit, though perhaps a few others also believed after the séance where he'd moved a scarf of one of the attendees when asked. With the revelation of the B&B's ghost, Gwen harbored no doubt that Betty – and Robert, too – would be the next Harbor Falls' residents to believe that Parker's spirit had returned from the afterlife.

Deciding it was too late to attempt a second connection with him, Gwen made the rounds of her first floor, checking that her windows and doors were locked. Safe and secure, she headed upstairs to her gable bedroom, nearly tripping over Amber as the cat bounded up the staircase beside her mistress.

Chapter Eight

...early morning, Thursday

Ben knocked on the door jamb of the police chief's office. Mike Brown lifted his head from the stack of documents littering his desk. "You look like hell, Ben. Late night at the B&B?"

"It shows, huh?"

"What have you uncovered so far?"

"Otis pointed out a cluster of hair caught on a tread, and I spotted a fresh dent. If that's where Mrs. Mueller's head made first contact, she would have been upside down."

Mike tapped his desk blotter with his pen. "So Otis thinks the woman had a little help?"

Ben nodded. "So does Peter."

"When's Otis performing the autopsy?"

"This morning. I'm heading over to his office after I'm finished here."

Mike pointed at Ben's hand. "Your witness statements?"

Ben held up his notebook. "The people in Mr. Owens' tour weren't much help. One of the guests – Charlie Brewster – is Mrs. Mueller's nephew. He swore he avoided his aunt all evening. There's no reason for a second grilling until Otis submits his conclusions."

"Makes sense," Mike agreed.

"After the autopsy, I'll interview the other B&B guests who weren't on Mr. Owens' portion of the house tour. One of them might have seen something relevant." Ben tucked his notebook into his pocket. "Guess who was there with the garden club?"

"I'm not up for guessing games, Ben. Just tell me."

Ben eased into the side chair. "Gwen Andrews."

A grin split the police chief's face. "Our favorite amateur sleuth? Was she a witness?"

"Not directly. I'm stopping at her place for her statement on my way to the B&B."

Mike focused on a point beyond Ben's shoulder. "You're making me wish I was still the lead detective." He indicated his cluttered desk. "I've become a glorified paper jockey."

"And doing a bang-up job, Mike."

"Thanks for that, but I'd rather be out searching for someone to lock up."

Ben laughed. "In that case, why don't you live vicariously through me?"

"I'll do that." The chief's chair snapped forward. "I have a suggestion for you."

"What's that?"

Mike leaned closer. "If Otis confirms that Mrs. Mueller's death was suspicious, Gwen's involvement with the garden club could prove useful. Why don't you sign her up now as your confidential informant?"

"Good idea, chief. I'll find out if she's willing. My guess is that she's already started forming ideas."

Ben's cell phone buzzed. After a short conversation, he ended the call. "That was Otis. He's finished the preliminaries and has something to show me."

"Keep me in the loop, Ben."

"Sure thing."

***

Ben was glad the medical examiner suggested a delayed

arrival. Not that Ben had a weak constitution, but lingering inside the autopsy suite was never pleasant. The smell of formaldehyde alone was enough to make him gag.

Standing next to Mrs. Mueller's draped body, Otis pulled off his gloves and picked up a folder. "Let's talk in my office."

In the enclosed space along one wall of the autopsy room, Otis shut the door and turned on a fan, dissipating an insufficient portion of the nauseating odors. "Mrs. Mueller did not suffer a heart attack, an aneurism, or anything similar that could have caused her to collapse or lose her balance. The location of her wound tells me her feet were above her head at the moment of contact with that wooden tread. I'm sure Peter's lab will confirm that the indentation plus the snatch of hair are hers. She actually died from a basilar skull fracture, an indication of her speed on impact."

"So you think she was airborne?"

"That's the only way her head could have connected at that angle. She had no broken nails, which tells me she never reached out to break her fall." Otis passed a photograph to Ben. "This is the upper section of Mrs. Mueller's left arm."

Ben squinted at the image. "What I am looking at?"

Otis pointed at several marks. "Older women bruise very easily. These black and blue marks were inflicted shortly before her death." Otis spread his hand and held his fingers above the photo. "You can see that the size, shape, and placement could be splayed fingers."

Ben studied the picture. "Are you saying someone shoved Mrs. Mueller hard enough to leave these bruises?"

"That's for you to determine. All I can tell you is that I'm ruling her death suspicious."

Ben held the photo at arm's length. "Is this actual size?"

"Not quite. Give me a sec to make adjustments." Otis turned to his computer, pulled up the digital photo, tweaked the height and width, and printed a page. "Let me compare this to her arm. Do you want to examine the bruises?"

Ben made no attempt to move. "No thanks. I'll wait here."

"Suit yourself." Otis passed through his office door into the autopsy room, admitting the unpleasant smell of death. Ben raised his hand to his nose as he gazed through the window and watched Otis hold his printout near Mrs. Mueller's bare arm. Making a thumbs-up gesture, Otis re-entered his office. "This is a perfect match."

Ben spread his own fingers and laid his hand atop the picture; his fingertips were too large. "This is either a man with smaller hands or a woman with larger ones. Thanks, Otis."

"You're welcome. By the way, I collected her clothing." Otis indicated a brown paper bag on the shelf behind him.

Ben gave it a brief glance before returning to his study of the bruise placement. "Isn't there a new technique that reveals fingerprints on fabric?"

"There is, Ben. The Scots developed it a few years ago."

Ben's cell phone buzzed. Caller ID indicated the crime lab. "Your timing is perfect, Peter. I'm with Otis now."

Otis made a signal for Ben to place his phone on speaker.

"You're on speaker, Peter, so Otis can hear what you say."

"Hey, Otis."

"Morning, Peter."

"What have you got for me?" Ben asked.

"The snatch of hair belonged to Mrs. Mueller. The lack of blood in the fresh indentation indicates that's where her head made first contact. Her prints were not on the side walls or the railing, so it appears she never reached out to stop her fall. Not a lot to go on, Ben, but this woman's death was no accident."

"Otis confirmed your opinion and ruled Mrs. Mueller's death suspicious. Let me ask you something, Peter. Does your lab have the equipment to reveal fingerprints on fabric?"

"We sure do. Ben. The fabric is fumed with a special liquid that clings to fingertip oils. The prints can't be lifted from the fabric, so we take a hi-res photograph through an infrared microscope. No guarantee we'll find anything, but forward her clothes with a written request of where to concentrate the search."

"Otis here, Peter. I'll send them over today."

Before disconnecting the call, Ben said, "Thanks, you two. You're both a great help, as always."

Ben hung up and made a run for the fresh air outside.

Chapter Nine

...mid- morning, Thursday

As Gwen wrapped gifts near the double-sided fireplace, the whispered conversation in the B&B's front parlor drifted into focus like a bad movie. She needed to call the police station and share the blackmailer's threat with Ben.

Although Gwen had told Officer Ed what she knew about the events at the B&B, would Ben need her official statement?

At the sound of a car engine rumbling to the curb, Gwen stepped to the front window and grinned. As if he'd read her mind, Ben climbed from his SUV and sauntered up her walkway. The white hair escaping his cap matched the glistening snow beneath his boots.

Before he reached for the buzzer, she pulled open the heavy oak door. "Hi, Ben. Get in here before you freeze."

He stomped his feet and stepped into the foyer. "Sorry we didn't have a chance to talk last night."

"No apology needed. Coffee?"

"Only if it's your special brew."

She led him to the kitchen where morning sunshine drifted through the bay window above the sink. Shadows created by the bare tree branches danced on the island's granite countertop. Pouring coffee from the carafe, she held out a mug.

Ben took a quick sip. "Even better than I remember."

Adding a spoon of raw sugar and a splash of light cream to her second cup, Gwen said, "I suspect you're here on official police business."

"Unfortunately." He swirled his coffee. "My interviews last night barely skimmed the surface. I understand you're the club's vice president this year?"

"Afraid so. They roped me into it at the June meeting."

"Then you're the perfect person to review this list." He reached into his jacket pocket, removed a photocopy, and handed it to her. "Is this everyone who attended your party?"

Gwen perused the list compiled by the young patrolman at the B&B door, mentally recalling who'd participated in the Yankee Swap. She counted the names. The total matched the numbered slips she'd created for choosing a gift. She extended the paper to Ben. "This is everyone."

He didn't reach for it. "The people in the lower section were on Mr. Owens' tour. They gave me their witness statements. Could you mark the rest to indicate who was with Betty's group and who stayed in the living room?"

"Sure. Were you told why those few didn't join either tour?"

Ben's light gray eyes studied Gwen. "I'd like to hear your explanation."

Assuming someone had already mentioned Theo, Gwen saw no reason to avoid the topic. "They were afraid they'd bump into the B&B's ghost."

Ben didn't move a muscle. "Do *you* believe in ghosts, Gwen?"

She didn't miss his dubious tone. Now was not the time to tell him that Parker's spirit had visited her more than once. And so she said, "Sorry, I don't discuss politics, religion, or the possibility of an afterlife. My personal beliefs are not worth losing a friendship."

Ben grinned. "That's a very safe answer."

"Safe or not, Betty and Robert have seen the spirit of a bride who died on those same servant steps." Gwen relayed Betty's list of Theo's recent pranks, along with possibly shoving Charlie from his bed. "When our president Holly Nichols suggested a tour, Betty warned everyone that Theo's been restless for the past few days. The women who stayed in the living room didn't want to risk an encounter."

"Do you believe this ghost had anything to do with Mrs. Mueller's fall?"

Gwen struggled to keep her tone even. "I can't say because I wasn't in Robert's group. But given Theo's recent unrest, Betty and Robert are worried about Theo's possible involvement. The rumor of an unfriendly ghost would devastate their bookings. I prefer to think Myrtle lost her balance or had a heart attack."

Ben took another sip of his coffee. "I hate to crush your optimism, but I met with Otis after the autopsy this morning. Mrs. Mueller died from a basilar skull fracture."

Gwen nearly choked. "So she didn't have a heart attack?"

"Far from it. The extent and type of her injury indicate she was airborne when her head hit the edge of the midway step. The medical examiner theorized someone shoved Mrs. Mueller hard enough to leave telltale bruises. His finding is all I need to initiate a full-blown investigation."

While Gwen absorbed this disturbing update, Ben kept talking. "I have another reason for stopping by."

Gwen looked at him directly. "What's that?"

He reached inside his jacket and pulled out a multi-page document. "After a shaky start, you and I made a good team last April. For this case, your connection to the garden club members could come in handy." He unfolded the pages and placed them in front of her. "This is a Confidential Informant Agreement. Take a minute to read through it."

After perusing the document, Gwen asked, "Does Chief Brown know you're offering this to me? He warned me to stay out of police business."

"This might surprise you, but Mike's the one who suggested we take advantage of your sleuthing instincts. Think of yourself as either a confidential informant or a cooperating individual."

Gwen preferred the latter but didn't say so. "We weren't this formal in April."

"You're right. But if you remember, I'd resigned from the police department, so this document wasn't necessary."

Gwen flipped the pages. "Are you sure about this?"

Ben pulled a pen from his pocket and held it out. "As sure as I can be."

"It says here I can't tell anyone that I'm your C.I."

"Correct. You'd undermine any details a witness might tell you. This arrangement needs to stay between you and me."

"So this document is our little secret?"

"Exactly."

Despite her unease, she accepted his pen, filled in the blanks, and signed on the final dotted line.

Ben folded the document and tucked it in his pocket. "Welcome aboard, Gwen."

She couldn't deny her energy spike at the possibility of solving another mystery. "What do you need me to do?"

"Share your observations from last night's party and your inside knowledge of the garden club members. Initiate conversations with them without being obvious."

"You want me to spy?"

"Don't think of it that way. Think of it as putting your uncanny instincts to work for a good cause."

"That sounds much better, Ben. Even if I wasn't your new C.I., there's something I'd already planned to tell you."

"What's that?"

"Last night at the party, I overheard a conversation in Betty's front parlor." Gwen paraphrased the confrontation between the whisperers. "I have no idea who they were. Do you think the threat is linked to Myrtle's fall?"

"I've always been suspicious of coincidences. Do me a favor and write down that conversation as accurately as you can remember." Pulling a notebook from his pocket, Ben scribbled. "Can you also create a timeline of last night's events? I need an understanding of who was where and when."

"I can do that. How soon do you want them?"

"As soon as possible. In the meantime, if you happen to bump into anyone who was at the B&B, pay close attention to what they say. In fact, start a notebook and keep a record of not only the conversation but your observations as well."

"I can do that, too."

Ben's smile lit up his gray eyes. "Our collaboration is off to a great start. But I'm curious. Now that Mrs. Mueller's death is labeled suspicious, will Mr. and Mrs. Owens ask you to help them disprove their ghost's involvement?"

Studying Ben's expression, Gwen attempted to judge whether he was mocking her or asking a serious question. Should she mention she'd be searching the family history binders with Betty that very afternoon for a connection between the bride-to-be's death and Theo's current unrest? Almost certain she should not reveal her ghost-related pursuits to Ben,

Gwen came up with what she considered a valid response. "I've never been very good at predicting the future."

Ben didn't seem offended. "Good policy. Can you squeeze in a daily update with me?"

"I can. Why don't you stop by around eighty thirty tomorrow and I'll feed you breakfast? You can review the confrontation and timeline while we eat."

"Breakfast reminds me of last April, Gwen."

"You're right, except back then you were warning me and my sister not to snoop. This time, you've invited me to join forces with you."

Ben lifted his mug in a silent toast before taking another sip then setting it down on the counter.

Gwen noticed it was empty. "Would you like another cup?"

He shook his head. "Thanks, but I've gotta run. I need to interview the other B&B guests."

"And tell Betty and Robert Owens that Myrtle's death was no accident?"

"Unfortunately." Ben picked up the now-coded list of garden club members and headed toward the foyer. He glanced into her living room and called over his shoulder, "Your Christmas tree looks great."

Ben's compliment made her smile. "Thanks."

"See you in the morning, Gwen."

Moments later, the rumble of his engine faded as he circled the village green.

While Gwen tucked their dirty plates and mugs into the dishwasher, her mind whirled to that whispered conversation. So many were gathered in the B&B last night; the guests, the garden club members, Betty and Robert, plus Gracie in the kitchen. Which two out of all those people had snuck into Betty's front parlor for the threatening confrontation?

Were those disturbing words related to Myrtle's tumble?

Or was there no connection?

Chapter Ten

...early morning, Thursday

Ben waited to hear footsteps from inside the B&B.

Betty Owens swung the door wide and gestured him into the entrance hall. "I'd say good morning, Detective, but that wouldn't be accurate. Myrtle's accident is very upsetting. One of our members dying was the last thing I expected during our club Christmas party."

"Dealing with a death on your property is not easy." Ben sympathized, knowing his next words would not make her feel any better. "Unfortunately, the medical examiner is calling Mrs. Mueller's death suspicious."

Visibly shaken, Mrs. Owens retreated to a corner chair and sat down, shoving her hands between her knees. "Oh, this is terrible, just terrible. It's distressing enough that Myrtle died, but to hear her death is suspicious is truly disturbing."

Robert Owens burst through a swinging door, skirted around the dining room table, and strode into the entrance hall. "I thought I heard voices. Good morning, Detective Snowcrest."

Looking down at his wife, Robert noticed Betty's pained expression and tossed Ben a challenging look. "What's going on here?"

Mrs. Owens turned her face up at her husband. "Detective Snowcrest just told me that Myrtle's death was not an accident."

"That's not what I expected to hear." Robert squatted beside his wife and grasped her hand, speaking sideways to Ben. "What happens now?"

Ben watched the couple as he answered. "I've initiated a full-blown investigation. First, I need to speak to your other guests. May I use the front parlor for my interviews?"

"Of course," Robert answered as he helped his wife to her feet. "Everyone is still in their rooms upstairs. Who do you want to interview first? I can bring them to you."

Ben didn't need to refer to his notebook because he'd memorized the names. "Mr. and Mrs. Pettigrew."

A few moments later, as Ben settled on the upholstered chair in the front parlor, Robert ushered in a stately gentleman and a neatly-coiffed woman. "This is Cyril and Lillian Pettigrew."

Ben gestured them toward the loveseat. "I have a few questions to ask you."

Cyril's nose lifted but he remained silent.

Ben opened his notebook to a fresh page. "Where were you last evening when you heard the scream?"

Lillian crossed her legs at the ankle and laid her hands in her lap. "I was coming out of the bathroom after a shower. Cyril was in his pajamas on the bed reading the local newspaper."

Ben jotted. "What did you do after you heard the scream?"

Cyril answered, "I opened our door a crack to see what was going on. With that boisterous party downstairs, I thought the scream was a garden club lady a bit out of control."

The couple's clipped British accents made Ben feel as though he were questioning Queen Elizabeth and Prince Phillip.

"What did you see?" Ben prompted.

"Some ladies running across the sitting room," Cyril answered. "Lillian and I weren't properly dressed, so I closed the door. We didn't want to get involved."

Lillian eased closer to her husband but didn't interrupt.

"There's really nothing else we can tell you, Detective," Cyril insisted. "We didn't know that a woman had died until your bobby forced us to the entrance hall in our nightclothes. The death was tragic, but Lillian and I can't provide any details beyond what we've told you."

Ben flipped his book closed. "Thank you for your candor."

After the Pettigrew couple exited, Robert poked his head in. "Who's next?"

"The Schuster family."

Robert returned with the young couple and their two children, all with winter coats tossed over their arms. The perfect American family: father and mother, both in their mid to late thirties; pre-teen son, perhaps eleven or twelve; younger daughter around eight.

Fritz Schuster turned to his wife. "I'll speak with the detective, Isabella. You stay out here with the kids." He walked into the parlor, sat on the loveseat, and glared at Ben. "I don't see any need for you to interview my wife or children. We were all in bed when Isabella and I heard that scream."

"Did you open your door?"

"We did not. In fact, I checked to be sure it was locked."

"So you have no idea who was in the sitting room?"

"None at all. I looked in on Waldo and Julie through the connecting door. The kids were both sound asleep. There's nothing more I can tell you."

Ben extended a business card. "If any other details come to mind, give me a call." Escorting Fritz Schuster into the entrance hall, Ben motioned to his wife. "You're next."

Fritz scowled. "Is that really necessary?"

Isabella moved forward. "Don't be overprotective, Fritz."

Ben slid the pocket door closed and waved her to sit.

Despite her willingness to provide a statement, Isabella Schuster repeated her husband's tally of events nearly word for word, adding nothing new or earth-shattering.

"Mrs. Schuster," Ben began, "because your children are under-aged, I need your permission to speak with them."

"I have no problem with that, Detective."

"Thank you. Please send in your daughter."

Ben listened from afar as Isabella convinced Fritz to allow the children to be interviewed.

Moments later, little Julie stepped into the parlor, turning to speak to her hovering father. "Daddy, I'm a big girl. I don't mind talking to the detective."

Julie couldn't manage to close the pocket door, so Ben stepped over and slid it the last few inches.

Her head held high, Julie murmured, "Thank you," and hopped onto Ben's empty chair.

"You're quite the young lady, Julie. I won't keep you long."

"I watch the TV detective shows, so you don't scare me."

Ben hid a grin at the girl's precociousness. "Can you tell me if you heard or saw anything after you went to bed last night?"

Julie scooted forward, clinging to the chair arms. "I heard a scream and then my brother opened our door to the hallway. I thought someone had seen the ghost."

"Do you believe there's a ghost in this B&B, Julie?"

The little girl's head nodded, causing her curls to bounce. "I sure do, because she shoved that boy Charlie from his bed. But I don't know if I want to bump into her myself."

Ben wouldn't encourage any more speculation about the

ghost. "What happened after your brother opened your door?"

"Not much. When Waldo heard our parents unlatching the connecting door, he jumped into his bed and pulled the covers over his head. So did I."

Ben made a note. "That's very helpful, Julie. After your parents returned to their room, did Waldo tell you if he saw anything?"

Julie pouted. "No, he didn't. He told me not to be so nosey and go to sleep."

Chapter Eleven

...mid-morning Thursday

Ignoring Fritz Schuster's evil eye, Ben waved the man's son into the parlor. "Have a seat, Waldo."

The pre-teen plopped into the side chair and leaned forward, his forearms resting on his knees, his wide eyes. "This is so awesome, Detective Snowcrest. Just like on TV."

"Unfortunately, Waldo," Ben lectured in his most authoritative voice, "this is not a TV show. A woman lost her life last night."

Waldo's face fell, his bubble burst.

Ben proceeded with the interview. "What did you see last night when you peeked out your hallway door?"

The boy's expression came to life, but with anger. "My little sister has a big mouth."

"Don't be too hard on her. She was just being truthful. Now tell me what you saw."

Waldo crossed his arms in a defiant posture. "Oh, all right. I was hoping the ghost had scared someone, but all I saw were some of those old women running across the sitting room. The others were hanging around near the back steps."

"Do you recall who was standing where?"

Waldo's face screwed up in thought. "The only one I remember is the tall lady in the elf costume with red-and-white legs. Then I heard my parents turning the doorknob, so I hopped into bed."

"Thank you, Waldo. You've been a big help."

The boy's excitement returned. "I have? That's great! Wait 'til I tell the kids at school."

Ben stood up. "You can join your family now."

Waldo exited the parlor to find his father holding his coat.

Fritz Schuster again scowled at Ben. "Are you okay, son?"

"More than okay, Dad. That was awesome."

As the Schuster family headed out the front door, Robert Owens re-appeared. "I'll go check on Miss Hammond."

While Ben waited, he leaned against the pocket door, pondering why some believed in ghosts and others didn't. Though Gwen hadn't said so directly, he suspected she harbored no doubt. What he didn't understand was why.

Robert returned alone. "Miss Hammond is lying down with a cold compress on her forehead. She asked if she could speak to you when her migraine has passed."

Ben wasn't thrown by this snag. "That's fine, Mr. Owens. Tell her I'll come back tomorrow for her statement."

"I'll let her know." Robert bounded up the staircase.

Ben mentally reviewed the additional witness interviews. Only Waldo provided the detail of an elf costume, complete with striped legs. That meant Holly Nichols was standing at the edge of the crowd after Mrs. Mueller screamed and fell.

The clatter of pots and pans gave a clear signal where he could find Betty Owens. As he circumvented the dining room table, he noticed a stack of platters and serving bowls.

As he entered the kitchen through the swinging door, she grabbed a towel and wiped her hands. "Did you learn anything new from our other guests?"

"Not a lot. Miss Hammond has a headache, so I'll have to take her statement tomorrow." Ben turned to leave.

"Wait, Detective. Is it okay if we wash down the servant steps and the landing?"

Ben did a double take. He'd given no thought to the clean-up. Evidence was collected and photographs taken. "You're clear to do whatever cleaning needs to be done, Mrs. Owens."

"Thank you, Detective. The residue of blood on the landing is quite upsetting."

***

As Ben drove toward the police station, his detective brain rekindled Gwen's whisperers. Motive and opportunity all rolled into one neat conversation. A coincidence Ben couldn't ignore.

If Mrs. Mueller had been the blackmailer – which fit the case like a glove – Ben would only have to seek out the adulterer, the person most likely to have pushed poor Myrtle down those servant steps.

His choices were limited to the people in Robert's half of the impromptu tour; the three Harvard students, the six club women, and Robert himself.

After Ben entered the station, he stopped at the chief's office and rapped on the doorframe. "Got a minute, Mike?"

"Sure, Ben, have a seat. What did Otis have to say?"

Ben made himself as comfortable as possible on the hard side chair. "Based on his autopsy findings and Peter's evidence, Otis is citing Mrs. Mueller's death as suspicious. He determined she was flying through the air when her head made contact with the midway tread." Ben passed Otis' printout of the bruises across Mike's desk.

"What am I looking at?" the chief asked, echoing Ben's initial reaction.

"Bruises on Mrs. Mueller's left arm. Otis says they were

inflicted shortly before her death, likely by the fingers of the person who shoved her with enough force to send the woman flying."

"If he's right, Ben, that person is diabolical."

"I agree. Peter called while I was at Otis's office. Are you aware of a new technique to reveal fingerprints on fabric?"

"Can't say I am."

"Well, the lab has the equipment for the test. Peter told Otis to send over Mrs. Mueller's clothes with a request to concentrate on the left sleeve."

"Is that an expensive test?"

Ben should have expected the question. "No idea what the lab will charge the department. I only know it might solve the case. You worried it will blow our budget?"

Mike shrugged and picked up a paperclip. "You can't imagine how tiresome it is to wrestle with the pencil pushers over every dollar we spend."

"In that case, I'll ask Peter for a discount."

The chief smirked. "What's your next move?"

"I'll continue to investigate. So far, none of them were very helpful." Ben shifted his weight on the uncomfortable chair. "There's another element I haven't mentioned."

Mike leaned his forearms on his desk blotter. "Tell me."

"The B&B owners claim to have a Carswell family ghost. Can't speak for you, Mike, but I'm a skeptic. According to Gwen, the Owens are worried their ghost pushed Mrs. Mueller."

"Any idea why they'd think that?"

"Because that's the same way the bride died on her wedding day. Plus Charlie Brewster claims the ghost shoved him from his bed the other night."

The chief leaned back, his expression solemn. "An interesting twist." He snapped his chair forward. "Keep this ghost connection under your hat for now. We'll deal with it later if we have to."

Before Ben could comment, a knock announced the arrival of Officer Ed Bells.

Mike waved him to enter. "Come in, Ed."

"Hope I'm not interrupting, but I saw Ben walk in here and wanted to tell him about last night's notification."

Ben's ears perked up. "How did Mr. Mueller take his wife's accident and death?"

Ed leaned his bulk against the door frame. "Well, it was one of the oddest I've ever delivered. First of all, he didn't invite me into his home. He stood in the shadows at the door, so I couldn't see his facial expressions. After I told him what happened, he closed the door. Hardly a reaction at all."

"That's curious," Ben said. "Mr. Mueller is on my list for an interview, so I'll have a chance to meet the man in person."

"I'd be interested to hear your reaction to him." Ed lifted his hand in a wave and turned on his heel. "See you both later."

Ben rose to his feet. "I'll head out, too, chief."

"Keep me informed, Ben."

As Ben approached his desk in the detective unit, he realized Mike hadn't said if he believed in ghosts or not.

Chapter Twelve

...late morning, Thursday

After Betty phoned that Detective Snowcrest had come and gone, Gwen walked to the B&B. Bright sunshine reflected off the snow, creating a deceptively cheerful winter scene.

"Thanks for coming over," Betty said.

Gwen stomped her boots on the welcome mat and stepped into the entrance hall.

"It's been a madhouse here this morning. Detective Snowcrest didn't stop by just to interview the other guests. He said Myrtle's death has been deemed suspicious, and he's launching a full investigation."

Although Gwen was fully aware of Ben's assignment, she had to pretend she was hearing this news for the first time. "Oh, my. That's upsetting."

"Robert and I were distressed enough that Myrtle fell to her death. And now this." Betty patted her eyes with a tissue clutched in her hand. "After my warning, the club ladies probably think Theo did it."

Gwen placed her arm across Betty's shoulders. "You can't assume they'll jump to that conclusion."

Tendrils of gray fell along Betty's cheek. "Oh, I don't know. If I were them, I might think the same thing."

As Betty led her toward the front parlor, Gwen's mind swirled with uncertainties about Theo. Charlie had blamed the B&B ghost for his fall from his bed, which seemed impossible to Gwen. Based on her experience with Parker's spirit and his

68

lack of physical strength, she doubted Theo's ghost could accomplish such a feat. Last evening, Betty had suggested either a bad dream or a fib to win the wager. Both were more valid.

Betty's concern that Theo might have pushed Myrtle down the servant steps was unlikely. Gwen was sure that the most Theo could have done was materialize and frighten Myrtle.

The medical examiner had concluded that someone had shoved Myrtle with enough force to leave behind those bruises. So a simple case of Myrtle losing her balance from fright was out of the question.

But if not Theo, who? That angry confrontation in the front parlor would only be relevant if the blackmailer had been Myrtle. The adulterer could have grasped the opportunity of the house tour to eliminate the threat of exposure. But surely, someone in Robert's group would have noticed the movement. Were they really too distracted? According to Ben's initial interviews, no one had seen anything out of the ordinary.

There were too many questions and too few answers. Gwen would have to do some digging to unearth the truth. For the first time, she was glad Ben had asked her sign on as his C.I.

She linked arms with Betty. "When we rushed across the sitting room last night after hearing the scream, did you notice if any of your guests were standing in their doorway?"

A pensive expression altered Betty's face. "Why?"

Gwen needed to blame her curiosity on something other than her partnership with Ben. "Just wondering if any of them noticed any unusual movement in Robert's group."

Before Betty could comment, the front door opened and Cyril Pettigrew rushed inside, a newspaper tucked under his arm, his expression sour. "Mrs. Owens, Lillian and I did not appreciate being interrogated this morning as though we are criminals." His British accent emphasized his indignation.

"I'm sorry you were drawn into the inquiry, Mr. Pettigrew."

"Well, I hope we are not detained past our checkout date. After we leave New England, we have reservations in three more destinations here in the colonies. We would be most upset if any of our plans are delayed."

Betty continued to placate her guest. "I can't speak for the detective, but if you have no details to share about the incident, your travel itinerary shouldn't be disrupted."

His expression softened. "Don't misunderstand me, Mrs. Owens. We do not fault you or your husband for that poor woman's accident. And by the way, our condolences on the passing of your friend." Without waiting for Betty's response, Cyril marched up the front staircase.

Betty helped Gwen shrug out of her winter coat and placed it on the loveseat. "What are Robert and I going to do if our guests have to stay past their booking dates?"

"What do you mean?"

"Last night, Detective Snowcrest told everyone not to leave town. Their rooms are reserved through Sunday morning. The next group is due Sunday afternoon."

Gwen eased Betty onto the loveseat. "Don't panic just yet. The detective has days between now and Sunday to dismiss your current guests."

Betty sniffed and wiped her nose. "I hope you're right."

Because they were seated in the front parlor, Gwen relayed the whisperers' conversation, watching Betty's reaction closely for signs of being caught.

Betty wrinkled her forehead. "Any idea who they were?"

Gwen chose her words with care. "Neither voice sounded familiar. I don't even know if they were male or female."

"But they were whispering. That would make them nearly impossible to identify."

"That's the main reason I can't attach a name to either voice. Those two could have been club members, your guests, even the Harvard boys. Or maybe the woman who was helping you in the kitchen."

Betty swallowed a laugh. "My cleaning lady Gracie? That would be impossible."

"Why do you say that?"

"The poor dear suffered a childhood illness that robbed her of her voice. There's no way she was one of your whisperers."

Gwen shifted her weight, debating how far to push the issue. "I wonder if Gracie noticed who entered the dining room from your front parlor after I overheard the threat. Can we ask her?"

Betty scrunched her eyebrows. "Unfortunately, no. Gracie was here this morning, but left before the detective arrived."

"When is she scheduled to return?"

"Tomorrow morning."

Footfalls on the staircase signaled someone descending. Cyril and Lillian exited through the front door without glancing into the front parlor.

"Unless they're skipping out without their luggage, I assume they'll return later." Betty tapped Gwen's knee. "I've got chicken rice soup bubbling on the stove and I need to stir the pot. Can you stay for lunch?"

"I'd love to. Smells delicious."

"Make yourself comfortable in the dining room. I'll join you in a sec."

As Gwen settled at the long table, she spied a pile of serving plates, bowls, and platters clustered at the other end. Given the turmoil after Myrtle's fall, the party containers – including Gwen's own deviled egg carrier – had been left behind.

Betty barreled through the swinging door and waved toward the assortment. "In case you're wondering, those have been washed. I need to contact the club members to pick them up."

Gwen surveyed the array of shapes, sizes, and colors. "Why don't I handle that for you?"

"You'd do that?"

"Of course. Your hands are full. Besides, as I reunite those dishes with each woman, I'll bring up the subject of members who need money or are having an affair."

"You be careful, Gwen. You might be chatting with one or the other of your whisperers."

Was that a subtle warning? Should Gwen be worried that Betty had been one or the other of them?

Betty tapped her finger on the table's surface. "If you want, I can ask Gracie if she noticed who came through that other door around the time of the confrontation."

"Wait a sec. Didn't you tell me Gracie can't speak?"

"I did, but she and I have a special way of communicating. It's a combination of sign language and writing."

In that instant, relief flooded Gwen that Betty had not been one of the whisperers. She wouldn't offer to ask Gracie who had exited the front parlor if she'd been one of them. For a brief moment, Gwen felt guilty that she wouldn't be questioning Gracie herself. Would Ben care who obtained the answer as long as there *was* an answer? "You wouldn't mind checking with her, Betty?"

"Of course not, Gwen. You're going out of your way to handle those party dishes. Asking Gracie one simple question is the least I can do."

"Thank you." Then, so as to not be suspicious, Gwen added, "There's nothing like a bit of gossip around the holidays."

Betty laughed then picked at a non-existent thread on the placemat. "It just occurred to me, Gwen. Should we form a garden club delegation and call on Myrtle's family?"

"Good idea. I'm sure they'd appreciate our condolences. Let's check with Holly first, make sure we don't duplicate any of her plans." Gwen pulled her cell phone from her shoulder bag and scrolled through her contacts. "Do you have something I can write on?"

Betty nodded and stretched over, pulling open the top drawer of the sideboard. She lifted out a legal pad plus a handful of pens.

When Gwen's call was picked up, she embarked on a five-minute conversation with Holly before pressing the red button and twisting toward Betty. "She likes your idea of a condolence call and suggested a monetary donation to the family rather than flowers, but she's out straight with holiday shoppers and asked if we can handle it. She said to come down to her gift shop and pick up a check she'll write from the club's account."

"Holly has the checkbook?" Betty asked.

"Veronica always leaves it behind when she's going out of town. Holly's on the signing card at the bank. I'll let Veronica know what we're doing. She's working a tradeshow, but she should have her cell phone nearby."

Dialing a second number, Gwen engaged in another five-minute dialogue before disconnecting. "Veronica is shocked about Myrtle's death and agrees with the donation."

Betty peered at Gwen's cell phone. "Do you have Alicia's number? As the club secretary, maybe she can go with us."

A minute later, Gwen ended a third call. "She's busy with sick kids, so she can't join us. That's it for board members. Looks like it's just you and me. I'll email the members and let them know what we did."

When a timer pinged, Betty pushed back her chair. "You stay put. I'll bring our lunch." In short order, she carried in a tray laden with soup crocks, sliced bread, and honey butter. "After we finish eating, we can walk to Serendipity and pick up that donation check."

Betty waved her napkin at the pile of plates, platters, and bowls sitting at the other end of the dining room table. "Any idea which one belongs to Holly?"

***

At his desk in the police station, Ben was busy adding his morning activities into the Myrtle Mueller digital case file when Chief Mike Brown strolled into the detectives' room.

"Hey, Ben. Anything from your morning interviews?"

Ben pulled his notebook closer and fingered through the pages. "I spoke to the Pettigrew couple and the Schuster family. Only the Schuster boy noticed anything, and all he remembers is the red-and-white legs of the elf costume."

Mike laughed. "I like that kid." He headed toward the door then reversed direction. "Did you convince Gwen to sign up as your C.I?"

Ben removed the folded agreement from his inside pocket and waved it in the air. "Didn't have to convince her. After I explained that someone in Mr. Owens' group pushed Mrs.

74

Mueller, Gwen was eager to help me identify the culprit."

"If I remember, Ben, most of the group were garden club women. Unless you think the Harvard student wanted his aunt out of his life."

Ben shook his head. "I've talked to that young man, and I don't think he shoved his aunt. But there's another piece of the puzzle I didn't learn until a little while ago."

"What's that?" Mike settled into Ben's side chair.

"This is gonna sound like the script from a soap opera, but here goes." Ben relayed the gist of the whispered confrontation, then waited for the chief's reaction.

"That's quite a coincidence, Ben."

"And you know I don't believe in coincidences." Ben tapped his notebook for emphasis. "My gut tells me there's a connection between those combatants and Mrs. Mueller's death. Based on her money complaints, she could easily slide into the blackmailer's role. I'm going to assign Gwen to search for an adulterer in the garden club."

"Good luck with that, Ben. Let me know how our Gwen makes out." The chief headed off to another part of the station.

Ben registered Gwen's agreement in the coded file before stashing the document in the evidence room.

No matter which path this case traveled, Ben would be seeing Gwen the next morning. She would no doubt brighten his day.

Chapter Thirteen

…early afternoon, Thursday

Arms intertwined, Gwen and Betty maneuvered the sloping sidewalk of Harbor Hill, avoiding store owners tossing salt crystals or shoveling. If one went down, they'd both go down.

Inside the Serendipity Gift Shoppe, a gaggle of shoppers wandered among the displays of locally crafted items: hand-painted holiday themes on driftwood, half-size stuffed Santas, snowmen sporting cheeky grins, knitted sweaters, hand-made quilts. A fascinating array of unique items.

"Wow," Betty commented. "Holly's right that she's busy."

Gwen noticed Holly chatting with a lady in the far corner and pointed. "There she is." They stood patiently until Holly's sales pitch ended and she spotted them.

"Hi, Gwen. And you, too, Betty. Thanks for taking charge of condolence call. Let me get that donation for you." She hurried to the register and withdrew a check from the drawer.

Glancing around, Gwen asked, "Do you sell gift cards?"

"Sorry. Only gift certificates for my shop. You can buy a VISA card at the grocery store or CVS."

Gwen tucked the check into her shoulder bag. "Thanks."

Betty extended a paper bag. "We think this is yours."

Unrolling the top, Holly peeked inside and nodded. "Yep, that's my platter. Sorry I forgot to grab it last night."

"Don't apologize. Everyone left their serving dishes behind." Betty pointed to the nearest aisle. "I'm going to take a quick look around, Gwen."

As Betty wandered away, Holly's face distorted. She dipped her hand into the pocket of her cardigan and withdrew a tissue, lifting it to her nose a nano-second before she sneezed. "Sorry. I've caught the cold that's going around."

Gwen stepped away. "Hope it's gone before Christmas."

"Me, too." Holly reached below the counter and came up with a bottle of hand sanitizer. After squirting a few drops in her other palm, she extended the bottle toward Gwen's outstretched hand and squeezed again. "This stuff is the best invention."

A display on the wall caught Gwen's attention. "Can you hold that quilt for me? I'll pick it up in the next day or two."

"Sure." Holly's eyes roamed the variety of designs and pointed. "The seaside motif?"

After Gwen confirmed, Holly stretched her hand upward. Despite her height and long arms, she couldn't reach. Glancing around the shop, she called, "Kristin, I need you."

A thirty-something young woman with a wild mop of red curls waved from a pile of embroidered linens near the front window and headed their way. "What do you need, Holly?"

"First of all, this is Gwen Andrews from the garden club."

Kristin extended her hand. "Nice to meet you."

"She wants us to put aside that quilt." Holly pointed. "I'm tall, but I can't reach quite that high. Would you bring the ladder and hand it down to me?"

"Sure thing." Kristen ducked into a room behind the sales counter, hauled out a ladder, and secured the legs before scrambling up. She touched the first in the group. "This one?"

"The next one to your right." Holly stretched her arms upward to catch it. "Thanks, Kristin. That lady at the front window has a question."

"Nice to meet you," Kristin said before bouncing away.

While waiting for the layaway slip, Gwen's eyes roamed the shelves adjacent to the register, landing on a set of snowmen mugs. "Those are adorable, Holly. I'll take them, too."

"The blue ones?"

"Yes. That motif will be appropriate all winter."

"Smart choice. My customers are buying mostly holiday themed items." Holly wrapped each before adding them to Gwen's quilt bag. "The glaze on these earthenware mugs will retain their color if you wash them by hand."

"Thanks for that tip. How much for the deposit?"

"No deposit. Pay the total when you pick them up." Holly added the mugs to the layaway slip and extended a copy.

Gwen tucked it into her shoulder bag next to the garden club's check. "Were you nervous answering the detective's questions last night?"

Holly went silent for a moment. "If I had to assign a word, it would be unsettling. I've never been that close to a detective. He didn't ask much. Where I was standing when Myrtle screamed. Who was near me. Those kinds of details."

A woman shopper approached, her arms full. Holly reached out to transfer the gifts to the counter.

Betty appeared and looped her hand through the crook of Gwen's arm. "We'll leave you to your customers, Holly."

Gwen soon found herself standing on the sidewalk. "Why the rush, Betty?"

"Holly has some nice craft items, but they're pricey." Betty pointed across the street. "I want to see what Fiction 'n Fables Book Stop is offering in the expanded store. Do you mind if we have a look before we drive to Myrtle's house?"

Because Gwen's best friend Liz owned the bookstore, she didn't mind at all. Crossing the birch-lined median strip of Harbor Hill, they scurried between the cars and trucks crawling past, the drivers mindful of the snow beneath their tires. The bare-branched shadows on the white snow created a slightly spooky effect.

The bell above the door jangled as they entered Fiction 'n Fables. Liz and her salesclerk Olivia looked over from the new releases kiosk.

Liz squealed, "Gwen!" and rushed over.

Disentangling herself from her best friend's embrace, Gwen indicated Betty standing beside her. "Do you know Betty Owens? She and her husband Robert recently opened the Harbor Falls B&B at the top of the hill."

Liz studied Betty. "You *do* look familiar, but I don't think we've ever spoken."

"That's because I'm always in such a hurry," Betty offered.

Gwen glanced at the kiosk. "What's the new book?"

Reaching over, Liz hoisted a heavy volume. "It's the latest story from Diana Gabaldon in her *Outlander* series."

Gwen flipped to the back cover and read the blurb. "She's an amazing storyteller. I'll buy this one for my collection." Gwen handed the thick book to Olivia. "Could you begin a pile for me at the register?"

"Sure," Olivia answered, her gray pigtails wiggling as she walked away.

Gwen turned to Liz. "Show us your enlarged store."

"Of course. I'm loving the extra display space. Come and have a look."

Peering through a newly constructed archway into the center

section of the building, Gwen commented, "I see you broke through to the old cigar bar."

Liz's face drooped. "Sorry I haven't had a chance to keep you updated, Gwen. I organized the aromatherapy offerings just yesterday." She escorted Gwen and Betty into the adjacent retail area where a dozen shoppers wandered.

The former dark paneling of the ill-fated cigar bar had been painted a creamy white with taupe accents on the framework and wall shelves. Liz waved toward a huge circular display dominating the center of the space and filled with dried herbs. "These are for my potpourri do-it-yourselfers."

Betty stepped closer and chimed in. "I need to refresh my guest rooms. Herbs provide such a welcoming aroma."

"They do," Liz agreed. "Each bin is tagged with the name of the herb, its origin, and description of its scent."

While Betty filled a bag with an assortment of the dried leaves, Gwen sniffed the air. "What else am I smelling?"

Liz waved toward the counter along the rear wall where a mist escaped from a faux wooden sphere. "Today's essential oil combination is cinnamon, blood orange, and frankincense."

"I love it," Gwen said. "I'll take a bottle of each, and I'll need an infuser."

"Not an infuser," Liz corrected. "A diffuser."

"What's the difference?"

"An infuser is dropping a tea bag into hot water, or dropping cut-up oranges and mint into cold water. You infuse the water with the flavors. A diffuser sends a cool mist of scented water into the surrounding air."

Gwen grinned. "In that case, I'll take a *diffuser.*"

Liz plucked the requested items from the wall display,

placed them in a wicker shopping basket, added three glass eye droppers, and handed it to Gwen. "There are lots of essential oils. It's fun to experiment with different combinations."

"I'd love to stay and learn more, but Betty and I need to make a condolence call, so we have to scoot."

"Sorry to hear that. Who died?"

"A garden club member. Her name is...was...Myrtle Mueller."

Liz's head tilted. "Don't think I know her."

Betty came up beside them. "I doubt she ever stepped foot in here. Do you sell VISA gift cards, Liz?"

"Sorry, I don't."

Waving her hand in dismissal, Betty went on. "That's okay. Gwen and I will stop at the North Street CVS on our way."

***

Gwen had never visited Myrtle Mueller's home. Even with the woman's self-proclaimed master gardener status, Myrtle had never once volunteered her property for the annual garden tour. Gwen took in the tired Cape-style house. Any gardening efforts along the front and sides were hidden beneath the snow cover.

A young blonde female answered. "Yes, may I help you?"

Betty took charge. "We're from the garden club and came to pay our respects."

From inside, a man's voice boomed, "Who is it?"

"Some ladies from the garden club, Uncle Fletcher."

A tall gangly man with a sad-sack expression blocked the doorway. "I'm Myrtle's husband. Appreciate you stopping by, but I'm on the phone with the Mayflower Society."

Betty looked up at the tall man. "If you don't mind me asking, what is Myrtle's connection to the Mayflower?"

"Her maiden name was Brewster. She has documents passed down through her family proving she's a descendant of William Brewster. I'm checking if the Society wants her papers for their archives. It's for sure our son has no interest, but future generations might. Sorry, but I need to get back to my phone call." With that, he closed the door.

Sitting in Betty's van, safely out of earshot, Gwen quipped, "Is it my imagination or did Myrtle's husband not seem all that upset that she's gone?"

"I noticed that, too. It could be the shock hasn't hit him yet." Gwen dug into her purse, pulling out the club's gift card. "And he didn't give us a chance to present him with this."

"Plus we forgot to return Myrtle's baking dish. Let's knock on the door again and see what happens."

When they delivered the two items, the second visit was equally abrupt, punctuated only by a grunt of thanks from Myrtle's sour-faced husband.

As they drove away, Betty said, "I'm surprised I didn't pick up on Myrtle's ancestry when she nearly suffocated poor Charlie. The name Brewster should have struck a chord."

"And I'm wondering why she hasn't seen her nephew since he was ten," Gwen added. "Must be a story there. Do you suppose the blonde niece is Charlie's sister?"

"Most likely, but I'd only be guessing," Betty answered. "What shocks me is that Myrtle never mentioned her Mayflower connection."

The return drive to the B&B flew by in relative silence.

***

Betty waved Gwen to sit at the dining room table. "Thanks for helping me figure out what's going on with Theo."

"My experience with ghosts is limited to Parker, but I'll help you search for reasons to explain Theo's restlessness."

Opening the lower door of the sideboard, Betty hauled out three thick scrapbooks. "After Robert and I signed the papers to buy this house from Clara Carswell, she entrusted us with these binders. She insisted the family history belongs with the house." Betty pushed one book in front of Gwen, choosing another for herself. "I never examined this family history in depth. Now that we're looking specifically for details about Theo, these binders should prove invaluable."

For the next half hour, they slogged through letters, pictures, and genealogical records. Gwen flipped to yet another page, announcing, "Here's something."

Betty slid her chair closer. "What is it?"

"A wedding announcement." Gwen read aloud:

Mr. and Mrs. Elias Carswell of Harbor Falls
have the pleasure of announcing
the marriage of their daughter
Theodosia Charity Carswell
to
Nehemiah Linus Brewster of Plymouth
on
Saturday, the Twentieth of December,
Nineteen Hundred Twenty-Four
Trinitarian Congregational Church
Harbor Falls, Massachusetts

After Gwen finished reciting the words, she turned her head to see Betty staring at her.

Together, they mouthed, "Brewster?"

"Oh, my gosh, Gwen. Do you think it's possible that Theo's beau was an ancestor to both Myrtle and Charlie?"

"If those three *are* related, Betty, do you think it's possible Theo recognized Charlie and Myrtle as descendants of her bridegroom? But why would she have gone after them?"

"I just don't know, Gwen. I hate to think Theo shoved Charlie from his bed or pushed Myrtle."

Having already discounted Theo's physical ability to do either, Gwen remained curious about their connection. To relieve some of Betty's distress, she said, "Only Theo knows."

Gwen didn't voice the similarity between the deaths of Theo and Myrtle on the same stretch of unforgiving wooden steps. No doubt Betty had already gone there.

As Gwen was letting her words settle, a wacky thought occurred to her. "I have an idea, Betty. But first, I need to share something with you."

For the next few minutes, Betty sat quietly, listening as Gwen retold the details of her reunions with Parker's spirit.

Betty looked up, her eyes sparkling. "That's amazing."

"You believe me?"

"Every word."

Gwen released a breath. "I was afraid you'd think I imagined Parker or that I dreamed up his appearances."

"Not at all. Because of my encounters with Theo, I'll believe anyone who admits they have a ghost. Parker's visits must bring you joy."

"Elation is more like it."

"Does your idea involve his spirit?"

"I'm wondering if he can appear somewhere besides our home."

"You're thinking you can call him here?" Betty waved to include the entire B&B.

"It's worth a try. If I'm successful, he can search for Theo and ask her the questions we've been asking ourselves."

"What an irresistible plan. I want to include Robert, and we should wait until our guests are out for the day."

"How soon should we make the attempt?"

"The sooner the better. How about tomorrow?"

Gwen checked her cell phone calendar, seeing only that she'd invited Ben for breakfast and an update meeting. "I've got errands in the morning, but I can stop over when I'm done."

"That works. Our guests head out after breakfast and usually don't return until later in the day."

Rising to her feet, Gwen said, "Sorry, but I need to get home and feed my cat. I'll call you when I'm on my way."

Gwen pointed at the pile of serving dishes taking up space on Betty's table. "I'll drive over tomorrow. After we hopefully bring Parker and Theo together, I'll load up my trunk."

Hugging Betty good-bye, Gwen strode across the village green, pondering the likelihood of Parker responding to her call from the B&B. It certainly would add a new twist to her personal collection of ghost stories.

Chapter Fourteen

...late afternoon, Thursday

Back home in her music studio, Gwen read the directions for her new diffuser, added filtered water and the essential oils of blood orange, cinnamon, and Frankincense, and plugged it in. When she pressed the 'on' button, a cloud of mist shot from the opening. The scent drifted past her nose, energizing her mood.

She recalled Ben's request that she keep a record of her interactions with garden club members. A stickler for detail – some would call Gwen a nitpicker or worse – she found an unused stenography pad tucked among blank recipe cards and post-it notes in a kitchen drawer. "Perfect."

Turning to the first page, she began with last evening's Christmas party, touched on the Yankee Swap game, the names of the members who participated in the house tours, and Myrtle's fall with minimal details.

Flipping to the next page to denote a new day, she wrote the date and time they'd returned Holly's platter, picked up the check for the condolence offering, and purchased the gift card at CVS. As an afterthought, she added their stymied visit with Fletcher Mueller.

The house phone rang.

"Want to meet me for an early dinner?"

Gwen leaned against the kitchen island, portable receiver to her ear. "I'd love to, Hal. You won't believe what happened at our garden club party last night."

"Why don't you meet me at that new pizza place south of

the high school and you can tell me what happened. I have some news myself."

"You're sounding very mysterious. Give me a half hour. I'll see you there."

***

As Gwen entered, the tantalizing smell of tomato pies baking in brick ovens enveloped her, heightening her appetite. Murals of Italian scenes covered three walls of the Pizza Palace.

Hal leaned against the counter, a big smile on his face as he watched her approach. Gwen had often toyed with the idea of submitting his photo to a talent agency as a slightly younger stand-in for her favorite actor Hal Holbrook.

Her Hal didn't speak until she was close enough to hear. "I called in our order before I drove over. They're cutting the slices now. Bacon and mushrooms on your half? Well done?"

"Perfect." She followed him as he carried their pizza to a nearby table. She smoothed the red and white checkered tablecloth. "You're very upbeat tonight."

His blue eyes twinkled as he transferred slices to their plates. "Is that a bad thing?"

"Not at all. What's your news?" Unlike most people, Gwen ate pizza with a knife and fork. While she waited for Hal to answer, she savored her first mouthful.

"You first. What happened at your party?"

She held up a finger until she swallowed, and then abbreviated the party events, ending with Myrtle's death.

Hal's light-hearted demeanor dissipated. "That's terrible. How did the other women react?"

"Everyone was upset. Some members stayed behind to give their witness statement. The rest of us were sent home."

Gwen purposely omitted the involvement of Ben Snowcrest. Last April, when she'd been working closely with Ben on the cigar bar case, Hal had acted like a jealous high school bully. She also omitted that Ben had asked her to be his C.I. She finished her story with, "Everyone left their serving dishes behind. I told Betty I'd reunite those pieces with their owners."

"Hmmm. You need to tell her to handle that."

"Why?"

As an answer, Hal reached inside his jacket pocket and extended an envelope, grinning like a ten-year-old boy. "Early Christmas gift, Gwen."

She lifted the flap and pulled out a ticket. "What's this?"

"Just what it says. You're flying with me and Jenna to Florida. We leave Saturday morning."

The printed details floated before Gwen's eyes. "Did you forget I invited you and Jenna to Tess's for Christmas dinner?"

Hal's eyebrows scrunched. "I never promised we'd go with you. I've been planning this trip for quite a while."

"And I've been planning the holidays with my sister and our relatives for quite a while."

"Hold on, Gwen. Any sane person would jump at this chance to escape the snow and ice."

"So you're saying I'm not a sane person." How insulting could the man be? Despite her commitment to help Ben with the case, she said, "Why don't you rebook after the holidays so I can go with you?"

"Can't do that, Gwen. I scheduled it during Jenna's college break so she can fly with us and offer her opinion."

"Her opinion about what?"

His expression softened. "I guess I need to explain."

"Please do." Gwen's stomach lurched. She wasn't sure she wanted to hear what Hal was about to say.

Pushing aside the cooling pizza, Hal leaned across the table and locked eyes with her. "I'm getting too old to be a slave to the nursery. Jenna's not interested in taking over the family business. I'll hire Oscar to manage the place until it's sold."

Gwen's ability to speak abandoned her. She couldn't picture Hal without his greenhouses, his fields of perennials, the seasonal flowers at his garden center. "When..." she stuttered, "...when did you decide to uproot your life?"

"If I have to pick a day, I'd say late summer."

"And you never said anything?"

"I didn't want to bother you until I was ready."

Gwen stared at this man she thought she'd gotten to know over the past year or so. He seemed more a stranger. "How is selling your nursery connected to your Florida flight?"

"I'm tired of Massachusetts winters and I want to move south where it's warmer." He reached over and enclosed her soft hands in his rough ones. "And I want you to move with me, Gwen. This trip is to find and purchase a suitable home."

Shock did not begin to describe Gwen's reaction. She recoiled, pulled her hands out from under his, and leaned as far away as the chair would allow. Since the day Hal asked for her friendship, they'd never once discussed living together.

And now Hal expected her to sacrifice her holiday plans for his last-minute flight to go house-hunting. Plus pack up her belongings and live with him in an as-yet-unpurchased home in an unknown Florida town. *Who at this table is insane?*

"To use a tired cliché, Hal, Florida's a nice place to visit, but I wouldn't want to live there."

"But you told me you enjoyed your Gulf Coast vacations with your husband."

"And that's true. Parker and I had a lot of fun. But spending a few weeks as a tourist during the winter months is totally different from living there as a permanent resident. I have no plans to move away from Harbor Falls." Gwen didn't mention she'd never leave her home where Parker's spirit appeared.

Hal snapped his fingers. "I know why you're resisting my plan, Gwen. I have no intention of forcing myself on you. I've accepted that you're not interested in a physical relationship."

On this point, Hal was exactly right. The one time Hal had tried to coax Gwen into his bed, she'd pulled away at the last second. After thirty-seven years of a nearly perfect marriage, she hadn't been willing to expose her aging body to another man. And she hadn't wanted to ruin her friendship with Hal for a brief – and potentially unsatisfying – roll in the hay.

Hal was still talking. "I can't imagine my life without you, Gwen. I'll buy a place with more than one bedroom, so you'll have your privacy." Without waiting for her to comment, he held up her ticket and shook it. "How can you refuse this?"

"You're not hearing me, Hal. I'm spending the holiday with Tess. I invited you and Jenna to join my family celebration. Seems to me *you're* the one who's refusing *me*."

He slapped the plane ticket on the table where it sat between them like the proverbial white elephant. "Can't you skip Christmas with your sister this year?"

Heaviness blanketed Gwen's heart. She'd extended her invitation to Hal and Jenna over a month ago. She now knew he'd already decided to book these flights, wrongly assuming Gwen would agree to his last-minute get-away.

Now here they sat at an impasse in a pizza parlor. "I don't know how to say this any clearer, Hal. I have no intention of skipping the holidays with Tess."

His fingers drummed the tabletop. "But you can visit your sister whenever you want. She's only a few hours' drive. How often are you invited to Florida during the winter months?"

Gwen's hackles rose in defiance. "This is Tess's first Christmas without Nathan. I wouldn't dream of not showing up. Besides, she's arranged for our last surviving aunt to join us, as well as cousins I haven't seen for years."

Hal again enclosed her hands in his. "You have to change your mind. I'm uncomfortable buying a place without you."

"Even if I'll never live there?" She glanced from him to the ticket. "If you can change the dates to January, I'll help you evaluate condos, double-wide homes, cottages, and houses. But I have no desire to move to Florida."

His salt-and-pepper head moved side to side. "No can do. Like I told you earlier, I have to take this trip while Jenna's on Christmas break. I expect you to meet us at the airport on Saturday morning."

Straining to remain calm, Gwen again pulled her hands out from under his. "Tell you what. You fly to Florida and house hunt with your granddaughter. I'll drive to the Berkshires to celebrate Christmas with my family." She nudged the ticket across the tablecloth. "You should request a credit for this."

Hal surged to his feet, his blue eyes turned stormy. "Keep it. When you come to your senses, meet us at the airport on Saturday morning."

Hal stalked out, leaving Gwen to stare after him.

Flabbergasted by his domineering attitude, she stared at the remaining slices of pizza, now stone cold. The temptation to eat even one more bite vanished.

***

That evening, Gwen wandered the rooms, her mind a jumble of conflict. Hal's unexpected flight to Florida. His assumption that she'd go with him. His disrespectful words when she turned him down.

Hal Jenkins had occupied a special place in Gwen's world for more than a year. He'd offered his companionship as she emerged from her mourning for Parker. She'd always hold dear the time she'd spent with Hal, but she wasn't willing to leave Harbor Falls for him.

Gwen squared her shoulders and drifted into her music studio. Flipping the switch on her new diffuser, she sent the scented vapor into the air for its soothing aromatherapy.

When a tail rubbed against Gwen's ankles, she looked down into Amber's green eyes. Picking up her pet, Gwen settled on the bench at her Steinway, a gift from Parker on move-in day more than ten years before. Burying her nose in the critter's sweet fur, she gazed out the mullioned windows, surveying her winter-weary gardens, lit only by the landscape lights.

She whispered into the cat's twitching ear. "You and I will never leave our wonderful home, Amber. We need to be here for Parker's ghostly visits."

As if the cat understood, she glanced around. When Gwen squeezed Amber's plump body, the cat squirmed to be released.

Gwen's angst about Hal's plans was replaced by her promise to prepare two reports for Ben. She retrieved her laptop and settled at her great-grandmother's maple table in the dining room. Her fingers flew across the keys as she typed a first draft of the conversation between the adulterer and the blackmailer. As their words floated past, Gwen adjusted the report. The project not only took her mind off Hal's plans, but wrapped her in the challenge of figuring out the identity of those whisperers.

Finally satisfied with her transcript, she requested copies on the wireless printer in the guest room. She closed out that first file, opened a second, and listed the sequence of events on party night. Using bulleted format, she included as much specificity as she could recall. If she was over-reporting, Ben could ignore the portions he deemed unimportant. Finished, she again requested printouts, saved the file, and went to bed.

***

A few miles north of Gwen's, Ben hunched over his desk in the deserted police station. He pulled up an email from Otis and printed the final autopsy report. Then he reviewed the scribbles in his notebook, puzzling over Myrtle Mueller's death until he yawned.

Ben headed to his apartment because he deserved a night of rest… if his subconscious didn't keep him twisting in his sheets until morning.

Chapter Fifteen

...early morning, Friday

Unsettling dreams wakened Gwen throughout the night.

Where had Hal gotten the idea that he could dictate her life? He'd bought her plane ticket without her knowledge or consent. He'd assumed she'd dismiss her plans to celebrate Christmas at Tess's in favor of his house-hunting trip. And what made him think she'd pack up and relocate to Florida?

Had she misunderstood Hal when he'd asked for her friendship last year? He'd assured her he wasn't looking for a commitment, suggesting they simply enjoy each other's company. And they had. Dinners, nature walks, local plays. Had he all along planned a more permanent relationship?

Gwen had wrongly assumed her buddy Hal would always be around. His rejection of the blustery chill of Massachusetts' winters in favor of Florida's sunshine and warmth had never crossed her mind.

Her thoughts were disrupted when the phone rang.

"Morning, Gwen. Thought I'd call before your day ran away with you."

Gwen recognized her sister's voice in a nanosecond and sat up in bed. "Hi, Tess. I was going to call you later today."

"You were?"

"Yep. Must be our sisterly ESP." Gwen plumped the pillows behind her and glanced at the clock. Not quite seven.

Tess chuckled. "Sorry to call so early, but I have a busy day ahead of me. I'm finalizing the sleeping arrangements for the family reunion next weekend." Tess hardly took a breath. "Most of the relatives made reservations at that motel at the bottom of my mountain. Aunt Nellie will sleep on my office daybed. You and Hal in my guestroom twin beds with a cot for Jenna."

"Sorry to upset your arrangements, Tess, but Hal and Jenna made other plans."

"They did?"

"They did," Gwen repeated. "Last night Hal invited me to meet him for pizza and handed me a plane ticket. Said I should skip your holiday dinner and fly to Florida with him and Jenna to shop for a new home."

Tess's silence spoke volumes. "Why does Hal need a home in Florida?"

Gwen's throat tightened. "He's selling the family nursery and moving south."

"Wow. That's a shock. Did you know about this?"

"Not a clue."

"Did you accept his plane ticket?"

"Just the opposite. I refused it. I wouldn't miss your Christmas reunion dinner for the world."

"Whew, that's a relief. I thought for a second you were going to tell me you decided to fly to Florida with Hal. How did he react when you told him no?"

"He bullied me, Tess. It's a side of him I've never seen, and I didn't like it one bit."

"Can't say I blame you, Sis. What happens now?"

"I guess our friendship has run its course. Hal's plans kept me up last night."

"Which part?" Tess asked. "The fact that he gave you no warning or his assumption that you'd fly down with him?"

"Both I guess."

The sisters remained silent until Tess spoke. "To be honest, I'm surprised something like this hasn't happened before."

"What are you saying?"

"I'm not sure how to phrase this. Hal's a nice guy on the surface, but do you remember how upset you were last spring when he broke his promise?"

"You're referring to his cigar-smoking?"

"Bingo. After you explained your aversion to cigar smoke because of our cigar-smoking uncle, Hal promised he'd give up cigars. The very next day, you caught him and his foreman Oscar puffing away between the greenhouses. I was there, Gwen. I witnessed your devastation. You avoided him for days until he promised a second time that he'd never smoke another cigar. You let him back into your life, but I've always wondered if you ever truly forgave him for his disrespect."

Gwen couldn't argue with Tess's interpretation of the incident and its effect.

Tess kept talking. "And now Hal insisted you give up your holiday plans with me to help him house-hunt in Florida. I don't mean to sound harsh, Gwen, but I'm not all that broken up that he's planning to move away."

Imagine Tess's reaction if she learned the rest of Hal's plan...that Gwen pack up and move south with him. Since she had no intention of leaving Harbor Falls, there was no need to mention that detail to her sister.

Tess's voice spoke into Gwen's ear once again, her tone charged with enthusiasm. "On the positive side, I'm glad you chose my holiday dinner over a last-minute trip to Florida. Christmas wouldn't be the same without you."

Inwardly, Gwen was relieved that the conversation had moved away from Hal and onto a more cheerful topic. She collected her senses and her voice. "I feel the same way, Tess. Christmas in the south doesn't feel right. I need snow and sleigh rides and chestnuts roasting on an open fire."

Tess laughed. "Can't say I blame you. Have you decided what day you're driving over?"

"Next Friday if that works for you."

"That's perfect. Do you mind picking up Aunt Nellie on your way?"

"Mind? Of course not. How did you convince her to join the family? She hardly ever leaves her little house."

Tess's laughter bounced through the handset. "Lots of cajoling. Told her she needs to make the stuffing because hers was always the tastiest. Convinced her she'd be the queen bee at the reunion since she's the last of her generation."

"Apparently your silver tongue is still in good form, Tess."

"We're going to have a full table for dinner, Gwen. I'll email a list."

For a brief second, Gwen considered mentioning Myrtle's death, then realized Tess had never met the woman. "I'll watch for your email."

"We'll talk again before next Friday." Tess broke the connection.

Gwen hopped out of bed, took a quick shower, and got dressed. Down in the kitchen, she put on a pot of decaf coffee. While it brewed, she pawed through her recipe collection until she came upon her dog-eared directions for Date Nut Bread. Tucking the recipe into her pocket, she began to prepare breakfast. Ben would be arriving soon.

97

***

On the other side of town, Ben knocked on the front door of the Mueller house. Muffled conversation came from inside and then a shuffling noise grew louder. The door flew open.

"Fletcher Mueller?" Ben asked the unshaven man.

"Yea, that's me. Who are you and what do you want?"

Ben held up his badge. "I'm Detective Ben Snowcrest. I've come with an update of your wife's death. My condolences, sir. Can I come in?"

Reluctantly, Fletcher opened the door just wide enough for Ben to squeeze through. The man didn't seem overjoyed to have a stranger inside his house. And the reason was soon apparent.

Behind the door, unopened boxes from QVC were piled high. In addition to the apparent buying addiction, there was evidence of hoarding. Stacks of newspapers, crushed cartons, cleaning supplies, baking dishes, empty jars and soda bottles littered every surface in a helter-skelter manner. Ben had heard about this OCD condition, but had never witnessed the residence of a hoarder. Had these compulsions plagued Fletcher or his wife Myrtle?

Mr. Mueller led Ben through the maze toward the kitchen. A young blonde woman leaned against the sink, looking none too happy. She nodded at Ben but didn't say anything.

"Have a seat, Detective," Fletcher mumbled, transferring a stack of papers to another chair. "Excuse the mess. My niece is here to help me get rid of all this stuff."

Ben wiped the chair's surface with his gloved hand and sat. "I won't stay long, Mr. Mueller. I'm here to tell you that the medical examiner ruled her death suspicious. I'm heading up a full-blown investigation."

Fletcher Mueller grabbed the edge of the stove where only a single burner was exposed. His face fell and a lone tear leaked from one eye. He quickly wiped at it with his sleeve. "So someone pushed her?"

"That's the working theory," Ben answered. "My job is to figure out who."

"She was there for the damn garden club party. Why was she at the top of those old steps?"

Ben shifted his weight on the chair, his neck kinking from looking up at the tall man. "Apparently the president of the club asked for a tour of the B&B, and your wife joined in."

"Figures. Myrtle's always had a nosey streak." Fletcher pushed himself upright. "Thanks for stopping by, Detective. I'll see you out."

***

Gwen handed Ben a mug of coffee as he settled on an island stool. He pulled out his notebook and flipped to a blank page, scribbling in his small script. She took advantage of his distraction to finish crisping the bacon and making pancakes embedded with banana slices.

Ben glanced up. "You're quiet this morning."

"I didn't sleep well last night."

"Mrs. Mueller's death bothering you?"

Debating how much of her personal life to share, Gwen decided Ben was fast becoming a good friend. "That plus a bit of unsettling news from Hal Jenkins." She shared Hal's decision to sell Jenkins Nursery, his flight to Florida on Saturday to hunt for a new home, and his plans to move south.

Ben stared at her. "That's the last thing I expected you to tell me. Will you be joining him?"

"Well, there's the rub, Ben. Hal bought me a plane ticket and expected me to change my Christmas plans with my sister, help find a house, and move there with him. No, I'm not going."

"Can I assume you won't be moving either?"

"You assume correctly. Relocating to Florida doesn't tempt me in the least. I've lived in Harbor Falls since I graduated college, and I plan to stay here for the rest of my days."

As had happened during her chat with Tess, Gwen was adjusting to the idea of life without Hal. She divided the bacon and pancakes onto plates and handed one to Ben.

He picked up his fork. "Thanks. This smells good."

Gwen continued her explanation. "I've had plans to celebrate Christmas with my sister for months."

"How is your sister?"

Gwen's head jerked up. She'd forgotten Ben had met Tess the previous April. "She's doing okay. This is her first Christmas without Nathan, so she organized a family reunion for the holiday dinner next weekend."

"Sounds like fun."

"I'm sure it will be." Suddenly famished, Gwen gobbled half her bacon strips before speaking again. "What are your Christmas plans, Ben?"

"The usual. You remember I'm divorced with no kids?"

Gwen nodded as she chewed.

"Most of my relatives live on the West Coast, so I rarely see them. For the past few years, I've organized dinner at The Wharf for the guys at the station with no local family. Five of us this year. It's become a tradition."

Despite Ben's prideful tone, Gwen suspected he missed a family-oriented celebration.

"So you'll be making the journey to Tess's by yourself?"

Though his question surprised Gwen, she answered, "Looks that way. At least until I pick up my aunt."

"The winter road conditions concern me. I'd be happy to be your chauffer."

Knifing through her stack of pancakes, Gwen considered his offer but stopped herself from accepting. Who was she to expect Ben to change his plans with the guys at the last minute?

"I appreciate your offer, Ben, but I don't mind the drive."

"If you change your mind, my offer stands." He pushed his plate away and flipped through his notes. "I stopped at the Mueller house earlier this morning."

"Are you the officer who informed the family of Myrtle's death the other night?"

"No, I was busy collecting witness statements. Officer Ed handled the family notification. He said Mr. Mueller hardly reacted and took the news with a straight face."

"Maybe he broke down after the officer left."

"Maybe," Ben agreed. "Everyone reacts in their own way."

Gwen let his theory register, recalling her crippling reaction to Parker's death. "Why did you stop there this morning?"

"To advise Mr. Mueller that his wife's death was not an accident. He could barely open the door, but when he did, I saw evidence of a hoarder. He noticed me glancing around and explained that he and his niece were clearing out the clutter."

Gwen rested her chin in her palm. "I had no idea."

"You wouldn't unless you went inside."

"Funny you should say that. I've always wondered why Myrtle never offered her home for a club meeting or volunteered her property for the year-end garden tour."

"Well, you mentioned that she blamed the financial burden of her grandson's college tuition on the fact that he didn't win the music competition scholarship."

Gwen flinched. "She never stopped blaming me that Jenna Jenkins won that scholarship."

Ben looked up from his notes. "Do you think that was true?"

"Not at all. As a music teacher, I prepared Jenna for the competition at Hal's request. When one of the three judges dropped out for medical reasons, the committee hired a prior professor at Baylies. When she met an untimely death, I was convinced to replace her."

"Didn't that create a conflict because your student was competing?"

"That's what I thought until they told me I'd be excused from the panel during Jenna's performance. The scores of the other two judges were averaged to replace mine. Jenna's talent won fair and square without any unfair advantage."

"But Mrs. Mueller never believed it?"

"No, she didn't. And she reminded me of her grandson's ruination every chance she got."

"Well, now that I've seen her shopping addiction, I'm wondering if the financial burden was self-inflicted."

"I'm wondering the same thing," Gwen agreed.

Ben flipped to a previous page. "Let me think out loud for a second. We're faced with potentially overlapping mysteries. First, there are your whisperers."

"Do you think they were guests?"

"Feasible, but doubtful. More likely local residents. They're only relevant to Mrs. Mueller's suspicious death case if she was the blackmailer."

Ben rested his forearms on the island granite. "Let's assume for the sake of discussion that she *was* the whispering blackmailer. With or without her husband's knowledge, she demanded money from the adulterer to keep the affair quiet."

When Ben paused to doodle, Gwen didn't interrupt, not wanting to break his train of thought.

"When the house tour paused near the top of those servant steps," he continued, "the adulterer took advantage and shoved Mrs. Mueller hard enough to leave those bruises."

Gwen leaned closer. "So Myrtle's fall couldn't have been planned ahead of time."

"Exactly. This was a crime of opportunity."

"Do you think the shove was a warning for the blackmailer to back off and not expose the adulterer?"

"Hard to say. I'd guess the adulterer was filled with rage and didn't consider the consequences. At least that's my theory until a better one comes along."

Ben closed his notebook. "None of the direct witnesses recalled the person next to them when Mrs. Mueller screamed. I'll re-interview each person in Robert Owens' group plus Robert himself. Maybe by now one of them has remembered some detail that's relevant."

Gwen cringed. "I refuse to believe Robert did it."

"I understand your resistance, but it's important to keep an open mind while we investigate."

Not wanting to argue with Ben, Gwen pushed aside her resolve about Robert's innocence.

Ben focused his gray eyes on her. "I need you to concentrate on the garden club members as potential whisperers. Are you still okay as my C.I.? Any second thoughts?"

Gwen shook her head. "None. The person who pushed Myrtle needs to be held accountable."

"Can you find a reason to visit your gardening friends?"

"Already have one. I told Betty I'd return the food containers everyone left behind."

"Perfect. Don't be obvious, but listen carefully to what each woman has to say."

"Even if she wasn't with Robert's tour?"

"Definitely. There's no way to predict the gossip each one might share with you."

Gwen reached for her steno pad and held it up. "I started a notebook like you asked."

"Good. A record of who, what, and when comes in handy."

Gwen remembered Cyril Pettigrew's complaint to Betty. "Will you be releasing any of the B&B guests?"

Ben ran his finger along the edge of the granite counter. "Except for the Harvard boys, the other B&B guests weren't on Robert's tour. Only Waldo Schuster peeked out his door and noticed Holly Nichols' red-and-white legs. I plan to tell the Pettigrew couple and the Schuster family that they're free to leave as they'd planned."

"Oh, that's a relief," Gwen commented. "I'm going to the B&B later. Do you want me to let Betty know?"

"Not something you should handle, Gwen. I'm stopping over there after we're finished here to interview Miss Hammond and update Mr. and Mrs. Owens."

Heat crept up Gwen's neck. She'd overstepped her role.

Chapter Sixteen

…mid-morning, Friday

Ben pretended not to notice Gwen's embarrassment. Although he appreciated her enthusiasm, he didn't want her to unwittingly reveal their partnership and ruin her chances of uncovering relevant information.

To Gwen, he said, "It's important no one suspects our collaboration. In fact, for our next meeting, I'll park nearby and enter from your deck."

Gwen nodded but said nothing.

"Did you write down your recollection of that front parlor conversation and the timeline on party night?"

"I did. I'll get the copies." Gwen strode to her music studio.

While Ben waited for her return, he contemplated Gwen's earlier news, ecstatic to hear that Hal Jenkins would be relocating to Florida. That man had made a big blunder assuming Gwen would move south. Hal's loss was Ben's gain. He was ready and willing to slide into the role of the new man in Gwen's life.

She returned, her hand clutching several papers, and handed the top sheet to him. "This is the whispered conversation. I'm aggravated that I didn't recognize either voice."

"Don't beat yourself up. We'll eventually figure out who they were."

After reading her account of the confrontation, Ben tapped the page. "Mention this whenever you talk to the club members. One of them is bound to have an idea who they might be."

"Can I ask a question, Ben?"

"Sure."

"How often do your C.I.'s get into trouble while they're gathering information?"

"Why do you ask?"

"Well, if you determine that Charlie, Shawn, Dylan, and Robert Owens weren't involved in Myrtle's fall, that would leave the six garden club members. If one of them is guilty, won't she wonder why I'm talking to the others?"

"Oh, I don't think so, Gwen. If you offer support for their shock at Myrtle's death, you'll enhance your role as the club's VP. Sharing your curiosity about these whisperers," he held up her printed page, "will be a juicy piece of gossip. None of them should suspect you're working with me. Even the guilty one."

"I hope you're right."

"But you bring up a good point. My C.I.'s have always been men. Why don't you text me before you head out? Let me know where you're going and who you'll be talking to. Then a second text when you walk in your door. Does that ease your mind?"

Gwen relaxed. "A little bit. If you're aware of my comings and goings, you'll always know where I am. What could possibly go wrong?"

"I can't imagine anything, Gwen."

They both sat in silence until Ben spoke again. "Here's another idea. Buy yourself a can of pepper spray."

"Isn't that illegal?"

"Not anymore. The law was changed a few years ago. Dick's Sporting Goods carries the Mace brand. Buy the one marked Police Model. Carry it in your pocket whenever you leave the house, and you'll always have a ready defense."

"I'll do that, Ben. Thanks."

He lifted his empty mug. "Any more coffee in the carafe?"

***

As they waited for a fresh pot to brew, Gwen handed Ben her bulleted printout of the timeline, feeling like a grade school kid waiting for the teacher's approval.

He glanced at the first page. "I'm going to read your summary out loud. Hearing the words might remind you of anything you overlooked." He cleared his throat and began.

- Holly Nichols interrupted Betty Owens' conversation with Gwen Andrews in the front parlor, asking Betty to open the buffet and begin the party.
- Myrtle Mueller stopped beside Gwen and remarked about the burden of her grandson's college tuition.

Ben stopped reading. "I'm glad you wrote this in third person. If anyone else in the department reads it, the details will be crystal clear." Returning to her report, he continued.

- The Schuster family came through the front door and chatted with the club for a few minutes before heading upstairs. The pre-teen son Waldo ignored his father's warning and raced up the staircase.
- The three Harvard students returned after beers and karaoke at The Wharf. Betty introduced the boys and Myrtle Mueller recognized Charlie Brewster as her nephew. She nearly strangled him with a bear hug. Charlie asked if there were any more breakfast muffins and Holly offered the club's buffet leftovers.
- A female barbershop quartet Betty had hired arrived and entertained for half an hour.
- After the singers departed, Holly announced the Yankee

Swap. She instructed everyone to toss their paper plates in the trash and take a bathroom break.

• As Gwen was tossing her plate and utensils, she remembered she'd left her swap gift in the front parlor and headed in that direction. The pocket door was not quite closed, and she heard angry whispers inside.

• *[see separate account of confrontation].*

Again, Ben stopped reading. "You listened to the entire conversation?"

Gwen felt her face warm. "I couldn't help it, Ben."

"I'm not chastising you. I just want to be sure you heard enough." He returned to reading:

• Gwen knocked on the pocket door, spoke, then slid it open to find the parlor empty. Earlier, she hadn't noticed an adjacent door into the dining room. She rushed through to see the club members milling about, but none of them seemed breathless or acted guilty.

• Gwen retrieved her gift from the parlor and returned to the living room.

• During the Yankee Swap, B&B guests the Pettigrews appeared in the archway wondering what the ruckus was about.

For a third time, Ben stopped reading. "Had the Pettigrews just returned, or were they already in the house?"

"Let me think," Gwen said, waiting for her memory to kick in. "They weren't wearing coats, so I'd guess they'd been upstairs in their room."

"You're doing great, Gwen. Let's keep going."

• The club members were showing the Pettigrews the swap gifts when Brooke Hammond came in from outside. She had a headache and went directly upstairs.

- At the end of the swap, Holly suggested the house tour.

After Ben finished reading the last entry, Gwen asked, "Were these details helpful?"

"Definitely," he answered. "I needed your reports in black and white for the file. But I also needed a clearer picture of who was in the B&B when you heard the whisperers. Based on your summary, Miss Hammond is the only guest who wasn't on the property." Ben flipped over the last page, looking for a continuation. "Am I missing a page?"

"No," Gwen answered. "I assumed you knew the rest from your interviews, so I didn't bother."

He handed her the printouts. "Could you keep going? You can stop when you left the B&B."

"Sure, Ben, that's not a problem." Gwen accepted her pages. "By the way, I've eliminated Gracie Tyler as a whisperer."

Ben held his pen in mid-air. "Who is she? She isn't on my list of witnesses. And, furthermore, why is that?"

"Oh, she's someone Betty has helping her at the inn. She was there while we were eating, refilling some bits of the buffet, but she left before the Yankee Swap began. Yesterday, I shared the whispered threat with Betty and asked if Gracie could have been one of them. Betty said Gracie can't speak. A childhood illness damaged her vocal cords."

"But she could have noticed who entered the dining room from the front parlor after you interrupted the whisperers."

"That same thought occurred to me. Betty offered to ask."

Ben shifted on the stool. "I'm not comfortable involving Mrs. Owens in our investigation. How did she react when she heard the blackmailer's threat?"

"Betty's as curious as I am, especially since they could be two of her guests."

Ben tapped his pen on the page. "I guess it won't do any harm for Mrs. Owens to ask this Gracie."

Gwen carried their plates to the kitchen sink, her back to him as she spoke. "On a related topic, I know you're skeptical about the B&B's ghost, but both Betty and Robert are worried that rumors of a destructive spirit will devastate their future bookings."

Ben watched as Gwen rinsed the dishes before tucking them into the dishwasher, her movements smooth and purposeful. He forced his eyes away to regain his concentration. "How are Mr. and Mrs. Owens going to disprove the involvement of..." he paused to remember. "Theo, isn't it?"

"That's right. Her full name was Theodosia Charity Carswell. Her portrait hangs at the top of the front staircase."

Ben didn't miss the fact that Gwen had side-stepped the first part of his question. How an intelligent woman like Gwen could believe that spirits walked among humans was beyond Ben's grasp. But he wouldn't insult her conviction. That would destroy any chance he had of becoming the next significant man in her life.

Keeping his reaction to himself, he changed the subject. "Tell me, Gwen, do you think any of the remaining six club women could be the adulterer?"

Gwen flexed her shoulder. "I truly have no idea."

Ben suddenly felt sorry for her. Unlike their April case, where most of the suspects were strangers, Gwen's involvement in this case placed her in an awkward position with her garden club friends. "I'm aware I'm asking a lot of you."

"Thanks, Ben, but don't worry. I want to help you find the person who pushed Myrtle."

Ben needed to tread carefully, but wanted his skepticism in plain sight. "Ghost or not?"

"Ghost or not," Gwen confirmed, her chin lowered.

Ben pictured Gwen wearing glasses, peering over the rims like a schoolmarm. Glancing at the kitchen clock, Ben pocketed his notebook. "It's nearly ten. Can you meet me at the B&B?"

"I didn't think you wanted me to go with you."

"Sorry if I gave you that impression. I'll come up with a reason to explain your presence to the Owens. Besides, I still need to interview Brooke Hammond and I'd like your reaction to her answers."

"Betty's expecting me later this morning to pick up the dishes for return to the other club members," Gwen responded. "I'll just be arriving earlier than she and I discussed."

Chapter Seventeen

...mid-morning, Friday

After parking her Sonata near Ben's SUV in the B&B's rear parking lot, Gwen walked beside him to the front porch. He lifted the heavy door knocker and let it drop.

They waited until Betty opened the door. "Good morning, Detective Snowcrest, and you, too, Gwen. I didn't expect to see you until later."

As Ben waved Gwen over the threshold, he said, "Let me explain why Mrs. Andrews is here. I had a second interview with her earlier and she shared your concern about your guests being detained. I asked her to accompany me while I provide you with an official update."

Gwen was impressed with Ben's clever explanation. After all, without knowing Gwen's C.I. status, or the fact that she'd served breakfast to Ben, Betty must have wondered why she'd arrived earlier than planned to call Parker's spirit.

"Let's make ourselves comfortable in the living room," Betty offered. "Robert's not here at the moment."

Ben waited until they were seated. "I came to release several of your guests."

"Which ones?" Betty asked, her forehead settling into grooves.

"The Pettigrew couple and the Schuster family."

"Oh, thank goodness," Betty said. "How about our three Harvard students? And how soon will you release Miss Hammond?"

Ben paused. "Let me address them one at a time. No one I interviewed noticed the boys when Mrs. Mueller screamed, so I'll be talking to all three again before I can let them go. Because Miss Hammond was ill yesterday, I need to get her statement while I'm here this morning. And I need another chat with Mr. Owens of course."

Betty stiffened. "I can tell you, Detective Snowcrest, with not a shred of doubt, that Robert would never harm a soul."

"You misunderstand me, Mrs. Owens. Your husband may now recall where the boys were standing when the incident happened. Are the Harvard boys here this morning?"

Seeming to ease regarding her husband's role, Betty answered in a calm voice. "Charlie went to his uncle's home to see if there was any way he could help. Dylan and Shawn went with him. I don't know when they'll return."

"That's fine. As long as they haven't left town. Call me they walk in." Ben removed a business card from a small leather case and held it out. "And where is your husband?"

Betty waved her hand to dismiss the question. "He's at Home Depot buying light bulbs. He won't be back for a while."

"Not a problem. I'll catch up with him later. How is Miss Hammond feeling this morning?"

"She's still battling a headache and is resting upstairs. Do you want me to go fetch her?"

"No," Snowcrest answered. "If you'll show me to her room, I'll interview her there. I'd like you to come with me."

Betty placed her hand on Gwen's arm. "Let's both go."

***

Miss Hammond's room above the front parlor was the furthest from the servant steps. Gwen determined that if the

113

other guests had been looking toward the rear wall, they wouldn't have noticed Brooke Hammond in her doorway.

After Betty knocked and asked permission to enter, a thin voice called out, "Come in."

Betty opened the door, followed closely by Ben and Gwen. The room gave off a welcoming vibe with its rose-colored linens, draperies, and floral scatter rugs.

"Excuse us, Miss Hammond, but Detective Snowcrest would like to ask you a few questions."

The young woman sat up, catching a damp cloth as it fell from her forehead.

"Ask me anything, but I have nothing to share."

Ben's questions elicited no useful information. Miss Hammond claimed her door was closed, that she'd been dealing with a raging migraine, and she hadn't even heard the scream. Ben advised her she was free to leave on Sunday, and they left her to do battle with her headache.

***

In the entrance hall, Gwen stood beside Betty, facing Ben. "I'm not leaving right away, Detective Snowcrest. I need to discuss garden club matters with Betty." Gwen used his official title to conceal their partnership.

"That's fine, Mrs. Andrews. Thank you for meeting me here and for your presence during Miss Hammond's interview. I'll be in touch if I need any further information."

After Ben closed the door behind him, Betty turned to Gwen. "Did the detective stopping at your home this morning mess up your errands?"

Gwen remembered her fib to mask her breakfast meeting with Ben. "He sure did. I'll handle them later."

Betty seemed to accept the bogus explanation. "He made me nervous until he said Miss Hammond can leave on Sunday."

Gwen took up the thread. "After the detective clears Charlie, Shawn, and Dylan, your house will be empty for your new guests arriving on Sunday."

"My fingers are crossed, Gwen."

"With each person he clears, the closer he comes to identifying the person who pushed Myrtle."

Betty's frown elongated her round face. "I'm so hoping Theo wasn't involved."

The rustle of bags in the dining room diverted their attention.

Robert placed several Home Depot bags on the table before joining them in the entrance hall. He kissed Betty on the cheek and nodded to Gwen. "Was that Detective Snowcrest pulling out of our parking lot?"

Betty wrapped her arms around his waist. "Yes, that was him. He released the Pettigrews and the Schusters. After he interviewed Miss Hammond, he released her as well. He wants to talk to you again though."

Robert scowled. "There's nothing more I can tell him."

Betty gazed up at him. "He wants to know if you noticed Charlie, Dylan, and Shawn just before Myrtle's tumble."

Robert waved his hand in dismissal. "Unfortunately, I can't help him. I was busy answering questions about a newspaper article. I'll call the detective and tell him so."

He turned to Gwen. "I wasn't surprised to hear Parker has appeared to you. Asking him to connect with Theo is inventive. How soon do you want to give it a try?"

***

Half an hour later, Gwen's voice was barely audible. "Let me try again." She reached for the hands of Betty and Robert before repeating Madame Eudora's chant and calling, "Parker? Parker? If you can hear me, please show yourself."

Nothing.

Gwen slumped in her chair. "I'm so sorry. I was sure I could reach him."

Betty patted Gwen's sleeve. "Don't fret. Maybe you can figure out another way to bring him here."

"Maybe," Gwen conceded. "We need him to search for Theo and ask about her mischief. Any other damage since the broken candles, spilled vase, and bunched runners?"

Robert shook his head. "Nothing we've noticed."

"That's good," Gwen commented. "We also need to know if Theo witnessed anyone near Myrtle just before she fell."

Betty tilted her head in a hopeful manner. "Are you willing to try calling Parker again on another day?"

"I'm not going to give up. What day works best for you?"

Betty and Robert looked at each other as if in an unspoken conversation until Robert spoke. "We have a lot of chores to take care of tomorrow. Sunday might be better between this week's guests checking out and the new guests checking in."

Gwen pulled up her cell phone calendar and maneuvered to Sunday. Other than her own chores, nothing was scheduled. Ben hadn't mentioned an update meeting during the weekend. "Sunday works for me. What time?"

"Between eleven and three," Robert answered.

Gwen blocked out those hours. "Done and done." Out of the corner of her eye, she detected a movement near the swinging door into the kitchen. "Is Gracie working this morning?"

"No, she's already come and gone," Betty answered. "Why do you ask?"

Gwen shrugged. "Oh, nothing. I thought I saw something move."

Betty's round face brightened. "You've just had your first glimpse of Theo."

"Really?" Gwen said, sensing her eyes had widened.

"Really," Betty confirmed, a grin forming. "Did you notice her white gown?"

"I didn't see anything specifically. It was just an unfocused motion."

"She might be eavesdropping on our conversation."

"Oh, dear," Gwen said. "Will she object to Parker's involvement?"

"Hard to say," Robert countered. "We'll find out after you coax his spirit to join us."

Without an answer to that ethereal quandary, Gwen could only hope she'd be successful on Sunday.

In the dining room, Robert lifted his Home Depot bags and headed for the basement stairs.

Gwen noticed the table was completely empty. "Where are the party dishes, Betty?"

"Robert moved them to the back hallway. More convenient to load them into your trunk. We can do that now if you want."

***

Gazing down at the pile, Gwen suggested, "If we both grab a few each time, I think we can carry everything to my trunk in two trips."

Betty reached for the nearest containers and balanced four in her ample arms. "Thanks again for returning these."

"My thank-you for your conversation with Gracie." After the second trip, Gwen closed her trunk lid. "I'll see you tomorrow afternoon."

Betty headed inside, waving as she disappeared.

Gwen was settling into her driver's seat when she remembered Tess's quilt and the snowman mugs on hold at Serendipity. *Might as well pick them up while I'm so close.*

Closing and locking her car door, Gwen trekked down the icy slope of Harbor Hill and entered the Serendipity Gift Shoppe without incident, grateful she hadn't fallen. An injury would have surely ruined her Christmas plans with Tess.

Chapter Eighteen

…late morning, Friday

"Hi, Holly," Gwen called as she approached. "I'm here to pick up those items you're holding for me."

Holly whirled around. "Sure thing. Give me a sec to retrieve them." She ducked into a small room behind the register.

Less than a minute later, Gwen was tucking her credit card into her wallet.

"You chose well," Holly commented as she hoisted the over-sized shopping bag across the counter.

Gwen reached inside to touch the supple fabric. "My sister will love the seaside motif. Who made this one?"

"A seamstress who lives up the coast. She creates three or four items every season and submits them for consignment. They're the first ones to fly out of here."

"I can understand why. I love those snowmen mugs, too. Can't wait to fill them with hot chocolate or spiced cider."

"I hope they bring you many hours of pleasure."

Gwen leaned on the counter. "Do you have time to hear the details of our condolence call yesterday?"

Holly glanced around her gift shop, finding no shoppers who needed immediate attention. "Now is good. And thanks again to you and Betty."

"We were happy to do it." As Gwen shared Fletcher Mueller's cool reception, Holly murmured appropriate comments, ending with, "I've never met the man, but if that's as friendly as he gets, it explains Myrtle's sour disposition."

119

Apparently Gwen wasn't the only garden clubber irritated by Myrtle's constant complaining. "Oh, I don't know. His wife had just died. Good manners were probably the last thing on his mind."

"You're probably right. I shouldn't be so quick with a snarky remark."

Gwen tried a sleuthing topic. "Myrtle dying like that was so upsetting to all of us."

"It was," Holly agreed. "Not that I was ever a big fan of hers, but I think she tripped over her own feet."

Knowing Myrtle hadn't simply tripped, Gwen let Holly's comment slide by.

***

Ben pulled open the door to the craft shop and walked in, not quick enough to mask his surprise to see Gwen chatting with Holly Nichols. He recovered as he approached. "Mrs. Andrews, what a pleasure to bump into you."

Gwen stretched out her hand in greeting as if they were only casual acquaintances. "Good to see you as well, Detective Snowcrest."

Holly interrupted. "Can I help you find a gift, Detective?"

Pulling his notebook and pen from the outer pocket of his jacket, Ben gave her a half-grin. "I'm not shopping today, although your store is charming." He glanced around, nodding his approval. "I'm re-interviewing everyone I spoke to at the B&B the other night."

"Why?" Holly asked.

"Mrs. Mueller's fall was not an accident."

Holly crossed her arms. "That's awful. But I can't tell you anything more than what I said after the party."

"That's a common misconception. Now that the distress of the incident has subsided, you might remember details." Ben again glanced around the shop. "Do you prefer talking out here or in your office?"

A shopper approached, her arms filled with a stuffed Santa and decorated driftwood. Holly reached out. "Let me help you with those." She half-glanced at Ben. "Be with you in a minute."

Ben sidled to the display of greeting cards along the side wall, out of earshot, subtly nodding for Gwen to join him. With no browsers near them, Ben said in a low tone, "You got here fast. I'm impressed."

Gwen selected a card and pretended to read it. "Strictly coincidence. I haven't had a chance to bring up the whisperers."

"No problem. Find a reason to talk to her after I leave. We can compare notes over an early lunch next door."

"Sharing meals with you is becoming a habit."

"A pleasant one, I hope."

Feeling eyes on the back of his head, Ben let out a laugh. "I like that one, Mrs. Andrews."

"Me, too," Gwen agreed. "Thanks for your opinion, Detective." As the lady shopper passed with her purchases, Gwen carried the unread birthday greeting to the counter. "I'll just add this card to the quilt and the mugs."

As Gwen tucked the card away, Ben noticed that Holly leaned over and said something to Gwen that he couldn't hear. Gwen nodded and made no move to leave. Holly must have asked her to stay. Perfect. Now Gwen didn't need to invent an excuse to hang around.

Ben sauntered up beside them. "Have you decided where

you want to chat, Mrs. Nichols?"

"It'll have to be right here, Detective. My assistant Kristen is out on an errand, and I need to be available to my customers."

Holly turned her head and sneezed into her elbow as her hand ripped a tissue from the nearly-empty box on the counter. "Excuse me. This damn cold won't let go. Better to put some distance between us."

Ben lifted an eyebrow in Gwen's direction. Holly was quick to notice, giving him the reaction he expected.

"I asked Gwen to stay while you and I talk."

"Fine with me." Ben flipped to a clean page in his notebook. "In the time between your statement after the party the other night and now, have you remembered any more details?"

Holly squirted hand sanitizer into her palms and rubbed with vigor. "It's all still a bit fuzzy. I was working my way along the sitting room walls, examining the photographs and reading the articles. When Myrtle screamed, everyone around me moved in a bunch toward the top of the steps." Holly's forehead wrinkled. "I wasn't chatting with anyone, so I have no idea who was standing next to me. Sorry I'm not more help."

Ben scribbled a few lines before closing his notebook. "I appreciate your candor. I'll be talking to the others in your group. If you remember any more details, give me a call." He extended his business card in case she'd misplaced the first one.

Holly accepted it without comment.

On his way to the exit, Ben touched a colorful wool scarf folded on a table. The subdued colors would blend perfectly with Gwen's hazel eyes and ash brown hair. He considered buying it as a Christmas gift, then thought better of it because the lady herself was standing not ten feet away watching his every move. He could always stop back in another day.

***

Holly reached for another tissue. "Thanks, Gwen."

"No problem." Gwen settled into her sleuthing mission. "I overheard the strangest conversation during our party."

"Why was it strange?"

Glancing around, she saw browsers inspecting potential purchases and paying no attention. "They were whispering in Betty's front parlor."

A wrinkle appeared on Holly's forehead. "Sounds intriguing. What were they saying?"

Gwen repeated the angry blackmail threat to keep the adultery a secret.

After another sneeze escaped, Holly blew her nose. "Do you know who they were?"

Gwen took one step sideways to be out of range. "No idea. I didn't recognize their voices. The whispering made it hard to even guess male or female."

Holly again rubbed sanitizer on her hands. "How about those Harvard boys? College students always need money."

Without waiting for Gwen's response, Holly kept talking. "Or two of the guests. Mrs. Pettigrew or Mrs. Schuster might be cheating on their husbands. If you couldn't distinguish man or woman, the other way around could be true as well. Husbands cheating on their wives. And that Miss Hammond was an odd duck. She's the only one who didn't interact with us."

Gwen didn't share that Ben had cleared Miss Hammond a few hours ago. Holly hadn't suggested any club women who were having an affair. Could be Holly wasn't aware of those personal secrets. Or maybe the blackmailer and adulterer

123

weren't connected to the garden club at all.

But Holly was the first member Gwen had approached. Others might be more aware of the seamier side of the club.

Holly continued to speak. "There was also that woman helping Betty in the kitchen. I didn't catch her name."

Gwen shrugged her shoulders. She knew Gracie's name, her position as cleaning lady, and the fact that she couldn't speak. Best not to admit those facts to Holly. Instead, Gwen said, "There were so many people in the B&B that night. Any two of them could have met up in that front parlor."

"I hate to suggest this, Gwen, but do you think the blackmailer was Betty herself? She's the only person who knew everyone else. Any idea if the B&B is doing well?"

Before Gwen could foil Holly's absurd suggestion, another customer placed items on the counter, looking hopeful for a rapid checkout.

Holly turned a megawatt smile on the woman, speaking to Gwen while she keyed in the purchases. "Let me know if you learn anything more. That conversation is fascinating, despite the sordid undertones."

"I'll do that, Holly. See you soon."

Chapter Nineteen

…mid-day, Friday

Gwen exited the gift shop, spotting Ben as he leaned against the outer wall of the Bayside Café, blowing on his hands, his breath disappearing in sharp puffs of coldness.

As she approached, Gwen asked, "Where are your gloves?"

Ben pushed himself upright. "In the front pocket of my other coat."

"Might be time to buy a second pair," she teased.

He opened the café door and waved her into the warmth.

"You should have waited inside, Ben."

"I didn't want to monopolize a table until you joined me."

"Very considerate of you."

He nodded toward the restroom sign. "I'll be right back."

"Mrs. Andrews?" a voice called.

Gwen turned, instantly recognizing the wild red curls. "Hello, Kristin. Your errands all handled?"

The younger woman nodded as she removed colorful knitted mittens. "Holly usually does the running around, but I think her cold has sapped her energy. She asked me to check on our crafters today."

"You don't seem unhappy about it."

Kristen grinned. "Not at all. It's refreshing to be outside in the crisp air. You here for lunch?"

"I am. Are you staying?"

"No. I'm picking up Holly's food order before I return to the shop. I'd better check if it's ready. See you, Mrs. Andrews."

As Kristin headed for the take-out counter, Ben strolled from the other end. The sign read '*Sit Anywhere*' so Ben guided Gwen toward an empty booth along the far wall.

Sliding across the bench seat and placing her gifts close to the wall, Gwen glanced up and saw Kristin waving from the doorway, a brown paper bag clutched in her arms, her face puzzled as she noticed white-haired Ben.

Smiling innocently, Gwen returned the gesture and waited until Kristen disappeared out the door before leaning across the table. "Isn't it a bad idea for us to be seen together in public?"

Handing her a menu, Ben shook his head. "Not at all. Now if a *criminal* noticed a detective meeting a citizen in a dark alley, *that* would look suspicious."

After a waitress took their orders. Ben focused on Gwen. "I'm impressed that you drove to Holly's shop so soon."

Gwen gave him a half grin. "Actually, I walked. After you left the B&B, I stayed to discuss garden club business with Betty." An outright lie, but Gwen wasn't about to confess her failed attempt to call Parker's spirit to the B&B.

"Let me guess, Gwen. You also discussed their ghost."

Gwen didn't respond to his cynical remark. Instead, she clung to the safety of her recent activities. "I decided to pick up a quilt Holly was holding for me. It's a perfect gift for Tess."

"Two birds with one stone." He made no further comments about the B&B ghost.

The waitress delivered broccoli bacon quiche and hot tea for Gwen, plus chowder, clam cakes, and soda for Ben.

Ben inserted a straw and drew a sip. "Did Mrs. Nichols volunteer any details after I left?"

Gwen swallowed her first bite of quiche. "She suggested

one of the guests might be cheating on her husband."

"So she didn't implicate any of the garden club ladies?"

Gwen shook her head. "Only that Betty could be the blackmailer. Or Gracie."

Ben popped a misshapen clam cake into his mouth. "Any idea how soon Mrs. Owens will have that chat with Gracie?"

"No specific date, Ben. I'll let you know as soon as Betty tells me Gracie's answer."

Ben lowered his voice. "Could Holly be right? Is there any chance Mrs. Owens was the blackmailer?"

"Despite Holly's opinion, I'll never believe Betty would stoop so low."

Ben leaned closer. "Don't be mad. We have to keep in mind that there might be no connection between your whisperers and Mrs. Mueller's fall. Anything else from your club president?"

"Holly said students always need money."

Ben licked grease from his fingers, crumbled his napkin, and reached for another. "True enough. Let's set Holly aside for now. I'm rethinking Mrs. Mueller's tuition complaint. Is she the type who would resort to blackmail?"

"I have no idea. In the interest of being open-minded, maybe Myrtle wasn't the blackmailer either."

"Touché. At the moment, she's our most likely candidate. The whispered threat is too much of a coincidence to ignore. Especially given all of the purchases someone in that house was ordering. I'm planning another visit with Fletcher Mueller under the guise of finding his wife's attacker."

Gwen glanced at the closest booth, cluttered with dirty dishes. "There's a third person we haven't considered."

Ben stared at her. "Who's that?"

127

"The adulterer's confidante."

Ben's cell phone buzzed and he clicked into the text message before tapping a response. "That was Mrs. Owens. Shawn and Dylan have returned to the B&B."

"Not Charlie?" Gwen asked.

"He's still at the Mueller home, which is fine with me. I'll question his friends now and catch up with Charlie later."

Getting to his feet, Ben tossed a twenty-dollar bill on the table, adding another five. "Sorry that I have to run. That should cover the tab and tip. I need to get over to the B&B before those boys scatter. I also want to print out the public records of everyone involved. Are you available to meet with me tomorrow around mid-morning?"

Gwen wasn't due at the B&B until noonish on Sunday, so didn't worry about double-booking. "Sure."

"I won't get to your place until at least ten, so you don't have to feed me breakfast." He grinned before saying, "We need to delve into that third person."

"Thanks for lunch, Ben."

"My pleasure. I'll see you in the morning."

***

Taking a page from Gwen's journey, Ben walked up Harbor Hill to the B&B instead of driving. As he moved along, he revisited his initial conversations with the three Harvard students on party night. Ben didn't expect Shawn and Dylan to reveal anything earth-shattering. He'd most likely release both boys after this second interview. Then a last chat with Charlie before giving him permission to check out on Sunday morning.

Despite his obligation to question Robert Owens, Ben didn't consider the B&B co-owner for either blackmailer or murderer, based in part on Gwen's perception of the man's sterling character, part on the fact that he was involved in a conversation when the incident happened. As before, Ben was placing his bet on one of those six garden club members.

***

A more deliberate eater, Gwen remained in the booth and finished her quiche, washing it down with the last few swallows of herbal tea. Her mind whirled around that third person...the adulterer's confidante.

Alicia walked through the door of the Bayside Cafe, spotted Gwen, and veered in her direction. "Hi, Gwen."

"Hello yourself. Doing some Christmas shopping?"

"I wish. My kids caught Travis's cold, and he took a sick day. I'm the only one who's not sneezing, so I escaped the house to buy chicken soup. What brings you here?"

Gwen indicated the Serendipity bag. "I picked up a quilt for my sister from Holly's shop."

Alicia made a face. "I have to admit she offers some unique gifts, but they're expensive, so I've never bought anything."

Gwen silently agreed that Holly's prices were on the high side but didn't consider them unusual for one-of-a-kind hand-crafted items.

Alicia waved her hand in a vague gesture. "I'd better get moving or Travis and the kids will wonder where I am. If I don't bump into you again, Gwen, enjoy the holidays."

"You, too," Gwen called to Alicia's retreating form.

Belatedly, Gwen realized she should have asked Alicia to retrieve her serving dish from Gwen's trunk. Too late now.

***

Once again, Ben guided a witness into the B&B's front

parlor. "So tell me, Shawn, have you remembered any more details from the other night?"

"Yes, sir. Charlie and Dylan and me had looked at every picture hanging on the walls and read every newspaper article. To be honest, we only skimmed the stories. I was getting bored and suggested we walk to The Wharf for a night cap."

"Do you recall where you were standing when you made that suggestion?"

"Yes, sir," Shawn repeated. "We had moved away from the club ladies because their chatter was driving us nuts and Charlie's aunt wouldn't leave him alone. He finally told her we were leaving and she turned away."

"When she rejoined the others, did you notice who she stood next to?"

"No, because none of us were watching her. Sorry I'm not being more helpful."

Ben had paid close attention to the boy's body language. He didn't avert his gaze during the questioning. He didn't fidget. He sat forward on the loveseat, forearms resting on thighs, implying interest in their conversation.

"By the way, Detective Snowcrest, I really admire you. My uncle's a cop up in Cambridge, and he's the coolest guy."

"Thanks, Shawn. I guess I don't have to tell you to call me if any other details surface?"

Shawn accepted Ben's business card. "No, sir, you don't have to tell me that. I'll definitely call you, but I don't think there's anything more."

Ben extended his hand. "Thanks, Shawn. Would you ask Dylan to join me?"

The next few minutes with Dylan revealed one more detail.

He'd argued against returning to The Wharf because they'd downed quite a few beers before the karaoke, and he wanted to get some sleep. His revelation did not affect the case. "Dylan, tell Shawn you're both free to check out on Sunday morning."

"That's great," Dylan responded. "Charlie, too?"

"I need to interview him one more time before I decide."

***

Ben leaned against the chief's open door and listened to his argument on the phone.

"What do you want me to say, Mayor?" Mike challenged. "We can't solve the crimes if we don't pay the detectives for the extra hours they devote to catching criminals. Either pay the time worked or hire more detectives. But consider this, sir. New men require training. Add costly benefits and the bottom-line payroll would be about the same, if not more."

Mike winked at Ben as he listened to the mayor's response. "I knew you'd see the logic. Thanks again for understanding."

Disconnecting the call, the chief focused on Ben. "How's the B&B case shaping up?"

"Slow but steady. I spoke again to two of the three Harvard boys and gave them permission to check out on Sunday. I'm still trying to catch up with Myrtle Mueller's nephew Charlie."

"How's our Gwen working out?"

"She's jumping right in. We met over lunch for an update. She's already chatted with club president Holly Nichols. She's the lady who owns the craft store near the waterfront."

"The one with the red-and-white leggings?"

Ben chuckled. "Your recall is as sharp as ever. Gwen is arranging visits with the other members under the pretext of returning their party dishes."

"I'm glad we agreed she'd be the perfect C.I for this case."

"I hate to give you credit, Mike, but it was your idea."

"I know that, Ben, but you're the one who had to convince her to work with you. You must be one charming guy."

"Wasn't all me, Mike. I suspect Gwen will be helping the B&B owners prove their ghost innocent. Agreeing to be my C.I. provided her with an inside track to our official activities."

"Do you think Gwen gave it that much thought?"

Ben shrugged. "Can't say for certain. I only know I'm glad she's working with me."

Mike's desk phone rang and he lifted the receiver. "Stay focused, Ben."

As Ben closed the chief's door, he pondered the undertone of that last comment. Was he so transparent that the chief sensed he was enchanted by Gwen?

Chapter Twenty

...mid-afternoon, Friday

Placing her laptop on the granite island, Gwen composed an email to the garden club members about retrieving their party dishes. If anyone couldn't pick theirs up by the following weekend, Gwen offered to deliver. Either method would provide her the chance to gather guesses about those whisperers and perhaps more observations about party night.

If the adulterer and blackmailer weren't connected to Myrtle's death, the reason behind her suspicious fall might be more difficult to unearth. But Gwen was determined to help Ben find the culprit. Beyond the loftier goal of seeking justice, she wanted desperately to prove that someone besides Theo had caused the accident and relieve Betty and Robert's worry.

While Gwen waited for responses from the email-savvy members, she recorded the details of her chat with Holly and Ben at the craft shop and then lunch with him next door. She added Kristen's puzzled expression when she saw them together and Alicia's unexpected appearance to buy chicken soup. Skipping a line, she noted the details of the group email.

Cheerful pings indicated incoming responses.

The first arrived from Alicia. *'If I hadn't rushed out of the Bayside Café earlier, I could have taken my cut-glass bowl off your hands. Unfortunately, my tribe is all napping, and I can't leave in case one of them wakes up and needs some nursing. Would you mind dropping it off? I'm not planning to go anywhere for the rest of the day.'*

Gwen typed, *'Sure. I'll wait for more replies.'*

The second email came from Evelyn. *'I wouldn't dream of putting you out, so I'll pick up my Pyrex baking dish after supper. Around six-thirty if that's convenient for you.'*

Since Gwen had no plans, she typed, *'That works for me. See you this evening.'*

Another ping announced the reply from the Hobart twins, penned from Zelda's address. *'Zoe and I would be grateful if you'd drop off our cranberry glass compote dishes.'*

Gwen typed that she'd be there within the hour. Perhaps the sisters would remember some small detail from party night. The likelihood that the spinsters would contribute any salacious details about club members having an affair was slim, but Gwen knew well that clues often surfaced where you least expected them.

***

As Gwen drove along North Street to Alicia's house, her thoughts drifted to Betty and Robert's concern that the spectral Theo could in fact be the cause of Myrtle's death. The similarity between Theo's tumble so many decades ago and Myrtle's fall the other night remained a disturbing parallel.

Gwen's attempt that morning to call Parker's spirit to the B&B for a conversation with the elusive Theo had failed miserably. Gwen needed to figure out why it hadn't worked. They'd used Madame Eudora's techniques. Holding hands to form a circle. Lighting candles. Speaking in a quiet voice. But Parker had been a no show.

Gwen racked her brain for alternate approaches without asking for the medium's assistance. Gwen wanted to reach Parker on her own.

And then, like an old cartoon, the proverbial light bulb glowed above Gwen's head.

Annabelle! Gwen stopped short of snapping her fingers, preferring to keep both hands on the steering wheel.

Annabelle was the staff photographer for the Harbor Falls Gazette, but it was the girl's connections with the local ghost-hunting group that interested Gwen. They'd provided the special equipment needed to record last April's séance. Perhaps Annabelle would share some helpful hints for Gwen's goal to summon Parker to the B&B.

Gwen pulled to the side of the road and dialed *The Gazette*'s local office. After several phone line clicks, Annabelle picked up. "Mrs. Andrews, is that you? My ghost hunter friends keep asking me to retell what happened at your séance."

Gwen tittered. "The credit goes to Madame Eudora. Is there any chance you can stop by my home after work today?"

"Sure. I'm not doing anything tonight. Why don't I pick up supper for us both?"

Gwen hadn't thought about Annabelle being hungry after a long day of following reporters to snap pictures. Gwen wasn't concerned if the young woman hadn't left before Evelyn arrived at six-thirty. "That's a great idea, Annabelle."

"What do you want me to bring?"

"Your choice. Surprise me."

***

After Gwen parked at Alicia's curb, she texted Ben. Lifting Alicia's cut glass bowl from the cardboard boxes in her trunk, Gwen climbed the front steps and pushed the button.

Coatless, Alicia opened her door, her arms wrapped around her torso. "I'd invite you in, Gwen, but it's germ haven in there, and I don't want to expose you." She lifted her bowl from Gwen's outstretched hands. "Thanks for dropping this off." The door closed with no further conversation.

Discouraged, Gwen wandered toward her car. So much for exploring the whisperers or affairs of club members. Gwen couldn't force a conversation and expose her partnership with the police. She'd have to catch up with Alicia when her brood was feeling better.

Gwen drove a short distance until she was out of sight of Alicia's house. Parking in the lot of a convenience store, she pulled out her steno pad, made a note of the failed visit, and then texted Ben. *'Leaving Alicia's with no results. Next stop is the Hobart twins.'*

Steering in a northwesterly direction, Gwen entered an inland housing complex called Oak Leaf Terrace, a picturesque village of condo units. Parking in the lot assigned to visitors, she emerged into the waning afternoon light and breathed in the brisk December air. Following the numbers mounted on each unit, she approached the Hobart twins' condo in the building nearest the wetlands. The warble of red-winged blackbirds broke the quietude, bringing a smile to Gwen as she knocked.

A tiny voice made its way through the door. "Who is it?"

"It's Gwen with your compote dishes. Is this Zelda or Zoe?"

Without answering, a little lady who didn't break five feet opened the door a crack and peered out.

In an instant, Gwen understood why Zelda didn't use the peep hole to identify the knocker. The security opening was at least three inches above the top of her head.

Pulling Gwen inside, Zelda closed the door and lifted the cranberry glass compote dishes from Gwen's gloved hands.

"Thank you for returning these. They belonged to our grandmother, you know." Zelda hugged the glassware in a protective manner. "As soon as we knew you'd be dropping over, Zoe started baking her special lemon cake. You must stay to have a slice with a nice cup of hot tea."

Gwen couldn't have arranged snooping time any better. "That sounds wonderful. I accept."

"Good," Zelda said, reaching over to remove Gwen's winter coat. "Come see our breakfast nook. It's our favorite spot."

In the kitchen, Zoe was upending the contents of a Bundt pan onto a cooling rack, the huge oven mitts nearly reaching her elbows. The scent of lemon cake filled the air, making Gwen's mouth water.

At the stove, Zelda lifted a glass whistling kettle and poured boiling water into a large ceramic teapot. "Hope you like fruity tea. This is a special blend from the tea house in Sandwich."

Gwen waved the steam toward her nose. "Smells delicious."

Zelda pulled out the chair facing the wetlands and waved for Gwen to have a seat.

The scene outside the window did not disappoint. With the most recent snow clinging to the marsh grasses, the panorama was worthy of a Christmas card. "Lovely," Gwen murmured. "Did you choose this unit for the view?"

Zoe placed her lemon cake in the center of the round table, saying, "I wish we could take the credit. We were lucky this unit was for sale when we were looking in this village."

Owning a condo in this upscale complex required a tidy bundle of cash reserves. Gwen had no personal knowledge of the twins' financial status. She'd heard inferences that they'd inherited family money. At club meetings, they never talked about their careers, if indeed they ever held jobs. Even if they had, the sisters were too old now to still be working.

Zelda arranged China cups and saucers, plates, forks, and napkins before taking a seat. "I'm so glad you offered to deliver our dishes, Gwen. We get so few visitors here. It's always nice to see a friendly face." She accepted a giant knife from Zoe's outstretched hand and cut a huge slice of the lemon cake.

Gwen's hand flew up. "Make mine half that size, Zelda."

Zoe clucked her tongue. "Forget your weight, Gwen. We should throw caution to the wind and enjoy each day. I promise you'll want a second slice."

Rather than argue, Gwen forked a morsel of the pale-yellow treat into her mouth. "This is delicious. What's your secret?"

The younger twin grinned wide. "I use a combination of regular and almond flour, liquid sugar cane juice, plus fresh squeezed lemon juice and grated lemon peel. Good, isn't it?"

"I'll say." Gwen slid another generous forkful onto her waiting tongue.

Little talk interfered as they savored the lemon cake and sipped the fruity tea. After finishing the predicted second slice, Gwen pushed her plate aside. "That was so good, but I can't eat another bite." Besides, she needed to pick the twins' brains and lit upon the perfect segue. "I'm surprised you didn't bring this lemon cake to the party the other night."

Zoe waved her hand, pooh-poohing the idea. "I only serve my specialty cake to good-natured people like you, Gwen."

"You don't think the other members are worthy of your baking skills?"

Zelda answered for her twin. "Oh, some are all right, like Betty, but we don't care much for the rest of them."

Carrying the leftover cake to the counter, Zoe spoke over her shoulder. "You must wonder why we bothered to join."

"I am," Gwen said, genuinely curious. "Are you going to tell me, or am I being too nosey?"

"Of course we'll tell you," Zelda promised as she stacked the dirty dishes. "After our parents passed away and left the family farm to me and Zoe, we opened our doors to an ever-changing parade of relatives who were down on their luck. We never turned anyone away. One day, years later, the last cousin moved out and we found ourselves rattling around that big old house all by ourselves. So we sold the farm and bought this condo. So much easier to keep clean."

"Oh, Zelda, you do go on so," Zoe chided and turned in Gwen's direction. "We maintained a large garden of both veggies and flowers. This complex provides a small patch of land for the gardening residents, but it's not very satisfying. So we joined the club to soak up their gardening activities."

Zelda interrupted. "And that's why we never have much to contribute at the meetings. We only listen to the chatter."

Gwen needed to shift this conversation to the case. "Speaking of hearing the others talk, I overheard a strange conversation at the party the other night."

The twins turned and spoke in unison. "You did?"

Watching their faces, Gwen relayed the words whispered in Betty's front parlor.

"Oh, my," Zoe remarked. "They were both quite angry. I wonder who they were."

This would be Gwen's only chance to learn if the twins had any knowledge of the speakers, but she needed to be indirect. "I didn't recognize their voices. It's keeping me up nights."

A slight exaggeration, but Gwen was determined to gain some insight from the sisters. She paused to give them a chance to ponder.

Zelda busied herself loading the dirty plates into the dishwasher. "You know, I did overhear a snippet at our November meeting. I was headed for the church kitchen and heard voices. Someone said, '*You need to call it off. And I mean now.*' I don't know who she was or who she was talking to."

Gwen tried to sound nonchalant. "You never saw them?"

Zelda shook her head. "Another member pulled me aside. When I finally entered the kitchen, it was empty. Sorry, Gwen, but I have no idea who was talking."

"Zoe?" Gwen challenged. "Did you see them?"

The younger twin's head swayed in the negative. "No, I didn't. I was handing out flyers for the speaker."

Although the kitchen scolding was not specific to an adulterer, it was too much of a coincidence to ignore, and like Ben, Gwen didn't believe in coincidences. Disappointed, she would nevertheless mention Zelda's story to Ben.

Thanking the twins for their hospitality, Gwen stood up and reached for her coat.

"Oh, you must take some of my lemon cake home with you," Zoe insisted, striding to the counter. She returned carrying an oversized Tupperware container protecting a good portion of the lemon cake. "I usually freeze whatever Zelda and I don't eat that same day, but it never tastes the same. Better for a nice lady like you to enjoy it."

Gwen accepted the gift. "That's very generous of you. I'll make sure it doesn't go to waste."

Chapter Twenty-One

...late afternoon, Friday

As Gwen came into her foyer, a ping echoed from the kitchen announcing the arrival of another email. Hurrying to the island, she placed Zoe's lemon cake on the granite counter and clicked on the message.

Ruby had typed from her cell phone, *'Gwen, I'm boarding a flight to Denver in a few minutes for a family holiday. Can you hold onto my metal platter until I return? Thanks.'*

Picturing the flaming redhead, Gwen typed *'No problem'* and clicked the send button. Wait a minute. Hadn't Ben told everyone at the B&B to stay in town?

Rather than text Ben, Gwen dialed his cell, swearing under her breath when it bounced to voicemail. "Ben, this is Gwen. I need you to call me. We might have a problem."

While waiting for his return call, she scrolled through three additional emails, all from the club members in Betty's group.

Although these women would have no input about Robert's tour, they might have heard gossip about members with financial problems or having an affair.

These three offered to pick up their dishes anytime the next day, so Gwen scheduled them all to arrive at nine in the morning. What better way to inspire gossip than to let them compete with each other for the juiciest tidbit?

***

After listening to Gwen's voice message, Ben dialed her cell phone. "Are you okay?"

"Sorry, Ben. I should have said I'm home."

"Good. So you must have learned something important."

"I think so, but let me read Ruby's email to you." Gwen recited the words verbatim. "Will you try to stop her from flying to Denver?"

"No," Ben answered, his tone sullen. "Unfortunately, most of that *'don't leave town'* warning is an idle threat. I'll have to interview Miss Cox after she flies home. Have you scheduled any more visits with your club friends?"

"Three are stopping by at nine tomorrow morning."

"That works. I wasn't planning to arrive until ten. They should be gone by then, and you can tell me what they said."

"Fine with me," Gwen agreed.

"Great. I'll see you in the morning. And don't lose any sleep over Ruby leaving town."

Ben's mood lightened as he disconnected. Spending any time with Gwen was a bonus, even if they only discussed the Myrtle Mueller case.

***

At half past five, Annabelle arrived carrying two paper sacks. "Hi, Gwen. I hope you like what I brought for supper."

Reaching out, Gwen opened one and sniffed. "Oh, my, something smells really good. Let's eat in the kitchen."

While Gwen retrieved plates and utensils, Annabelle provided a running commentary about the food. "Beef and green beans in garlic sauce. Sesame chicken with broccoli and pea pods in orange sauce. White rice. Pork fried rice. Duck sauce. Mustard sauce. Chinese fortune cookies."

Gwen licked her lips. "All my favorites, Annabelle. Give me a few minutes to brew a pot of Chinese tea." Setting the filled kettle on the stove, Gwen retrieved a red-patterned Oriental tin from a nearby cabinet. She dropped four flow-thru bags in a cast iron teapot and waited for the water to boil. "Which restaurant prepared this feast?"

"It's a new place between *The Gazette* building and Baylies' campus." Annabelle located a paper menu. "Here's the name. Golden Express Chinese Take-Away. They don't have a dining room, but their cooks are top-notch. Lots of staff members walk over there to pick up lunch and eat at their desks."

"Can't say I blame them." The kettle whistled and Gwen set the oolong tea to steep.

"Should I fix you a plate?" Annabelle asked, holding a serving spoon in the air.

"Sure. I'll take a little of each." Gwen cut off the green bean tails before taking her first bite. "Ummm. This beef is tender and the sauce is divine."

"I thought you'd like it." Annabelle licked a finger. "You sounded very mysterious on the phone, Gwen."

"Why don't we eat first while everything is hot?"

"Fine by me." Annabelle served herself a second helping of pork fried rice and covered it with the sesame chicken.

Gwen lifted the cast iron pot. "This tea should be ready."

Ten minutes later, Annabelle handed Gwen one of the fortune cookies. "You first."

Gwen broke it open, slid out the tiny piece of paper, and flattened it with her finger. *"You will find what you seek if you are clever."* She laughed. "The person who dreams up these words of wisdom is the clever one."

"That's for sure," Annabelle quipped. "Somehow these sayings always apply to some part of my life. My favorites are collected in my desk drawer at *The Gazette*." She picked up the remaining cookie and broke it into pieces. Holding up her fortune, she flipped one hand in the air and recited with flare. *"You are never selfish with your advice."*

"I like the sound of that," Gwen commented, "because that's exactly why I invited you over."

Grinning, Annabelle tossed the cookie bits into her mouth, chewing and swallowing before she commented. "Let me guess. You found another ghost and want me to take more pictures."

Gwen stared at the young woman. "How did you know?"

Annabelle's hand flew to her mouth to catch the last of the cookie crumbles. "You're serious? There's another ghost in your life?"

"Not exactly mine." Gwen needed only an instant to decide how to proceed. "Are you aware of Theo, the ghost who haunts the Harbor Falls B&B?"

"No, I'm not. They haven't requested our ghost hunters group that I know of."

"The current owners bought the Carswell House from the last remaining member of the family. Betty and Robert Owens were delighted a ghost was included. Theo is a major component of their marketing plan. But lately she's been restless." Gwen listed Theo's recent shenanigans.

"Hang on a second." Annabelle straightened. "Wasn't there an incident at that B&B a few nights ago?"

The girl had switched gears from her ghost hunting hobby to her newspaper job.

Annabelle continued without waiting for Gwen to answer. "Someone fell down a run of steps and died. Shirley's working on a story for next week's edition."

Gwen panicked. She could only hope that Shirley Knapp would not discover the possible involvement of the B&B ghost.

Quick-witted Annabelle didn't miss a beat. "Do you think there's a connection between their ghost and that incident?"

Gwen's best bet was to downplay Theo's potential. "Do you think a ghost could physically push someone down a stairs?"

Annabelle went silent for a moment. "I'm just not sure."

"Well, the incident at the B&B is not why I invited you over, Annabelle. I need your advice on another matter."

Seeming to drop her curiosity, Annabelle said, "Tell me."

Gwen rested her forearms on the cool granite. "I called Parker to join us at the B&B, but he didn't materialize."

"I'm sorry, Gwen, I'm not following."

"We're hoping Parker's spirit can locate Theo's ghost and ask her some questions."

"Hmmm. That's a fascinating idea. Have you seen him since the séance?"

"Not until the night of the party. I'm wondering if this old library is the only place he can appear."

Annabelle's expression softened. "Have you considered contacting Madame Eudora?"

"Not yet. I'd rather connect with Parker myself, no matter where I am when I call him."

"Did you use any of the medium's techniques?"

"We did. Lit candles, dimmed the lights, held hands, but nothing seemed to work."

"Maybe you should add the smoldering herbs," Annabelle mused. "Fiction 'n Fables expanded their aromatherapy section. I only know because *The Gazette* sent me over there last week to take photos for the business spotlight section."

Gwen felt like an idiot. "You're right. When I was in there the other day, Liz was quite proud of her new herb selection. My brain didn't make the connection."

"Don't beat yourself up, Gwen. I'm sure you have a lot on your mind."

Annabelle had no idea how right she was. Even with the young woman's instant suspicion of a link between Myrtle's fall and Theo, Gwen wasn't going to confide the real reason for calling Parker to the B&B – so he could ask Theo if she'd seen who pushed Myrtle. No sense in risking a premature newspaper article based on supposition and unsubstantiated facts.

Again, Gwen felt torn. In order for Betty to prove Theo's innocence, the finger of guilt had to point to a garden club member, for it surely hadn't been Robert. Separating her task of identifying the whisperers from Ben's job to arrest the person who pushed Myrtle was becoming near to impossible for Gwen.

Annabelle stared at Gwen across the island counter. "Are you all right? You drifted away there for a second."

"Sorry, Annabelle. I'm a bit distracted. Tell me, would any of your ghost-hunting experiences help me entice Parker from the other side?"

"Not so much from my group, Gwen, but I have a personal story to share with you."

Chapter Twenty-Two

...late afternoon, Friday

Gwen shifted on her stool to a more comfortable position, prepared to listen to Annabelle's every word.

Annabelle took a deep breath. "What I'm going to tell you began three years ago. I'm not sure when these visits will end, if ever." She peered into her empty cup. "Is there any tea left?"

Gwen lifted the cast iron pot and refilled both of their cups.

"Thanks. You wouldn't know this, Gwen, but on weekends, I volunteer as a docent at several historic sites on Cape Cod." Annabelle stirred a small amount of raw sugar into her tea and took a sip. "On this particular day, I arrived at a 19th century house on Route 6A to prepare for a tour group. As I approached the front door, I sensed someone watching me and caught a glimpse of a man looking out the front window. The house was supposed to be empty, so I unlocked the door and went in."

"That was brave of you," Gwen commented, in awe of Annabelle's spunk.

"Not really. I'm a black belt in karate, and I always carry a knife. Anyway, there was no one inside, so I naturally assumed he was a ghost. He wasn't the first apparition I'd bumped into during a historic house tour. Cape Cod is full of ghosts. I pushed him out of my mind and proceeded with the tour."

Annabelle paused and took another sip of her tea. "After the tour, I walked to an outbuilding to lock up and he showed himself again. That second time, he was full body, clean shaven, wearing a cap and a fitted dark coat."

"Were you afraid of him?"

"For some reason, I wasn't. He didn't give off a threatening vibe at all."

"Did you see him again?"

Annabelle wrapped her hands around the cooling cup as she nodded. "More than once. A few weeks later, I was scheduled for another tour in that same house. I arrived before they did, so I sat in my car and listened to music while I waited. Out of the corner of my eye, I saw a movement in my rear-view mirror, and there he was. When I turned around, he disappeared."

Gwen's jaw dropped. "Wow, that's quite a story."

"Wait, there's more." Draining her cup, Annabelle held it out for another refill. "Three months later, I was booked for a third tour. I got out of my car and looked up, and there he was, standing in the second story bedroom. He smiled at me."

"Wow," Gwen uttered. "I had no idea you were so experienced with ghosts. I thought your group was mostly for hunting and usually didn't find much."

"Others have similar stories. You should attend our next meeting." Annabelle continued without waiting. "I've seen this same man during every tour at that house on 6A. He even followed me to a convenience store and appeared in my rear-view mirror. And I swear he thumped my car bumper."

"Did he ever speak to you?" Gwen recalled her many conversations with Parker's spirit during his ghostly visits.

Annabelle toyed with her teacup handle. "I think he called my name once, but that could have been my imagination."

"Did you ever find out who he was?"

"I did, but not until months later. During a tour in the neighboring house on 6A I spotted a portrait on the parlor wall and nearly fainted. It was the same man, Gwen! The artist had caught the twinkle in his eye and his mischievous grin."

"Who was he?"

"It took me a bit of research through the historical society records, but I finally identified him. He was a sea captain and very good friends with the family in the first house."

"Wow," Gwen whispered. "That's quite a story."

"I get goose bumps every time I tell it, Gwen. But here's why it might help you bring your Parker to the B&B."

Gwen's interest was fully engaged. "Go on, I'm listening."

"The captain followed me from that first house to the outbuilding, and another day to the convenience store. If you can call Parker here," Annabelle waved her arm to include every corner, "maybe he can follow you to the B&B."

Gwen stared at Annabelle. "You are one smart cookie. I'll make a trip to Fiction 'n Fables first and hope Liz stocked the sage and sweet grass." Gwen glanced at her wristwatch. "She's about to close up for the day, so I'll pop down there tomorrow."

"I hate to admit this, but I'm jealous of you, Gwen. I wish my sea captain had spoken to me." Annabelle's shoulders dropped imperceptibly. "Listen, I need to scoot. I'm scheduled for a tour tomorrow morning."

"At the sea captain's house?"

"No, an entirely different location, not even on 6A. Let's get together after you attempt to lead Parker to the B&B."

"We'll do that. Thanks for bringing dinner. Can I offer you any money to pay for my portion?"

Standing on the threshold, Annabelle shook her head then turned at the last second. "Listen, Gwen, I won't breathe a word of you bringing two ghosts together without your permission."

"I appreciate that. Good night."

Annabelle bounced along the front walk, seemingly unconcerned about the snow beneath her boots.

Because Annabelle wasn't in the garden club, her visit and their conversation wasn't logged into Gwen's steno pad.

Chapter Twenty-Three

...early evening, Friday

Ten minutes after Annabelle left, Gwen admitted Evelyn Woodley.

"Good evening, Gwen. I'm here to pick up my Pyrex pan."

"There are several. Come on back and choose yours."

Gwen slowed her usual hurried pace to allow Evelyn and her trusty cane to keep up. Step, thump, step, thump.

Skimming the four Pyrex dishes Gwen had brought in from her trunk, Evelyn pointed. "That's mine, the rectangular glass with handles on both ends."

"I remember that one," Gwen said. "You had prepared a cheesy broccoli bake. Delicious."

"Thank you. We all settle on a favorite recipe for gatherings. I'll grab my dish and leave you to your evening."

"Oh, can't you stay for coffee and cake?"

"If you're sure it's no bother, I'd enjoy that." Leaning her cane against the island, Evelyn maneuvered onto a stool.

Gwen's only knowledge of Evelyn involved their garden club conversations about annuals, perennials, and landscaping. No idea if the woman was married with children and grandchildren, whether her life was happy or sad. Perhaps she wasn't anxious to go home tonight. "Coffee or tea, Evelyn?"

"Coffee would be nice. Do you happen to have decaf?"

"That's all I drink."

While Gwen set the coffee maker to brew and sliced the lemon cake, she and Evelyn chatted about the never-ending snow showers and looking forward to spring gardening. Gwen needn't have worried how to bring up party night.

Evelyn took her first cautious sip of coffee. "This is good."

"It's hazelnut crème. Glad you like it."

Evelyn lifted her eyes. "I can't believe Myrtle's dead."

"It was quite a shock," Gwen commented. "Are you aware the police are investigating her death?"

"How do you know that?"

"I was at Holly's craft shop when Detective Snowcrest stopped by. He said Myrtle didn't fall by accident and asked Holly if she remembered anything."

"Do you think he'll want to interview me again?"

Was Evelyn anticipating a second interview or dreading it? "You were in Myrtle's group, so it makes sense that he would." Gwen needed to be careful with her next question. "On party night, did he ask who was standing next to you?"

"He did, but I couldn't think clearly. After the scream, everyone surged toward those steps. I was too busy trying to stay on my feet. Now that you ask, the Hobart twins were on my left. Zelda was reading the newspaper articles out loud to Zoe. I'm embarrassed to admit I almost told Zelda to shut up."

Unless Evelyn was fibbing, she'd just confirmed the sisters were nowhere near the top of the steps. Though Evelyn hadn't confirmed her own position. Gwen didn't want to blow her cover, so she simply waited for Evelyn to keep talking, but the woman volunteered no more details.

"This cake is delicious, Gwen. Can I have your recipe?"

"I confess I didn't bake it. This afternoon, when I delivered compote dishes to the Hobart twins, Zoe had baked this and insisted I take a piece home with me. It's quite good, isn't it?"

"Sure is. She needs to bring this to our next meeting."

Gwen resisted the urge to share Zelda's opinion that most of the garden club members were unworthy of Zoe's lemon cake, simply saying, "I'll suggest that to her." Circling the conversation back to party night, Gwen surged ahead. "I overheard a curious conversation before our Yankee Swap."

Lowering her fork to the plate, Evelyn tapped her lips with a napkin. "Why curious?"

Once again relaying the words of the blackmailer and the adulterer, Gwen asked for Evelyn's opinion.

Evelyn sat in silence a moment too long. "I'd rather not guess who they were." In the next instant, she reached for her cane and slid off the stool. "Thanks for the cake and coffee, Gwen. I won't take any more of your evening."

Thinking Evelyn's departure rather abrupt, Gwen retrieved the rectangular Pyrex pan from the stack atop her stove. "Let me carry this to your car."

"That's thoughtful of you." Evelyn began her arduous retreat to Gwen's front door. Step, thump, step, thump.

After Gwen placed the glass dish on the passenger floor, Evelyn fastened her seat belt without looking over. "See you at the January meeting."

"I'll be there," Gwen responded, perplexed.

Without so much as a backward glance, Evelyn drove away.

Evelyn's rush to leave begged the question: What did she know about those whisperers that she wasn't willing to share? Did she know the identity of one, if not both?

***

After non-stop activity, the abrupt silence of the old library surrounded Gwen like a warm blanket. Grabbing her steno pad, she noted the return of Evelyn's Pyrex baking dish plus the woman's odd behavior at the mention of the whisperers.

Sensing she'd be going to bed early, Gwen trudged out to her car trunk and carried the remaining party dishes into the kitchen. The next morning, Eunice, Frankie, and Nadine would be retrieving theirs.

Gwen located Ruby's silver platter and set it aside to wait for the woman's return. Once again, Gwen wondered if Ruby shoved Myrtle. Was her flight to Denver planned or a last-minute escape? Would she ever return to Harbor Falls?

When a furry body rubbed against Gwen's ankle, she glanced into Amber's upturned face. "It's been a long and busy day, my pet. Let's head up to bed."

Chapter Twenty-Four

…early morning, Saturday

Just after eight on Saturday morning, Ben parked in the lot behind the Carswell House and made his way to the front porch of the B&B. Although he'd given no warning that he'd be stopping by, the lights blazing inside the magnificent home told him that some of the guests were out of bed. If Ben's luck held, Charlie Brewster would be enjoying a hardy breakfast.

As soon as Betty opened the door, the smell of sizzling bacon and fried eggs wafted to Ben's nostrils. What was that additional smell? French toast? Waffles? Ben's belly growled.

"Good morning, Detective Snowcrest. I didn't realize we'd be seeing you again so soon."

"And to you, Mrs. Owens. It occurred to me that Charlie is due to check out tomorrow morning and I have yet to catch up with him for a second chat. Has he left for the day?"

Betty gestured Ben inside. "He's in the dining room. If you haven't eaten, you're welcome to join the boys."

When Ben entered, Shawn and Dylan jumped to their feet. The Schuster family, the Pettigrew couple, and Brooke Hammond were nowhere in sight.

"Hey, Detective," Shawn said, giving him a little wave.

Dylan nodded but said nothing.

Charlie poked the last piece of toast into his mouth and held up one finger. "Good morning, Detective Snowcrest. I guess you're here to talk to me again."

"That's right, Charlie, but I'll wait until you've eaten."

Betty barreled through the swinging door and set a plate in front of Ben. Steam rose from the waffles. The side of bacon sizzled. She hefted a carafe and filled his cup.

"Thank you, but you didn't need to go to all this trouble."

"No trouble at all, Detective. You need to eat before you go off to find Myrtle's attacker."

Ben didn't miss Mrs. Owens' crystal clear message that her husband should not be a suspect. Ben had come to the same conclusion. Robert's hand appeared too large to match the bruises. But it was too soon to say as much to her.

Flitting around the table, Mrs. Owens added, "You'll find clotted cream, strawberry jam, and genuine maple syrup from western Massachusetts. Let me know if you want more waffles. I hate to waste perfectly good batter."

She glanced at the Harvard students. "You boys want seconds, or is it thirds?"

"No, ma'am," Shawn answered. "Me and Dylan are stuffed. I can't speak for Charlie."

Charlie held up a hand, shaking his head as he chewed.

Betty turned to Ben. "Robert and I are debating whether to reveal our recent tragedy to our new batch of guests. What would you suggest?"

Ben resisted giving advice that could easily backfire. Still, he said, "If you think they'll find out some other way, it might be better if you and your husband are the ones to explain. The decision is entirely up to you."

"I'll give that some thought." Betty gathered used dishes before bustling through the swinging door.

During the interchange, Charlie had cleaned his plate. Ben took another minute to finish his unanticipated meal before rising to his feet. "If you're ready, Charlie, let's talk in the front parlor." Ben carried his coffee cup with him. The brew was good but not nearly as tasty as Gwen's. But then Ben had to admit he was prejudiced.

As he slid the pocket door closed, Ben glanced at Charlie. "This is just a curiosity question, but how sure are you that the ghost pushed you from your bed the other night?"

"That was my impression, Detective. I don't know how else I could have ended up on the floor. Why are you asking?"

"Like I said, just curious."

"You don't believe in ghosts?"

Ben eased into the upholstered chair. "Let me say it this way. My job's complicated enough dealing with mere mortals. I can't grasp the concept of ghosts."

"That's understandable, sir."

Ben launched into what he expected would be his final interview with Charlie, urging the young man to remember something, anything, that would point the finger at someone on Robert's tour. But the attempt proved pointless, as it had with every other witness.

Charlie confirmed the discussion with Shawn and Dylan about a night cap, maintaining he'd been facing away from the steps when his Aunt Myrtle tumbled down. Ben had no option but to tell Charlie he was free to check out the next morning, wishing him luck with his studies at Harvard.

***

As the morning light found its way into Gwen's bedroom, she was awakened by Amber's feline nose nuzzling her cheek. The bedside clock glowed half past eight. Either the alarm had failed or Gwen had punched the snooze button once too often.

Panicking, she jumped out of bed, took a quick shower, and dried her feathered hair into its usual tousled hairdo. Before she finished, the doorbell echoed up the staircase and she rushed to the first floor to greet the three club members.

"Good morning, Gwen," the first woman said, her tone a bit snippy. "If we had known you asked us all to arrive at the same time, we could have car-pooled."

"Sorry, Eunice. Very inconsiderate of me."

Eunice huffed and pushed past Gwen. Behind her, Frankie tossed Gwen an apologetic look, while Nadine gazed at her feet, clearly embarrassed by Eunice's criticism.

"The party dishes are in my kitchen. Follow me and you can hunt for your piece. Would any of you like coffee?"

Frankie and Nadine answered together. "I'd love a cup."

"None for me," Eunice snapped. "Too much to do before relatives invade my house for Christmas. I'll just grab my salad bowl and be on my way." After pawing through two boxes, Eunice pulled out a crystal dish from the third. "Where are my silver tongs?"

Gwen dug to the bottom of the first box. "They must be here somewhere. Betty gave me everything that was left behind the other night."

Stepping close to the second box, Frankie rummaged around. "Here they are, Eunice."

Eunice seized the tongs. "I wouldn't be surprised if that woman in Betty's kitchen swiped my grandmother's tongs. They're solid sterling you know." She clicked the tongs as if that proved their metal quality.

Given Eunice's lack of a charming disposition, Gwen doubted the woman ever had an affair, and further doubted that any club members would confide in her. Since Eunice couldn't provide any insight into Myrtle's tumble, Gwen opted not to detain her. "Let me walk you out, Eunice."

Minutes later, Gwen served the coffee. She sat on the stool opposite Frankie and Nadine and took her first sip, sighing with contentment. "Nothing like that first taste of morning coffee."

"Not my first cup of the day," Frankie confessed.

Nadine spoke in her timid voice. "Do either of you want to discuss poor Myrtle?"

Frankie wrapped her hands around the warm mug. "I'm still in shock. Did you know Detective Snowcrest went to Holly's shop and told her Myrtle's death was no accident?"

"How do you know that?" Nadine asked, echoing Evelyn's question to Gwen the evening before.

"I stopped in to buy a few gifts and she told me." Frankie stirred her coffee. "Holly *was* in the upper hallway when it happened. The detective asked if she remembered where everyone was standing."

Nadine drew in a sharp breath. "What did Holly say?"

"She was studying one of the pictures and didn't notice."

Gwen stood silently at the stove, waiting for them to share some new details.

"Is that detective going to question everyone?" Nadine wanted to know.

"Yep," Frankie confirmed. "I'm glad I picked Betty's group."

"Me, too," Nadine's tiny voice agreed.

When the silence became uncomfortable, Gwen brought up the whisperers. "Something else occurred that night. Let me tell you what I overheard in the front parlor during the party. Maybe you can make some sense of it."

Frankie and Nadine's eyes grew larger with each word.

"And you didn't recognize the voices?" Frankie asked, sounding disappointed.

"No, I didn't. They could have been either male or female."

"Well," Frankie sputtered, "if I had to speculate, I'd say the blackmailer was Myrtle. Her only topic of conversation at every club meeting is the burden of her grandson's education. She goes on and on like a broken record."

Nadine piped up, "Don't be too harsh on her. I heard she has shared custody of the boy. I don't know what happened to his parents. Myrtle and her husband are paying his tuition."

"I heard that, too," Gwen added. "But that doesn't prove she was the whispering blackmailer."

Frankie shook her finger in the air. "Your whisperers weren't necessarily members of the garden club."

"That's true," Gwen agreed, knowing she and Ben both assumed they were connected. "There were lots of others at the B&B on the night of our party."

Nadine studied the ceiling. "You're right. All those guests, plus that woman helping Betty in the kitchen. If those two in the parlor *were* club members, I don't know of any of us having an affair. How about you, Frankie?"

After a moment, Frankie shook her head. "If that adulterer belongs to the club, she sure knows how to keep a secret."

***

As she closed the door behind Frankie and Nadine, Gwen's cell phone buzzed and made her jump. Reading the caller ID, she hesitated before answering. "Hello, Hal."

"How close are you to the airport," he barked. "We board in

an hour, and you still need to get through security."

Gwen plunked herself on the bottom step of her staircase. "Like I told you the other night, Hal. If your trip didn't conflict with Tess's dinner, I might have flown down with you."

"And I told *you* I had to schedule this trip during Jenna's break. Where are you right now?"

"At home."

"You can still make it if you hurry."

Increasingly irritated with the man's tunnel vision, Gwen dropped her forehead into the palm of her other hand. "I'm not changing my holiday plans with Tess."

"So you've decided not to fly down with me and Jenna?" His voice mixed disbelief and barely-disguised anger.

"You're not hearing me, Hal. I'll be in the Berkshires for Tess's Christmas reunion dinner."

"You're a fool, Gwen. Any sane person would jump at this chance to escape the snow."

The past year or so with her buddy Hal flashed through Gwen's mind at lightning speed. He'd never been so inconsiderate, so pushy, so mean.

Was this flight to Florida for house-hunting Hal's underhanded way of separating his life from hers? Had he grown weary of her refusal to fall into his bed? Was he so calculating that he risked the price of her ticket, knowing she'd refuse his last-minute invitation? Add to that his supreme offense of once again implying she was not only a fool, but insane as well. Didn't he realize name-calling wasn't the way to change anyone's mind?

Gwen glanced at her watch. Ten o'clock. Ben would arrive any second. "Have a safe flight, Hal." She wished she had the house receiver in her hand so she could slam it in the man's ear. Instead, she pushed the red button on her cell phone and ended his aggravating call.

She wandered to her music studio and flipped the switch of her new diffuser, the mystery of her disintegrating friendship buzzing in her head like a nest of angry wasps. Up to the point of refusing his plane ticket, she and Hal had been very compatible, apparently giving him the false impression that she'd follow along with whatever he suggested.

Gwen was suddenly saddened by Hal's life-altering decision, but she wasn't about to leave Harbor Falls to retain their friendship. She had no choice but to wish the man well. Although Hal would be disappearing from her life, Gwen nurtured a close circle of friends. Every once in a while, a new one came along.

Moving into the living room, she glanced out the front windows. Low grey clouds hovered to the south. Visions of Hal and Jenna in Florida took shape. They'd find no ice or snow in the Sunshine State.

Gwen didn't let the weather in either state get to her. Harbor Falls would always be her home, including whatever Old Man Winter blew her way.

***

At quarter to nine, Ben left the B&B, crossed North Street, and strolled along the sidewalk until he reached the Sugar 'n Spice Bakery on the southern edge of the village green. He nabbed a window table for an unobstructed view of Gwen's property on the opposite corner.

Her three visitors arrived promptly at nine. Within five minutes, one of them drove off. Ben finished his cup of coffee and accepted a refill. Thirty minutes passed before the other two women emerged and sped away. He jammed his arms into his winter coat, picked up his briefcase, and walked the remaining distance to the northwest corner.

Before he reached the brownstone and brick structure of Gwen's home, he detoured up her driveway, crossed the rear deck, and knocked on the doorframe of the French door. Through the glass, he watched her approach. She flipped the lock, opened the door, and waved him inside.

Stomping his boots on the deck boards to un-stick the snow, he said, "Good morning, Gwen. Looks like more snow."

"So it seems. You can leave your boots on the mat if you'd like." Gwen's tone held no energy. As she helped him shrug out of his coat, she asked mechanically, "Coffee?"

"No, thanks. I nursed two cups at the Sugar 'n Spice until your visitors left." He sniffed the air. "Smells good in here."

Gwen gestured toward her music studio. "My new diffuser."

"I like it." No reaction from Gwen. "Why did one club member leave before the other two?"

"I'm sorry, Ben. What did you say?"

He repeated each word in slow motion. "Why-did-one-club-member-leave-before-the-other-two?"

"Oh. Eunice had to go home." Gwen led him into the living room and gestured toward the sofa before settling herself at the opposite end, pulling one leg beneath her.

Placing his briefcase on the floor, Ben retrieved his notebook and pen, poised to write. "Did those three women have anything to contribute?"

"Not really."

Puzzled by Gwen's lack of conversation, Ben kept talking.

"Why don't we review your notes?"

"I'm sorry, Ben, I haven't made any notes."

Ben lowered his pen. "I don't mean to find fault, but you don't seem all that interested in meeting with me."

She looked him straight in the eye. "I apologize. Hal just called me from Logan Airport."

"Oh." Ben tried to make his tone sympathetic, hoping she wouldn't notice he didn't sound all that sincere. "Isn't this the day he's flying to Florida with his granddaughter?"

Gwen nodded and hugged a pillow to her chest. "He still expected me to cancel my Christmas plans with Tess and shop Florida real estate with him."

"Are you sorry you said no?"

"Not so much sorry. More sad that I'm losing a friend I used to cherish."

"That explains why you're preoccupied." Ben rested his forearms on his knees, notebook and pen dangling. "I have an idea that might take your mind off him for a few hours."

"What's that?"

"On Saturday evenings, the Lucky Lobster features musicians in their lounge. Why don't we head up there later for an early dinner, then stay and listen for a while? I'll bring you home whenever you say you've had enough."

"I don't know, Ben. Loud bands give me a headache."

"Not a loud band. This month's musician is a female singer who also plays the piano. Her songs bring back memories of my younger days."

"You've heard her?"

He nodded, sensing Gwen might relent. "Last weekend. I'm sure you'll enjoy her. What do you think? Are you game?"

"I don't know, Ben. Should we be seen together in public again? I'm already concerned that Kristen noticed us eating lunch at the Bayside Café the other day."

Ben wasn't giving up. "The chances of someone from Harbor Falls seeing us at the Lucky Lobster are slim. We'll be ten miles up the coast."

"But isn't going out socially against department policy?"

Ben shook his head. "Not at all. You weren't a direct witness to Mrs. Mueller's fall. You're only helping me collect behind-the-scenes information. At the suggestion of the police chief, I might add."

Gwen seemed to ponder his rationale. "Well, if you're sure, because your suggestion sounds like an evening I'd enjoy. I haven't listened to live music for eons."

"Great. I'll pick you up around five thirty."

Ben could barely contain his euphoria that Gwen had accepted his invitation, struggling to re-route his brain to the Myrtle Mueller case.

Chapter Twenty-Five

...mid-morning, Saturday

Gwen welcomed the evening out Ben offered. She needed a break from stressing over Hal's decision to upend his life, and in the process upending hers as well.

Retrieving her steno pad from the kitchen counter, she rejoined Ben in the living room. "I'll write my notes while I tell you about my morning visitors." Locating the next blank page, Gwen suddenly flipped to the previous. "No, no, wait. First, I need to tell you about Evelyn Woodley's visit after supper last night." Gwen didn't add that she'd eaten with Annabelle while discussing Parker's potential walk to the B&B.

"The lady with a cane?" Ben asked, settling against the leather couch cushions.

"That's her. She came by to pick up her Pyrex baking pan. I invited her for coffee and lemon cake, and we commiserated over Myrtle's misfortune. When I brought up the whisperers, Evelyn grabbed her cane and hobbled out my door. I think she knows more than she's willing to say."

Ben's expression turned thoughtful. "Sounds like she could be hiding something. She was in Robert's tour group, so she's on my list for a second interview." He rested his arm along the back of the sofa, facing Gwen. "I want you to know I'm very pleased with your efforts as my C.I."

"But I haven't brought you any significant information."

"Not true. Your personal connection and input about the garden club members will round out my official reports."

Ben hefted his briefcase onto his lap and flipped the latches to expose a sheaf of stapled documents. "I printed background checks for most of the people at the B&B on party night. Since we're talking about Evelyn, let's begin with her."

"What sort of information do you have there?" Gwen asked, peering inside.

He recited the categories. "Education, addresses, eviction notices, town census, traffic violations, arrest records, credit card report, civil suits."

"Wow, that's impressive. I didn't know you had access to all that detail."

"These reports only provide a person's documented history, but there's nothing remotely personal in here. That's where you come in. Your perspective will provide insight into each one's potential beyond these black-and-white facts. Let me find Evelyn's report while you fill me in on the lady." Ben selected a printout before sliding his attaché onto the couch cushions between them.

Gwen gathered her impressions of the woman before saying them out loud. "Evelyn is somewhat of an enigma. Whenever I've spoken to her at club meetings, she always turns our conversation to me. She's never shared any portion of her life story. I don't know the barest detail. Don't even know the reason behind her cane."

Ben concentrated on the first document, the town census. "Here are her basics. Evelyn has lived in a small bungalow north of town with three cats for more than thirty years." He flipped to the next. "This state police report explains her cane. Twenty-one years ago, she and her husband were in a serious car accident. She was driving. Her husband died at the scene.

Her right leg is severely scarred and slightly shorter. Charges were filed against the drunk driver who crossed into their lane."

Gwen murmured, "I didn't know she's a widow."

Lifting a third piece of paper, Ben scrutinized the details. "She received a generous insurance settlement." A fourth report: "She invested that money and lives on the dividends plus her social security check." Ben looked over at Gwen. "Do you think she could have pushed Mrs. Mueller?"

"I can't imagine Evelyn pushing anyone, Ben. With her dependence on that cane, the effort to shove another person would throw her off balance. In fact, she told me that when everyone rushed forward after the scream, it was all she could do to stay on her feet." Gwen jotted a notation. "Your background check eliminates her as the adulterer since she doesn't have a husband and she doesn't seem to need money. She might have left so abruptly last night because she has an idea of who the whisperers could be."

"A distinct possibility," Ben agreed. "But I'll keep her on my list until we've gathered as many facts as we can find. Let's move to your morning visitors."

Feeling totally involved in the investigation, Gwen said, "These three women were in Betty's group with me, so they had no input about Myrtle's fall."

"That's fine. What's the name of the woman who left first?"

"Eunice Flint. She hurried out before I had a chance bring up the whisperers."

Ben again rummaged in his briefcase. "Here she is. Do you think she could be either the adulterer or blackmailer?"

Gwen mulled over his question. "Given her unpleasant attitude this morning, I can't see Eunice having an affair. But people can fool you. You have her financial report there?"

Ben pulled another sheaf of papers, reciting Eunice's history as he flipped from one document to the next. "High school graduate, no college, married young, still married to the same man, living in the same house. She's never worked outside her home. Her husband won't retire for another ten years. Two sons, a daughter, all college-educated with good jobs, all three living close enough to visit. Four grandchildren from the sons, daughter unmarried. Several speeding tickets, no arrests, a single civil suit twenty years ago with a minimal settlement. No major illnesses. On the surface, a typical American family."

"So no indication that she could be the blackmailer?"

"Nothing that sticks out at least. Give me the other names."

"Frankie Peterson and Nadine Alexander." Gwen waited until Ben rifled through his briefcase and separated their histories before sharing the morning discussions. "Frankie thinks Myrtle was the blackmailer because of her constant complaints about her grandson's tuition bills. I supposed it's possible Frankie was taking the spotlight off herself, but I don't think so. Anything there to indicate she's desperate for cash?"

"Again, nothing obvious," Ben answered without reciting Frankie's history. "She's not married, so doesn't qualify as the adulterer either." Ben passed the packet to Gwen before balancing the second set of papers on his lap. "Anything interesting from Nadine Alexander?"

"Not a lot. She pointed out that everyone in the B&B on party night were potential whisperers. She said that Myrtle and her husband are paying Herbert's college tuition because they share custody with the boy's parents but didn't know any other details. Neither Nadine nor Frankie claimed to know of a club member having an affair. I'm afraid their input wasn't much help."

"Solving a case doesn't happen in an hour like it does on TV, Gwen." Ben shifted Nadine's document from his lap to the couch beside him. "We'll follow each detail and see where it takes us. Eventually, something will click."

"I'll take your word for it." Gwen glanced at the paperwork threatening to engulf Ben. "Would you like to move to the dining room table?"

He grinned at her. "I thought you'd never ask."

Chapter Twenty-Six

...late morning, Saturday

Pushing the placemats to the other end of the dining room table, Gwen made a space for Ben's documents. "How long did it take you to gather and print all these details?"

"Hours, but I find the research satisfying. I suppose it gives me a false sense of progress."

Gwen grinned. "That's an interesting opinion of your efforts. Before we tackle these, Ben, are you hungry? I can fix us sandwiches."

"I'm always hungry, but I think you figured that out already. I'll have what you're having. What can I do to help?"

***

As Gwen prepared tuna salad with celery, tarragon, and mayonnaise, Ben popped slices of sourdough bread into the toaster oven.

"Do you like green olives, Ben?"

He scrunched up his nose.

Gwen laughed. "Okay, okay! No green olives for you. That leaves more for me. Can you grab the bag of potato chips from the cabinet above the stove?" She placed the quartered and plated sandwiches on the island counter before adding a can of soda for Ben and a bottle of peach iced tea for her.

Ben took his first bite. "Umm, good. You're the only woman I know who makes tuna salad like my mom. She swore tarragon was the magic ingredient."

"An intelligent woman, your mom. Is she still alive?"

"No. She passed eight years ago after battling cancer. She was the glue that held the family together for the holidays. That's why I rarely see my relatives."

Again, Gwen was tempted to invite Ben to Tess's for Christmas dinner but resisted the urge.

***

Returning to the dining room, Ben sat in front of his papers and Gwen eased into the adjacent chair. Ben tried to control his attraction to her because they had work to do. She was no help when she leaned closer and he got a whiff of her vanilla scent.

"Who's next?" she asked, unsuspecting of her effect on him.

Forcing his mind to focus, Ben selected a packet from the array on the table. "Zelda Hobart. You visited the twins yesterday, didn't you?"

Gwen nodded. "I did. Zoe baked that lemon cake and insisted I bring half home with me. Would you like a piece?"

Ben patted his flat stomach. "Maybe later."

Gwen shrugged and continued. "The twins are spinsters, so that eliminates them as the whispering adulterer. A few years ago, they sold their family farm and bought the condo where I met them yesterday. I saw no indication they're hurting for money, so I think they're both out as the blackmailer."

Ben flipped through the reports for the twins. "Nothing here refutes your analysis." He passed it to her.

Gwen took a quick look. "When you interviewed them on party night, did they remember anyone's location?"

"Nothing that points the finger at a particular person. Zelda insisted they be interviewed together."

"I'm not surprised. Zelda always speaks first. She's very protective of Zoe, who's five minutes younger."

Ben flipped to an earlier page in his notebook. "They both claimed they were on the far side of the sitting room. It was all I could do to keep them from telling me what they'd learned."

Gwen sat up. "I just remembered something Evelyn said last night. During the tour, the Hobart twins were standing next to her reading every word out loud. Maybe the twins are the ones who bumped Evelyn as they rushed toward Robert."

"That's good," Ben commented. "If Evelyn's memory is accurate, she's confirmed that the Hobart twins weren't close enough to push Mrs. Mueller. Anything else?"

"Yes. Zelda overheard a conversation in the kitchen at the November club meeting."

Ben lifted an eyebrow. "More eavesdropping?"

Gwen gave his arm a playful slap.

He faked injury. "Sorry, I couldn't resist. We're both getting a little punch-drunk after slogging through all these reports. Tell me what Zelda overheard."

Gwen located her notes from the day before. "Here's what Zelda heard. *'You need to call it off. And I mean now'.*"

Resting his chin in his palm, Ben tapped his cheek. "That's very telling."

"Maybe it was the confidante warning the adulterer to end the affair?"

"Possibly. Did Zelda see who was talking?"

"Of course not. That would be too easy. Unless Zelda was making this up — and I don't think she was — that tidbit confirms the adulterer is very likely a garden club member."

"Along with her confidant," he added, filing the Hobart packet. "We're making steady progress, Gwen." He pulled the next pack of paperwork. What's your input on Ruby Cox?"

"Other than observing she's a big flirt and has a green thumb in her rose beds, I don't know much."

Ben clicked his pen. "Her flirting seems to be on automatic pilot. I thought she was going to wink at me while I was taking her statement."

"I'm not at all surprised, Ben. Whenever we've had a male speaker at a club meeting, Ruby manages to drape herself all over the poor man. And I swear she winked at Robert when she joined his group for the B&B tour."

Ben sifted through Ruby's documents, sharing details as he read them. "She doesn't seem to have any financial problems. A good paying job as a researcher at a tech company on the ring road around Boston. She spends her money on clothes." Ben turned to the final page. "She filed for divorce last week."

"I wonder why?" Gwen speculated out loud. "If she's been having an affair and she's found out, that could ruin any alimony she's chasing from her soon-to-be ex-husband."

"Did she attend the November club meeting?"

Gwen sat quietly for a few seconds. "Yes," Gwen confirmed. "Ruby was there. I remember her asking the female speaker about preserving berries for door wreaths. She's a prime candidate as the adulterer who shoved Myrtle. Now I'm even more curious about her flight to Denver."

"Don't get me wrong, Gwen. I'm not happy that she left town, but there's nothing we can do until she returns."

"Can't you interview her over the phone?"

Ben shook his head. "I prefer face-to-face so I can gauge the person's honesty."

"How do you do that?"

"Reading body language and facial expressions."

"That could come in handy. Can you teach me?"

"I'll share what I've learned, but not right this second."

"Okay." Gwen eyed the packets. "Who's next?"

"Alicia Reed and Holly Nichols." He separated two files and slid one set of stapled papers in front of him. "Let's review your club president first. What's your input on the lady?"

Gwen thought first before speaking. "She owns the Serendipity Gift Shoppe. I don't know if it's a money maker or not. I think her husband is involved with a tech company on Rt. 128 west of Boston."

Ben scanned his research. "Mrs. Nichols' store turns a nice profit. Most of that cash is reinvested. Her husband Kyle not only works at a Boston tech company, he owns it. He gifts Holly with a generous chunk of capital each quarter. Unless she resents his money, I can't see her blackmailing anyone. They live in one of the historic homes near Powder Point Bridge."

Gwen quieted. "Parker and I used to walk across that bridge on our way to Duxbury Beach."

"Small world, Gwen. Powder Point Bridge is one of my favorites. The day I take my Corvette out of storage each spring, I always take a drive there. You interested in going with me?"

Ben watched her debating her decision, not knowing what she was thinking.

Gwen finally spoke. "I'd like that, Ben." Without saying any more, she glanced at his documents. "Sounds like Holly's not hurting for money."

"Any chance she could be the adulterer?"

Gwen shrugged. "Unless a club member tells me some salacious details, there's no way to find out. I can't just walk up to Holly and ask her."

"Point taken. We'll wait and see if someone suggests Holly is having an affair." Ben slid Holly's packet aside and brought forward the fourth set. "Alicia Reed and Travis."

Gwen didn't wait for him to ask for her input. "She's the club secretary and a stay-at-home mom. Her husband Travis landed a new job recently after being downsized last year. Money must have been tight, but Alicia's never complained …not to me, anyway."

Ben reviewed their bank statement. "They drained their savings until checks from Travis's new job bolstered their balance last month."

"That must have been a relief," Gwen said. "I don't think Alicia has the temperament to blackmail anyone. And I can't imagine her cheating on Travis either. With the kids, she doesn't have the time or opportunity."

"You're entitled to your opinion. Gwen. We won't know if you're right until this case is solved." Ben pulled the final two packets. "Let's begin with Mrs. Mueller and her husband Fletcher. By the way, I stumbled on the family arrangement."

Gwen gripped her mug. "What was that?"

"Mr. and Mrs. Mueller share custodial rights of their grandson with their son and daughter-in-law. This Caregiver Authorization Affidavit doesn't explain the reason."

"So Nadine heard right," Gwen murmured.

"As the boy's guardians," Ben continued, "they can make health and education-related decisions on his behalf."

"So Myrtle and Fletcher also took on the burden of paying for Herbert's college education," Gwen added. "I had no idea that losing the music competition and the scholarship money placed such a financial burden on them."

"You shouldn't feel responsible for their money problems, Gwen. Let's take a look at the Mueller financials."

Gwen peeked over Ben's arm as he progressed through the various documents. "They don't pay off their credit card bill each month, so the interest fees are piling up on top of new charges from QVC, eBay, and Amazon."

"Baylies College sends an invoice for tuition, so that won't show up on their VISA bill."

Ben pulled a different document. "Checking account statement." His finger stopped at an entry. "Here we go. A check to Baylies in the amount of nine thousand dollars."

Gwen gulped. "That's a lot of money, but it's only a portion of the yearly cost. That financial burden is a good reason for Myrtle to blackmail the adulterer."

"Possibly," Ben agreed, "but that assumes she was one of your whisperers." He tapped a packet. "Last file."

"Who's left?"

"Robert and Betty Owens."

Gwen glared at him. "I thought I convinced you Robert can't possibly be guilty of pushing Myrtle."

Ben wasn't ready to release the man. "Didn't you say that when you and Betty reached him, he was looking down the flight of steps?"

Gwen stiffened. "Yes, along with everyone else on his half of the tour. Nobody saw Robert push Myrtle."

Ben's frustration flared. "Nobody saw anyone push her, Gwen. They were all reading the damn articles and looking at the family pictures. At least that's what the immediate witnesses keep telling me. Obviously, one of them is lying, and I intend to find out which one."

Ben scratched his eyebrow with the back of his thumb, bringing his anger under control. "Forgive my outburst, Gwen. You seem to be good friends with Mrs. Owens. Has she mentioned how well they're doing with the B&B?"

"Well, they only opened a few weeks ago," Gwen answered. Betty mentioned two rooms on the second floor are empty this week. We didn't discuss future bookings."

Ben read the Owens report in sections. "They're carrying a substantial mortgage for the purchase of the Carswell House plus a construction loan for the B&B conversion."

"What are you implying?"

"If Mrs. Mueller wasn't the blackmailer, Betty or Robert Owens could have been. You did say you couldn't tell if the whisperers were men or women."

Gwen clasped her hands so tight her knuckles to turn white. "I disagree, Ben. I've known Betty and Robert for years through the garden club. They're hard-working people with kind hearts. If they can book the B&B to capacity, I'm sure they'll pay off those loans on schedule. I see no need for them to sink into blackmail. Plus they love each other, so adultery is out of the question. Aren't we leaning toward Myrtle as the blackmailer?"

"Because Mrs. Mueller was attacked, she's the most likely candidate, but it's always possible we're wrong."

Gwen sat up straight. "If the blackmailer wasn't Myrtle, does it matter who was?"

"Yes." Ben insisted. "Even if we determine your whisperers weren't connected to Mrs. Mueller's death, the threat is hanging out there. We don't know what the adulterer might do to prevent exposure. I sure as hell don't want another murder case on my hands."

"Neither do I," Gwen agreed. "But I'd hate to see two marriages ruined if the affair is over."

"So you'd prefer the adulterer pay up?"

Gwen jolted. "I guess so."

"Payment is no guarantee that the blackmail ends." Ben stacked his jumbled paperwork in a pile and slid the packets into his briefcase.

Seemingly at a loss for a comeback, Gwen asked, "Did you ever catch up with Charlie?"

"Yes, this morning at the B&B."

"With your skill at reading facial expressions, did you believe his claim of innocence?"

"I did. I gave all three boys permission to check-out tomorrow morning. If I need to speak to them again, Harvard is not that far of a drive."

"You've already excused the Pettigrews, Miss Hampton, and the Schuster family. How soon will you eliminate Robert from your suspect list?"

"Based on the lack of evidence to implicate him, it won't be long now."

"So we're almost back to the six garden club members on his half of the tour?"

Ben took a deep breath, relieved they were no longer disagreeing. "It's looking that way, Gwen. You still arranging the return of the party dishes?"

"I am," she confirmed. "Do you happen to have the patrolman's list of the members who attended the party?"

Ben pulled a piece of paper from his notebook. "This list?"

Gwen took it from him, her eyes traveling from one name to the next. "Can I make a copy to keep track of my activities?"

"Sure."

"My copier's upstairs in the guest room. I'll be right back."

"No need to rush. Give it to me when I pick you up later."

Ben wasn't sure, but he thought Gwen blushed.

She stepped away from him. "I'd rather do this now."

As she headed for the curving staircase to the second-floor mezzanine, Ben's excitement resurfaced that she'd agreed to dinner and the lounge singer at the Lucky Lobster that evening. She'd balked at first until he convinced her their outing wasn't against department policy.

He considered her more than his sleuthing partner. Gwen was becoming a close friend. With Hal Jenkins planning to move south, any claim the man had on her was fast evaporating. Ben might mail Hal Jenkins a thank-you note.

A few minutes later, Gwen returned and handed over the original list.

"I need to get back to the station, Gwen. I'm glad you agreed to dinner tonight. I hope I haven't oversold the singer. I'll be back at five-thirty to pick you up. See you then."

As he headed down Gwen's front walkway, Ben foolishly imagined her leaning against her front door, hand to her heart, the anticipation of his return sweeping over her like a teenager.

Chapter Twenty-Seven

…mid-afternoon, Saturday

Ben's earlier-than-expected departure gifted Gwen with free time for other projects. Turning her thoughts to her hope of leading Parker to the B&B the next afternoon, she decided a brisk walk to Liz's shop would be refreshing. Gwen pulled on her boots and opened her front door. A burst of snowflakes blew in. The earlier threatening clouds now loomed overhead, spilling their chilly contents to the earth.

Gwen opted to drive. As she cleared the snow from the windshield of her Sonata, she decided that having a garage built next summer seemed like a good idea.

Tossing her scraper onto the back floorboard, Gwen dropped into the driver's seat. Only then did she remember to send a quick text to Ben. Not that she was meeting a club member, but it wouldn't hurt for him to know where she was.

After buckling her seatbelt, Gwen inched around the village green on the snowy cobblestones of Library Lane.

*****

"Gwen, you're back so soon?" Liz stretched her arms wide for their usual hug.

"I'm on a mission, Liz. Does your new herb display include sweet grass and dried sage?"

"As a matter of fact, I'm stocking both tied bunches and loose leaves. If I hadn't witnessed Madame Eudora's séance with you, I wouldn't even be aware of them. They sell out fast, but I think there's a bit left. Let's go check."

Grateful Liz hadn't pursued the reason Gwen wanted those particular herbs, she followed her friend through the newly-constructed archway and paused beside the circular bin. Liz lifted a hinged lid and handed Gwen clear Mylar bags printed with the logo of Fiction 'n Fables. "Here you go. You might find others that tickle your nose, so to speak."

Gwen chuckled as she selected a braid each of sweet grass and sage. "Clever, Liz."

"This aromatherapy section is a magnet to my customers. Have you set up your new diffuser, Gwen?"

"Sure have, and I love the mix of frankincense, blood orange, and cinnamon. How did you know which oils to combine?"

"Easy, peasy," Liz's impish grin was effortless. "The suppliers provided those suggestions." Liz indicated a colorful poster on the wall. "And there are websites with other scent combinations for all sorts of mental health challenges."

"I'll check them out. Listen, Liz, I'd love to stay and catch up, but I have some errands to run." Gwen didn't dare mention her non-date with Ben later. Liz would beg for the details and Gwen didn't have the energy to explain Hal's exodus as the reason for Ben's invitation.

"No problem, Gwen. We'll get together after the holidays. You still driving to Tess's house for Christmas next weekend?"

"I am. Did I tell you she's hosting a mini family reunion?"

"No, but that sounds warm and fuzzy. Give Tess my best."

"I'll do that."

Before moving to another shopper, Liz gathered Gwen into another warm embrace. "Merry Christmas, my friend."

Gwen carried her herb bags to the register. While she waited for Olivia to punch up her purchases, Gwen glanced across busy Harbor Hill to the Serendipity Craft Shoppe on the other side. On the sidewalk, Holly stood coatless as she spoke to Veronica. Their hand gestures suggested a disagreement.

Gwen considered interrupting them, then changed her mind. Best to stay out of it. Holly and Veronica were best friends. But even best friends clashed once in a while.

***

When Gwen turned the ignition key, Ben's suggestion of pepper spray popped into her mind, so she drove to the mall on Rt. 3. A taped sign hung across the front of Dick's Sporting Goods announced, '*This location closed. Please visit our store at the Westgate Mall in Brockton.*'

Deflated, but refusing to delay the purchase of that little can of protection, Gwen registered the mall's address into her GPS and requested back roads. If there was going to be a snow-related accident, it would most likely happen on the highways.

Finally entering the Brockton store, she asked a man where she could buy pepper spray.

He grinned at her and bellowed, "I can help you with that." He led her into the fishing and hunting section and indicated several packages hanging on the wall behind the register.

"I heard permits are no longer needed to buy pepper spray."

"That's right," the jolly salesclerk confirmed. "Which one do you want?"

Gwen racked her brain to remember Ben's recommendation, and finally pointed to the package labeled *Police Model*. "That blue one, please."

***

The snow continued to pile up as Gwen drove home. The

storm clouds masked the sun, ushering in the low light of dusk.

As Gwen stepped into her foyer, the grandmother clock bonged four. She placed the pepper spray and bags of herbs on the dining room table and texted Ben. *'I'm home. See you at five thirty.'*

Not fond of last-minute decisions, she headed upstairs to her alcove bedroom and sorted through her fancier clothes. Amber sat nearby, providing a non-stop soliloquy of feline opinion. When the chime of the front doorbell echoed up the staircase, Gwen dropped several ensembles onto her queen-sized bed and hurried to the first floor.

Her visitor was an unexpected surprise.

"Good afternoon, Veronica. Please come in."

The garden club treasurer stomped her feet before stepping into the foyer. "Sorry to barge in, Gwen, but I need to finalize the donation to Myrtle's family."

"Of course. Can you stay for a cup of tea and a slice of lemon cake?" Gwen didn't expect this impromptu visit to last long enough to interfere with getting ready for her non-date.

"Tea would be nice. I'll pass on the lemon cake." Veronica stepped out of her boots, revealing socks embroidered with snowmen. When she saw Gwen staring, Veronica laughed. "These are from Holly's store. They're so warm."

"They're also cute. Let me have your coat and hat." Gwen reached up as the girl slid her arms from her L.L. Bean jacket.

Veronica lifted the fur hat from her head, releasing her wavy brown hair to tumble down her back. "The temperature's dropping, Gwen. Snow is still falling. I won't be surprised if we get a few more inches than the weather gurus are predicting."

Following Gwen to the kitchen, Veronica eased onto a

counter stool and unlatched her leather tote. "Holly appreciated you and Betty delivering the club's donation. If I hadn't been out of town, I would've handled it myself."

Gwen filled the kettle and set it on the stove. "It was no trouble. What do you need from me?"

"Let's take care of the paperwork first. Do you have the receipt for the gift card?"

"It's in my shoulder bag. I'll go get it."

Thirty seconds later, Gwen placed the receipt in Veronica's outstretched hand.

"Thanks. You won't believe how many members buy items for a club function and toss the paperwork. Makes my bookkeeping nearly impossible."

Gwen chuckled. "As I grow older, I'm becoming just the opposite. Consider me a pack rat. I rarely throw anything away until I'm absolutely sure I won't need it."

"Not a bad habit." Veronica filed the receipt, her banter turning more serious. "I wonder if I'd been here for the Christmas party, maybe Myrtle wouldn't be dead."

The young woman's premonition-in-reverse brought Gwen up short. "Why would you think that?"

"Oh, I don't know, Gwen. Another person could have changed the group dynamics. Maybe Myrtle wouldn't have stood near the top of those steps. Maybe Holly wouldn't have suggested the tour in the first place."

Gwen retrieved her new snowman mugs from the cabinet. "Have you heard that Myrtle's fall wasn't an accident?"

Veronica didn't blink. "Yes. Holly told me."

"Was that you in front of her shop earlier? I was across the street at Fiction 'n Fables."

"Why didn't you come over and say hello?"

"I was in a hurry. Besides, you two were talking up a storm. In fact, you and Holly appeared to be arguing."

"She's a good friend, but I don't always agree with her decisions."

"Care to elaborate?"

"Not really. What happened at the party?"

Gwen found this request odd. "Didn't Holly tell you?"

"She did. But Holly was part of Robert's tour. You were in Betty's group, weren't you?"

Unsure how her account would differ from Holly's, Gwen countered, "That's true. I was at the top of the front staircase when we heard the scream. By the time we reached the far wall, Robert and his group stood in a cluster. It wasn't until I came up beside him that I glanced down the steps at a body and recognized Myrtle's brown polyester suit."

Veronica shuddered.

The teakettle whistled and Gwen added water to the mugs.

Veronica slid off the stool and came around the island. "Let me help you with that. Where are the tea bags?"

Gwen pointed the other side of the sink. "That canister contains a variety of flavors."

Pulling off the lid, Veronica peered inside. "Can I have this Constant Comment?"

"Of course." Gwen placed the steaming mugs on the countertop. "Grab two. I enjoy the orange and spice combination. Do you prefer raw sugar or honey?"

Lowering her teabag into the hot water, Veronica answered, "Honey, please."

As they waited for the tea to brew, Veronica said, "Holly

said you were at her shop when that detective stopped by for a second interview. She said you seemed to know him." Veronica paused, apparently waiting for Gwen to confirm or deny.

Gwen removed her tea bag and tossed it in the trash. Her initial connection to Ben last spring was public knowledge to anyone who'd read the Harbor Falls Gazette. However, her new role as his C.I. was not for public consumption. "Only casually," Gwen fibbed to Veronica now. "I met him during a police investigation earlier this year." Her name had been mentioned in the news article as a helpful citizen.

Veronica straightened. "Then you can ask him who the police think was responsible for Myrtle's fall."

"Did Holly suggest you ask me that question?"

"Not directly, but we're both curious. Does the detective think a garden club member did it? Is that why he's re-questioning everyone who was in Mr. Owens' group?"

Gwen needed to be careful not to reveal how much she knew. "Several of the B&B guests had joined Robert's group, too."

"That's right. Holly mentioned the three Harvard boys. So I guess the police are talking to them as well."

Though Veronica seemed sidetracked, Gwen tossed out another diversion. "I'd like your input on a conversation I overheard in Betty's front parlor earlier that night."

"Sure." Veronica took a delicate first sip. "What did you hear?"

After Gwen finished her story, she gazed at Veronica. "Do you know any club members who could be the whisperers?"

Veronica's face froze. "What makes you think they were garden club members? You said yourself that there were other people in the B&B that night."

Worried she'd pushed too hard, Gwen lowered her chin. "They were whispering, so I have no idea *who* they were."

Veronica glanced at her designer watch. "I'd better be going. Such a lot to catch up on after being away all week. Thanks for the tea, Gwen."

In her rush to leave, Veronica nearly lost her balance while shoving her feet into her boots. "Enjoy the holidays."

Gwen watched Veronica drive away in her Tesla sedan. The young woman's job obviously paid well. Like Evelyn's quick exit, Veronica's sudden rush to leave didn't sit right either. Was it possible both women knew the identity of the whisperers?

More than ever, Gwen wanted to learn the techniques of spotting a fib. Not willing to wait for Ben to share his knowledge, she pulled out her laptop for a quick online search, and printed several articles about reading facial expressions and analyzing body language.

Chapter Twenty-Eight

...early evening, Saturday

At the Lucky Lobster, Gwen ordered baked haddock with Ritz cracker topping. Ben requested a rib-eye steak with mushroom sauce.

He leaned across the table. "I thought the storm would pass before I picked you up."

"So did I," Gwen agreed. "The snow is obscuring our view of Massachusetts Bay." Out their waterside window, only the palest glimmer implied distant buoy lights.

The waiter appeared with Gwen's White Zinfandel and Ben's draft beer. After the man walked away, Gwen said, "Veronica showed up on my doorstep this afternoon."

Ben tilted his head. "I don't recall that name."

"That's because she wasn't at the party. She's the garden club treasurer but was out of town at a tradeshow last week."

"Was her visit relevant to either of our mysteries?"

Gwen took her first taste of the wine, savoring the sweetness before replying. "Sort of. I mentioned seeing her and Holly in a heated discussion outside Serendipity. Veronica downplayed their disagreement. As soon as I brought up the whisperers, she left. Like Evelyn, I think Veronica knows something."

Ben rested his chin in his palm. "I trust your instincts, Gwen, but I have no reason to interview Veronica. Do you have any reason to meet with her again?"

"I'll come up with some excuse." Gwen pulled out her website research. "I found these tips about reading faces."

Ben extended his hand. "Let me see what you've got."

She handed over the printout and waited.

His focus traveled from one guideline to the next. "These cover basic human reactions: happiness, surprise, contempt, anger, disgust, and fear. They relate more to a job interview. What you really want to know is how to determine if someone is lying. That's different. More like poker game tells."

Gwen reached for the page, turned it over and pulled a pen from her beaded evening bag. "You talk, I'll write."

"Okay," Ben agreed. "My biggest tell is when the person looks away. It doesn't matter if it's right, left, or down. They're avoiding eye contact. A second tell is the person talking too quickly, indicating nervousness. On the flip side, if they take too long to speak, they're deciding how much to reveal. They could be hiding something, but it's not necessarily connected to your basic inquiry."

He paused while she jotted notes. "If their hands begin to shake from excess adrenalin, the person might tuck them out of sight. The last tell I watch for is attention span. A person avoiding a question might pretend their cell phone vibrated. I've had suspects fake an entire phone call."

"Wow, that's amazing. Do you think Evelyn or Veronica's quick exits qualify?"

"Hard to say, Gwen. These tips are only indicators, not a guarantee that the person is fibbing or hiding details. Those two women could be hiding something unconnected to your whisperers or Mrs. Mueller's fall. I can't guess at what Evelyn didn't want to discuss. Veronica could have been embarrassed that you caught her arguing with Holly in public."

The waiter arrived with their meals, curtailing their

conversation. By mutual unspoken agreement, they suspended serious discussion while they savored their dinners, exchanging only comments about the delicious food.

When their waiter appeared and removed their emptied plates, he asked, "Any dessert for you folks this evening?"

Gwen drew in a deep breath. "I'd like a cup of decaf tea."

"I'll pass on the dessert, too," Ben agreed, "but I'll take a cup of coffee, black, and the check, please."

Stepping to a service area less than ten feet away, the waiter returned with their requested beverages. "If you decide you'd like dessert, I'll be close by." He scurried away with Ben's credit card and returned with the slip for signature.

Gwen sipped her tea. "My brain is tired, Ben."

"That's understandable. Let's drop the case for now."

As they topped off their meal, they exchanged small talk until the tickle of piano keys floated in from the lounge.

Ben placed his napkin on the table and reached for her hand. "Ready, Gwen?"

***

Seeing that the lounge was packed, Gwen's spirit deflated. And then Ben spotted an empty table, found her hand, and led her through the crowd.

From the first song, Gwen's foot swayed with each melody. With her private music students on hiatus during the holidays, topped with the non-stop activities surrounding those whisperers and Myrtle's death, Gwen hadn't played her flute or tickled the keys of her Steinway for nearly a week. After the holidays, she'd make amends.

Gwen leaned closer to Ben. "You're right. This singer is as wonderful as you promised."

191

The female crooner sang the first words of "At Last", the classic Etta Jones song about finding love. Ben extended his hand. "May I have this dance?"

Not expecting his invitation, Gwen found herself flustered until her fondness for play-acting kicked in. "My dance card is empty at the moment, sir."

Joining the other couples on the parquet floor, Ben whirled Gwen into his arms, placed his hand on the small of her back, and spun her into the crowd. She couldn't deny the clutch in her stomach at his nearness.

"Your outfit is very becoming," he whispered in her ear.

Gwen felt her cheeks warm. She glanced down at the lapis blue beaded top with flowing chiffon sleeves worn over black harem pants. Parker's favorite ensemble. She'd been relieved the garments still fit. "Thank you, Ben. Allow me to return the compliment. Your suit jacket fits your shoulders perfectly. Plus you're a very good dancer."

"I have to give my dance partner some of the credit. You've followed my every lead."

For the rest of the evening, Ben remained the consummate gentleman. As they danced, he didn't pull Gwen too close. When she rested her temple against his cheek, she stopped short of snuggling into his neck. Although she now considered Ben a good friend, he was far from her lover, and he was foremost a detective chasing a murderer. She was merely his CI.

The magical hours passed unnoticed until Ben glanced at his watch. "Whoa. I'd better get you home before your carriage turns into a pumpkin." He paid the bar bill and escorted her to his SUV. The storm had passed, but his windshield was caked with frozen sleet.

***

Stepping into her foyer, Gwen turned to say goodnight and found Ben leaning against the iron railing, his arms crossed. "Well, did my plan work?"

Confused, Gwen countered, "What plan?"

"Have you thought about Hal during the past few hours?"

Shocked at the truth of his statement, she chuckled. "As a matter of fact, I haven't. Your intention to distract me was a great success. Thanks for dinner, Ben. And I thoroughly enjoyed the lounge singer and the dancing."

"Then we'll have to do it again." Once more, Ben made a motion as if to leave, then turned back. "If you're available, let's meet Monday. I'm thinking ten o'clock again."

If he'd suggested Sunday, Gwen would have had to invent bogus plans so she could decline. She had no idea how much of her day would be devoted to connecting with Parker and walking him to the B&B, followed by his hunt for Theo. "Monday at ten is fine."

He set the appointment in his cell phone calendar. "Hope you don't mind me coming here for our meetings."

"Not at all. We're less likely to be caught together here than anywhere public."

"I agree. Goodnight, Gwen. See you Monday. Enjoy your day off from the case."

For a brief moment, she thought Ben was going to kiss her, but he didn't. Instead, he made his way along the front walkway, waving his hand backwards.

Gwen closed the door, replaying the evening. She hadn't enjoyed herself this much since she and Parker had danced the night away years before.

193

***

Ben drove away from Gwen's home with a lightness he hadn't felt for decades. That past April, they'd shared a few casual meals plus an abbreviated ride in his Corvette.

Her acceptance of his invitation for a second ride to Powder Point Bridge would no doubt be another pleasant outing.

But holding Gwen in his arms on the dance floor for the past few hours had been an unparalleled treat.

Chapter Twenty-Nine

...early morning, Sunday

Gwen wasn't due to bring Parker to the B&B until last week's guests had checked out. To be safe, she'd call Betty before trying to contact Parker. If he appeared, their walk across the village green would take five minutes or less. She could only hope his spirit could remain by her side. He'd have a few hours to find Theo and ask the important questions before the next guests checked in at three. Hopefully, Theo's ghost wouldn't hide from Parker's spirit.

Not a fan of idleness, Gwen looked around for a task or two to fill the time and spotted the cardboard boxes on her kitchen counter. Time to re-visit the final returns of the party dishes.

Retrieving her copy of the patrolman's list, she reviewed the names. The first members to leave were the three who'd refused to join the tours. Gwen didn't know those women well, suspecting they didn't participant in many club activities. At least they'd attended the Christmas party.

The next batch of names were the women who chose Betty's tour, ending with Gwen.

The final names below the line...those in Robert's group...were added after Ben's initial interviews.

Gwen flipped open her steno pad and rifled through the pages of her garden club activities. Next to the name on the patrolman's list, she transferred the details of each return, whether picked up or delivered. She then emailed the remaining women. If she didn't receive responses before she headed over to the B&B – hopefully with Parker in tow – she'd call those ladies later when she returned.

After hitting the 'send' button, Gwen wandered to her music studio and plunked a few keys on her Steinway. The instrument was perfectly tuned, thanks to the man who arrived like clockwork with each change of season.

Inspired by last evening's lounge singer/piano player, Gwen made herself comfortable on the padded bench seat. Dropping her fingers to the keys, she played the first few measures of Mozart's "Moonlight Sonata."

In a single spritely movement, Amber landed on the piano bench, snuggled against Gwen's thigh, and began to purr. The cat often exhibited her preference for the classics. Without losing a beat, Gwen played Beethoven's three-part composition, each section touching different emotions. Finishing his creation fifteen minutes later, Gwen lifted her hands from the keys and cradled Amber in her arms.

As if on cue, Gwen's cell phone buzzed on top of the Steinway. She picked it up, noted the caller ID, and tapped the green button to answer.

"Good morning, Gwen."

Surprisingly, the sound of Hal's voice didn't make her cringe. She found she was no longer reeling from his plans to sell his family nursery and relocate to Florida. Her initial dumbfounded reaction to his announcement at the pizza parlor had dissipated. Gaining perspective first from Tess and then spending the previous evening with Ben, had taken the sting out of Hal's impending departure.

The old saying was so true: *Nothing stays the same.* Many friends had strayed in and out of Gwen's circle during the decades of her life. Hal would become simply another friend to move on. He'd soon be swept up in his new lifestyle and make friends in Florida. So there was no need for Gwen to be rude to the man. "Did you and Jenna have a nice flight?"

"Non-stop is the only way to travel," he answered, his tone upbeat. "We viewed a few places yesterday afternoon."

"Anything promising?"

"Nothing so far, but Jenna and I will be down here until we fly back on New Year's Eve."

Hal hesitated, as if deciding what to say next.

Gwen closed the cover over the piano keys and waited.

"Listen, Gwen, I'm sorry I lost my temper at the pizza parlor. When you refused my ticket, I forgot my manners."

Hal's apology didn't change the fact that she was forever disenchanted with the man. However she wasn't going to let his rudeness slide by unchallenged. "I've never seen that pushy side of your personality, Hal."

"Yeah, well, it's too late to take it back, Gwen. You know what they say. You can't un-ring a bell. I apologized. Isn't that enough?" When she didn't answer, he forged ahead. "Are you sure you don't want to book the next available flight? The weather's perfect. Beautiful sunsets."

Gwen struggled to regain her calm nature. "You need to stop, Hal. I'm celebrating Christmas at Tess's."

"You're breaking my heart, Gwen." Hal's voice belied a cynical tone. "Well, let me know if you change your mind. You can easily rebook the ticket I left with you."

The man wore blinders. Gwen didn't comment. Flying to Florida after Christmas was hardly worth the hassle. "What's on your list for today?"

"Two condos and a beach cottage."

"What does Jenna think about the choices so far?"

"To be honest, Gwen, she's bored. I explained that I wanted her to be comfortable with my new home for when she visits."

"That's a valid reason to request her opinion."

"Jenna said whichever place makes me happy is fine with her. All she wants to do is stretch out and soak up the sun."

"Maybe you should let her. You don't want her cranky while you're down there."

"You're right. I'll have to make a decision without Jenna's input. Makes me wish you were here even more."

Avoiding another pointless argument, Gwen said, "I have to hang up, Hal. I'm involved in a new project." She wasn't going to reveal she'd be summoning Parker's spirit to locate Theo's ghost at the B&B. Nor would she mention her involvement in another police investigation. And bringing Ben into the conversation was an even worse idea.

Hal didn't ask about her project. "Can I call you again?"

"Sure. Good luck with your house search."

Hal mumbled something and broke the connection.

Chapter Thirty

...mid-morning, Sunday

Gwen's music studio darkened. She moved from the piano bench to the mullioned windows, peering out to gaze skyward. Dark clouds settled above the old library. Mother Nature and Old Man Winter appeared to be atoning for their winter storm tardiness. Were they in cahoots? Rather than mid-morning, the atmosphere mimicked the evening dusk of December. Even Gwen's light-sensor landscape lights had blinked on.

Not a bad atmosphere for performing a private séance.

Gwen made a quick call to Betty, who confirmed all the guests had checked out. "I'm calling Parker now, Betty. If I'm successful, we'll be there soon. If I'm not, I'll let you know."

Gwen drifted into the dining room, expecting to see both packets of herbs, startled to also see the bag from Dick's. She'd forgotten all about the pepper spray.

She ripped open the package and read the directions. Seemed simple enough. Point and spray into the assailant's eyes from a short distance. Try not to position yourself upwind from the target, as the fumes would drift back into your own face.

Gwen pondered that scene. She envisioned holding up her hand and asking her attacker to trade places. Chuckling at the idea, she carried the canister to the foyer table. She'd grab it on her way out.

Returning her attention to Parker, she duplicated Madame Eudora's sequence during the April séance. Gwen retrieved the same three candlesticks, positioned them on the table, and lit the tapers. Having no colorful scarves to toss on the chandelier or windows, she hoped those were more to encourage the proper attitude from séance attendees than to invite spirits.

Removing the sage from the Fiction 'n Fables packet, Gwen touched a match to the bundle and blew on the flame until it dwindled to spirals of smoke. She circled the dining room table, waving the smoldering herb, then repeated with the sweet grass. All the while, Gwen recited an edited version of the words chanted by Madame Eudora.

"May the light and energy of these candles remove all fear, negativity, and doubt. May these herbs attract positive energy to the one gathered here. For the highest good of all and for the good of the universe, so be it, so be it, so be it."

Resting the smoking herbs on ceramic dishes, Gwen clasped her hands together to form a circle and called Parker to join her.

She glanced around for a glimpse of his spirit but sensed no response. Maybe Parker hadn't heard her. Waiting a few beats, she said his name a second time, and then a third.

"Gwen, Sweetheart?"

She jumped at the sound of Parker's spirit voice as he materialized at the far end of the table. "You heard me?"

"I did. I thought you called my name yesterday, but when I got here, I couldn't find you. I checked upstairs, downstairs, even in the basement and the third-floor loft."

Gwen laughed until a stitch tweaked her side. "I did call you, but I was at the B&B with Betty and Robert."

His translucent face split with a big grin as he glided toward her. "Well, that explains it. Let me guess. You lit candles, burned herbs, and held hands like you did just now?"

If he'd had a solid arm, she would have slapped it. "Don't

tease me, Parker."

"Sorry, Sweetheart. I couldn't resist."

"Yesterday I hadn't bought the sage and sweet grass from Liz yet. But if you showed up here after I called you from the B&B, it appears the herbs aren't a necessary part of the ritual."

"Apparently not," Parker agreed. "I heard you say my name just now clear as a bell. Why did you call me from the B&B?"

"Betty and Robert and I were going to ask you to search for their ghost and ask her a few questions. Are you willing?"

"Sure. How do you plan to get me over there?"

"Annabelle gave me the idea." Gwen shared the story of the sea captain's ghost. "Do you think it'll work for us, Parker?"

"We won't know until we try. Slip on your coat and gloves, Gwen, and let's get this show on the road."

"Hold on. I need to text Detective Snowcrest and let him know where I'm going."

Parker smirked. "Will you include why?"

She chuckled. "No way. Ben doesn't believe in ghosts. My message will only say I'm walking to the B&B to visit with Betty and Robert."

As she headed out the front door, Gwen spotted her can of pepper spray on the foyer table. Though she doubted she'd need it at the B&B, she tucked it into her coat pocket.

"What's that?" Parker asked over her shoulder.

She turned to face him. "Pepper spray. Ben suggested I buy a canister and keep it handy whenever I leave the house."

Parker's pale smile indicated approval. "Your detective is watching out for you. I like the man."

***

As Gwen walked beside Parker's spirit across the village

green, snow began to fall…again. With each break in their chatter, she glanced at his spirit to reassure herself he hadn't disappeared. Such an odd sensation to watch the snowflakes cascading through his transparent body.

Gwen whispered, "If anyone comes near us, I'll stop talking to you, so they won't think I'm ditzy."

"Nah, Gwen. They'll assume you're on your cell phone. Besides, we're the only ones in the village green."

As if to contradict him, a horse-drawn sleigh glided by on North Street, the hoofs clopping, the bells jangling.

Traffic was light so they didn't wait long to cross over to the B&B. Knowing Parker didn't have the strength to lift the heavy brass knocker, Gwen took care of it.

Betty's anxious face appeared in the opening. "Come inside before you freeze, Gwen. The temperature has dropped."

"I'm fine, Betty. The walk over kept me warm."

Betty scanned the area on both sides of Gwen. "Where's Parker?"

Gwen looked up at his spirit. "He's right here."

Betty peered closer. "All I see is a slightly wavy area. Maybe if you move, Parker, you'll be more obvious?"

He waved his arms. "Can you detect me now?"

Betty stumbled backwards, her hand moving to her chest. "Oh, dear. I still can't see you, but I heard you perfectly."

When they entered the B&B, Robert approached from the dining room. He focused on Betty, then Gwen, and finally to an area on her right. "Hey, Parker."

"You can *see* him?" Betty challenged, her eyes wide.

"I can. He's standing next to Gwen, honey. A bit pale, I might add, but clear as day." Robert tossed a thumbs-up in

Parker's direction. "Who knew this was possible? It's like an episode from *The Twilight Zone*."

Parker moved to a spot beside Robert. "Hi, Robert. Long time, no see."

When Robert didn't react, Parker shrugged.

Gwen repeated the greeting.

Robert shifted his stance to face Parker. "Sorry, old man, I didn't hear you. But I learned how to read lips in the service decades ago."

A hearty laugh escaped Betty. "This is a hoot. I can hear Parker, but I can't see him. You can see him, Robert, but you can't hear him. The four of us make a fine team of paranormal investigators."

"Well said, Betty," Parker commented. "Where should I begin my search for your ghost?"

"Follow me." Betty led him up the front staircase, speaking over her shoulder. "Theo came to the dining room the other day, but we usually encounter her upstairs near the servant steps."

At the top of the staircase, Parker turned around and faced Robert. "Theo might be more willing to show herself without an audience. Why don't you three wait downstairs?"

As they retreated to the living room, Parker repeatedly called Theo's name until his voice faded.

"What do you think?" Betty asked, breaking their silence. "Has his spirit moved too far away, or has he located Theo?"

"No idea."

For the next half hour, Gwen, Betty, and Robert didn't say much to each other. When Parker's spirit descended the stairs, Gwen and Robert pushed themselves up off the couch. Noticing their action, Betty stood up as well.

"Did you find her?" Gwen asked.

Parker grinned and nodded simultaneously. "I did, in a closet on the third floor. She was a little shy at first. I convinced her I'm not here to chase her out. She relaxed and listened to the reasons you asked me to seek her out."

"And did she answer you?" Betty asked.

"She did."

***

Settling at the dining room table, Gwen asked, "Is that legal pad handy, Betty?"

"Sure is." From the sideboard, Betty retrieved the legal pad covered with notes she and Gwen had made while perusing the family history binders. Flipping to a clean page, Betty clicked her pen. "I'm ready."

Sitting across from Betty, Gwen patted the adjacent chair. "Have a seat, Parker."

"I think better on my feet, Sweetheart, so I'll just hover."

"Very funny," Gwen snickered. "I'm so glad you retained your sense of humor."

Parker smiled at Gwen, his love for her unmistakable.

"I'll sit next to you, Betty," Robert said, "so I can read what you write as Parker talks."

Parker began. "Before I share Theo's answers to your questions, there's something she wants you to know, Betty."

Betty focused on the area of his voice. "What's that?"

"She heard you complain about the overturned vase, the rumpled rugs, and the broken candles. She wants you to know she didn't do any of that. The mischief maker was the young boy from the family in the connecting rooms."

Betty threw her hands in the air. "Waldo Schuster. I should

have guessed after he ignored his parents' warning not to run up the front staircase." Betty swiveled in her seat. "Theo, I don't know if you're listening to us, but thank you. Sorry we blamed you for the mischief."

They sat in silence until Gwen resurrected their purpose. "Parker, was Theo on the second floor the night of the party?"

He placed his feather-light hand on her shoulder. "She was in Charlie's room when Robert brought his group to the third floor. She had planned to touch Charlie again and give him another thrill and was quite upset when the boys joined the tour, so she followed them to the second floor."

Betty asked the next question. "Was she still on the second floor when Myrtle screamed, and did she see anyone push the poor dear?"

Parker's faded salt and pepper head wagged. "No and no. Theo couldn't handle all the chatter from the club ladies, so she retreated to Charlie's room and waited for him to return."

Betty stopped taking notes. "I'm so relieved. If Theo was on the third floor, she couldn't have been involved in Myrtle's fall." Betty's hand covered Robert's. "You and I need to assure our guests that Theo didn't scare or push Myrtle, though I'm at a loss how to justify our claim."

Robert stared up at Parker's see-through self. "Did Theo mention if she pushed Charlie from his bed a few nights ago?"

Parker remained where he stood so Robert could lip-read. "Actually, Theo giggled when she told me. She developed a crush on blonde Charlie because he reminds her of the man she would have married if she hadn't died on her wedding day. She swears she didn't push Charlie out of bed. She merely sat on the mattress and touched his shoulder. He must have panicked and rolled out on his own."

"Well, I'll be," Robert said. "So the boy didn't invent it."

Gwen waved her hand to get Parker's attention. "Did you ask her about the day she died?"

"I did. On the morning of her wedding, Theo called down the servant steps for someone to help her into her wedding dress. She felt someone's fingers on the small of her back. The next thing she remembers is floating above her body. She's wandered around this house ever since looking for the person who pushed her. Theo wants us to figure out who did it. She thinks her diary might help."

Nearly in unison, Gwen, Betty, and Robert yelped, "Diary?"

Chapter Thirty-One

…early afternoon, Sunday

The three of them stared at Parker's spirit. Gwen was the first to find her voice. "Parker, did you say Theo's diary?"

"That's what she told me," he confirmed. "Each night, she hid it beneath a loose board in a closet on the third floor."

Robert leapt to his feet. "Let's find that diary and see where it takes us."

***

Half an hour later, the four of them returned to the dining room empty-handed.

Resettling at the table, Robert focused on Parker's spirit. "Are you sure that's where Theo hid her diary?"

"That's where she told me. Maybe someone found it."

"Oh, I hope it wasn't thrown away," Betty fussed.

"Hold on," Gwen said. "There's someone who might know about Theo's diary."

Robert stared at her. "Who's that?"

"Clara Carswell. She lived here for decades before you bought this house."

Betty gazed across at Gwen. "You're brilliant. Do you realize Clara is turning one hundred years old this month?"

Gwen did a quick calculation in her head. "She would have been seven years old in 1924."

Betty sat forward. "If her mind hasn't faded, Clara might remember not only Theo's diary, but maybe details about the wedding day incident."

"That's a long shot," Robert chimed in. "Coaxing details from Clara all these years later would be an amazing feat."

Betty's fingers drummed the table's surface. "We need to visit Clara right away."

Robert held up both hands. "I think you and Gwen should go without me. Too many people might confuse Clara."

"That's a good point." Betty again glanced at Gwen. "I'm busy today with the new guests. Are you available tomorrow?"

Gwen opened her cell phone and checked her online calendar. "I have an appointment in the morning." She couldn't reveal that Ben was stopping over for an update meeting on Myrtle's case. "The afternoon is open."

"In that case, I'll pick you up around one." Betty smoothed her ever-present apron. "If anyone is hungry, I can heat up chicken and dumplings."

***

Satiated, Gwen rested her soup spoon beside the bowl. "That was delicious, Betty." She glanced to her right and left. "Have either of you seen Parker lately?"

Robert gathered their bowls. "Not since we started eating. Where do you suppose he went?"

Gwen shrugged. "Hard to know. Maybe he wandered upstairs to find Theo again. Or he could have disappeared. He does that without knowing it's about to happen."

Robert grinned at Betty. "If you pass before I do, will you come back and visit me?"

Her face brightened. "Of course I will, Robert. We already have one ghost in this house. Why not add a second?"

Amused by their playfulness about the afterlife, Gwen got to her feet. "Betty, can I look at the family portraits again?"

Robert reached for bowls and glasses. "You go with Gwen, Betty. I'll clean up before our next guests arrive."

***

At the top of the staircase, Gwen squinted at the portrait one down from Theo's. Dark eyes, pale skin, and black hair defined the lady. "Who's this?"

Betty moved to stand even with Gwen. "That's Winifred Sophia Carswell. She was the second child."

"And Clara was the youngest daughter. Were there any other children?"

"No. Mrs. Carswell miscarried the only boy." Betty descended a single stair tread and waved toward the painting below Winnie's. "Here's Clara."

Gwen studied the third portrait. A cloud of blonde hair surrounded the young woman's face, her expression more sad than serious. "Any idea when this one was painted?"

Betty lifted the frame from the picture hook and flipped to the backside. "The label reads December 18, 1937. That was Clara's twentieth birthday."

Leaning away from the wall, Gwen toggled her focus from Theo's portrait to Winnie's to Clara's. "Gosh, the three girls don't look anything alike."

"I noticed that, too," Betty commented, "though I never gave it much thought."

A movement caught Gwen's eye. Thinking it might be Theo, she turned to see Parker's translucent self moving toward them through the sitting room.

"Did you think I'd disappeared, Sweetheart?"

"You've done it before." Gwen chuckled. "Now I don't have to hunt for you."

When the clanging of the front door knocker echoed up the staircase, Betty changed directions and started down. "That must be the first of this week's guests. I'll see you tomorrow afternoon, Gwen."

***

During their return trek across the village green, Parker shared more details about his encounter with Theo. Her facial expressions, the way she moved, her general demeanor. When he stopped talking, Gwen glanced sideways, confirming that she walked alone. No choice but to accept his abrupt departures. She was grateful he'd stayed on terra firma long enough to complete the task of contacting Theo and reporting back.

Standing in her foyer, Gwen removed the pepper spray and placed it next to Parker's photo. After touching her fingers to his face, she texted Ben that she'd returned from the B&B.

Unable to keep her adventure to herself, she tossed her coat and gloves onto a dining room chair before dialing Annabelle.

A sleepy voice answered. "Hello. Who's this?"

"Annabelle, this is Gwen. Did I wake you?" She couldn't believe the girl was still in bed on a Sunday afternoon.

"You did." A yawn interrupted. "I was out late with the ghost hunters and didn't get home until four this morning."

"I'm so sorry. I can call you later."

"No, no, I need to get out of bed. What's up?"

"First of all, remember that I called Parker from the B&B yesterday and he didn't show up?"

Annabelle yawned. "I remember."

Gwen heard the rustling of bed covers. "Well, he told me today that he materialized here and couldn't find me because I was over there."

Annabelle chuckled. "You're collecting the most interesting ghost stories, Gwen. So you succeeded in contacting him?"

"I did. He walked across the village green to the B&B."

Annabelle's intake of breath traveled through the phone. "Fantastic. So my tale about my sea captain wasn't wasted. I'm impressed you were able to maintain your connection."

"I have to admit it was exciting. I had to let you know. Thanks so much for your suggestion."

"Glad to help." Annabelle sounded wide awake. "Do you mind if I tell my ghost hunting group?"

"Not at all. I'll let you get on with your day."

"Thanks. If I stay in bed much longer, I won't sleep tonight. Keep in touch, Gwen."

"I will. Take care."

Only after Gwen ended the call did she realize Annabelle hadn't asked if Parker located the B&B's ghost. And a good thing, too, for Gwen would have certainly blurted the news about Theo's diary. Though the girl was the photographer at the Harbor Falls Gazette and not a reporter, she might not be able to keep an important element like Theo's diary to herself.

After all, if the details Theo had written helped solve a nearly century-old murder, the revelation would certainly be newsworthy.

But it was way too soon to predict where this mystery would end.

Chapter Thirty-Two

...early evening, Sunday

As Gwen finished her gift-wrapping, the doorbell chimed.

"Hello, Evelyn, I didn't expect to see you again so soon. What can I do for you?"

"I owe you an apology, Gwen. May I come in?"

Gwen swung the door wide. "Of course. Where are my manners? Let's make ourselves comfortable in the living room."

Maneuvering up and across the threshold, Evelyn made steady progress, her cane keeping time with its rhythmic step-thump-step-thump.

As Evelyn approached the leather couch, Gwen asked, "Would you like something to drink?"

"Thank you, but no. I won't be staying long."

Settling at the other end, Gwen filtered through Ben's body language tips, working hard to apply them to Evelyn. "Why do you think you owe me an apology?"

Evelyn propped her cane against the end table. "I'm not usually so rude. When you brought up your whisperers Friday evening, all I wanted to do was get out of here."

"Why was that?"

Evelyn did not avert her eyes. "I can't abide people who gossip. They usually haven't got a clue."

Gwen recalled Ben's report detailing Evelyn as the driver when a drunk slammed into the family car and killed her husband. Had the town gossips gotten the facts all wrong and tormented Evelyn all those years ago? Without revealing how much she knew, Gwen said, "You sound like you've been the target of skewed gossip."

"I have, but it's in the past and not something I care to discuss. Let me get to the reason I stopped by."

Gwen watched and waited for Evelyn to continue.

"I think you expected me to offer my opinion about your whisperers. I'm telling you now that I have no idea. Because I don't gossip, nobody tells me anything, especially at the garden club meetings. That's all I came here to say."

When Evelyn struggled to push up from the cushions of the leather couch, Gwen stood up and extended her hand.

"You're such a kind woman, Gwen."

"I appreciate you stopping over to explain your hasty exit the other night."

Holding her front door open, Gwen stepped aside to make room for Evelyn to exit.

"I owed you that much. Goodnight, Gwen. Enjoy the holidays."

Before Gwen knew what was happening, someone raced up the granite slab steps and bumped into Evelyn, sending her cane skittering to the front walk.

Holly reached up and grabbed Evelyn's arm to steady her. "I'm so sorry. Are you okay?"

Evelyn righted herself, adjusted her coat and hat, and squinted at Holly. "You should watch where you're going. Please hand me my cane."

"Of course." Holly retrieved the wooden stick and handed it over. "Love the duck head."

Evelyn made no remark, but simply hobbled away in her uneven cadence.

Gwen waved Holly inside. "What brings you by?"

"Hate to drop in without warning, but it occurred to me that we should have included a signed card from all our members with the gift card for Myrtle's family." Holly reached into her handbag. "I brought a card from my shop."

Gwen waved the club president into the dining room, and reached for the card. "I'm curious to read it."

The front cover read *One life lived, many lives touched.* The words were surrounded by a garden of flowers in pastel colors. Gwen flipped to the inside. *Find strength and take comfort in the memories you shared.*

Holly switched her gaze from Gwen to the card. "Maybe I should have brought several to choose from. Do you think this one's appropriate?"

"It's perfect. The garden image represents the club."

Holly visibly relaxed. "Oh, good. I hate to ask, but could you do me another favor?"

"What's that?"

"My store is so busy with Christmas shoppers. I don't have time to chase all the members for their signature. Would you mind taking care of it?"

Without knowing it, Holly had provided Gwen with the perfect excuse to revisit all the club members. Not only to sign the card, but to have another chance to identify those whisperers. And maybe they'd remember a detail relevant to Myrtle's tumble. "Sure, I'll handle that for you."

Holly dropped her hand onto Gwen's shoulder. "Thanks so much. You're a terrific VP." As she turned to leave, Holly hesitated. "Kristen saw you having lunch with a white-haired man the other day. Was that Detective Snowcrest?"

214

Thrown off guard by the question, Gwen strained not to ooze guilty signals and struggled to not break eye contact. No way to deny it. "Yes, it was."

"When he stopped by the shop on Friday, you acted like you already knew him."

The truth was Gwen's only option. "That's because I met him last spring during his investigation of the cigar bar murder across the street from your shop. I was trying to prove to the police that my friend Liz was innocent."

Desperate to move Holly to a less volatile topic, Gwen turned the tables. "Speaking of Liz, I was over at her bookstore yesterday and noticed you and Veronica on your front sidewalk. Is everything okay between you two?"

Holly waved her hand. "Oh, that? It was nothing. I recommended a handyman who didn't do a job the way she wanted. We're good now."

"I'm glad to hear it. Nothing worse than being on the outs with your best friend." Gwen held up the condolence card. "You may as well sign this now."

As Holly rummaged in her purse, it slipped from her hands and the contents skittered beneath the dining room table. When Gwen made a move toward the floor, Holly held up her hand and dropped to her knees. "I can manage. Thanks."

A minute later, Holly emerged from beneath the table, brandishing a wooden pen. As she scribbled a short note on the inside flap of the card, she asked, "Have any of the members shared their thoughts about Myrtle's accident?"

Not an unreasonable question, Gwen decided, especially from someone who'd been part of Myrtle's group. "Not that they've mentioned to me." Not a lie. Not one gardener had shared any case-solving details, much to Gwen's disappointment. And Ben's.

Gwen seized the opportunity to dig deeper. "Have you remembered anything else?"

"Not a thing," Holly answered, handing over the card.

Considering Holly a dead end, Gwen slid the card into the envelope. "This was a good idea."

"I could have saved you extra effort if I'd thought of it earlier. Thanks again, Gwen, for collecting the signatures. I have to get back to the shop. We're open late tonight."

After Holly closed the front door behind her, Gwen re-read the soothing words on the condolence card. Would the person who pushed the unfortunate woman ever be uncovered?

Chapter Thirty-Three

...early morning, Monday

Twice Ben pushed the doorbell button at the Hobart twins' condo. No response. He knocked. And knocked again. Still no answer. The sisters were either heavy sleepers or had gone out for breakfast. He'd try again another day.

Fifteen minutes later, on the other side of town, as he raised his hand to Alicia Reed's door, it flew open to reveal the garden club secretary. On her left hip, she balanced a baby. A toddler clung to her leg. "Good morning, Detective."

"How did you know I was here?"

Alicia chuckled. "Travis installed a security camera. It lets us know if someone comes up the walk."

Ben stomped the snow from his boots, expecting to be invited inside and out of the cold.

But Alicia kept a firm grip on the door. "I'd invite you in, but our house is filled with germs. What can I do for you?"

"I'm hoping you've remembered more details since we spoke after the party."

Alicia shifted the baby to her other hip. "Like what?"

"Who was next to you when you heard the scream?"

Alicia shook her head. "Like I told you the other night, I was reading about the Carswells. I still have your card. If something occurs to me, I promise I'll call you."

With that, she closed the door.

Ben's frustration mounted as he sloughed through the snow toward his SUV. Like all the others, Alicia hadn't noticed the person standing next to her, let alone seen anyone make a physical move in Mrs. Mueller's direction.

With the engine running, Ben considered the unthinkable. Had Otis misinterpreted his autopsy results? The position of the head wound. The supposition that Mrs. Mueller was airborne before impact. But how about those bruises? Peter from the crime lab had agreed with Otis's findings.

Ben located Otis's printout and studied the marks. They appeared to be fingertips as Otis suggested. The bruises niggled at Ben's detective gut, and he admitted he wasn't qualified to question their professional credibility. Someone had shoved Mrs. Mueller, and Ben was hell bent to find out who.

Shifting into drive, he pointed the SUV in the direction of Evelyn Woodley's cottage. Unlike Alicia, Evelyn invited him inside and offered a cup of tea, which he refused. Evelyn repeated the same information she'd told him on party night, adding no new details.

Just like every other witness, neither Alicia nor Evelyn had seen a damn thing. At least nothing she was willing to share with Ben. Would Gwen do any better?

***

At mid-morning, Gwen waved Ben into the dining room.

"Sorry I'm late."

"It's only a few minutes past ten," she said.

"I made a few stops. First, the Hobart twins didn't answer their doorbell or my knock. Next, Alicia Reed, and finally Evelyn Woodley."

"Did Alicia or Evelyn remember any more details?"

Ben snorted. "Nothing worth adding to my notebook."

"Do you think they're hiding something?"

"They're hard to read. I don't know if they're protecting each other or truly have nothing to share."

Settling next to him, Gwen reported her own update. "Evelyn paid me a visit last night."

"That's funny. She didn't mention it."

"No reason she would, Ben. She doesn't know I'm working with you."

"Why did she stop by?"

"Not to share any insights. She wanted to apologize and explain why she left so abruptly the other night."

"And what was her explanation?"

"Nothing case-related. Evelyn refuses to gossip. She didn't go into detail, but I'd guess it's based on nasty rumors after her car accident and her husband's death. She at least told me she has no idea who the whisperers could be."

Ben's expression sagged. "Still, I need additional interviews with the rest of Robert's group. Someone must have seen something. I just need to convince that person to tell me."

He turned his gray eyes on her. "I need you to continue your concentration on identifying those whisperers, even though Mrs. Mueller is the most logical blackmailer. After you return the rest of the party containers, can you find a reason to revisit the members you've already seen?"

"Actually, Holly Nichols provided a perfect excuse."

"What's that?"

"A condolence card signed by all the members."

"Terrific." Ben made a move to leave. "Anything else?"

Gwen debated whether to tell Ben what she and Betty found in the Carswell family binders, deciding he'd be interested. "I have news from the B&B."

Ben smirked. "You're declaring their ghost innocent?"

"No need to be snide, Ben. What Betty and I discovered is more of a mystery. In the family binders, we came upon Theo's wedding announcement. Her bridegroom was a Brewster, which may or may not connect him to both Charlie Brewster and Myrtle, who was a Brewster descendant."

"I've never gotten into ancestry research, but you're piquing my interest. What year did you say Theo died?"

Though his question bewildered Gwen, she said, "1924."

"I don't know if I've mentioned this, but I've solved a few cold cases during my career."

The idea of a cold case hadn't occurred to Gwen, but that explained Ben's renewed interest. He might not believe in Theo as a ghost, but the tragic bride's death remained unsolved.

"How long are the records kept in storage, Ben?"

"That's exactly what I'm going to find out."

Elation buzzed through Gwen. If Ben located Theo's cold case file, Gwen itched to see it. Would he let her?

"Let's call it a day, Gwen. I want to get back to the station and have a look around the evidence room."

"Given you're a skeptic about ghosts, I'm surprised you want to follow-up on Theo's case."

"Skeptic or not, if I can close a cold case, I will." He made a second move to get up.

"Wait a minute, Ben. There's more."

"You're a fount of information this morning. What else have you uncovered?"

"Nothing connected to Myrtle's murder. Theo kept a diary, but we haven't found it yet." Gwen resisted telling Ben that Theo revealed this clue to Parker's spirit.

Ben's white eyebrows lifted. "A diary? What do you think that will tell you?"

"Maybe details surrounding the people living in the Carswell House while Theo was alive. Maybe point us to someone who held a grudge, wanted Theo out of the picture."

"If you find that diary, Gwen, I'd like to read it."

"We hunted for it yesterday without success."

'Too bad the family is all gone," Ben commented. "No witnesses to interview."

A thrill coursed through Gwen that she could share one more piece of news. "That's not true, Ben. There's one living Carswell."

"There is?" Ben's expression became animated.

"There is," Gwen confirmed, pleased with herself. "Her name is Clara Carswell. She's nearly one hundred years old and was seven when Theo died. Betty and I are planning to visit her this afternoon."

Chapter Thirty-Four

...late morning, Monday

As soon as Ben headed back to the police station, Gwen checked her laptop for emails. To her dismay, she found no responses from the two other women in Betty's group or the three who refused the tour. Realizing not everyone was prompt in checking for or answering emails, Gwen set aside her irritation and delayed her follow-up phone calls until she returned from Clara's retirement facility.

For the next hour, Gwen vacuumed and dusted before fixing herself a light lunch. Promptly at one o'clock, Betty pulled up at the curb and tapped her van's horn.

As Gwen clambered into the passenger seat, Betty hitched her thumb toward the back. "I brought one of the binders. I thought looking through those mementos might make it easier for Clara to discuss Theo."

"Clever, Betty. How far is the ride?"

"Less than fifteen minutes."

Gwen tapped out a text to Ben: *Riding with Betty to visit Clara Carswell. Hopefully, we'll learn details to help us locate Theo's diary.*

***

In the evidence room at the police station, Ben stared at the file cabinets along the near wall plus rows of shelving jammed with cardboard boxes filling the remaining space. Theo's case – if it still existed – would have been stored long before the digital cross-reference system was initiated.

As Ben debated where to begin, his cell phone buzzed. After reading Gwen's text message, he grinned. Would her positive attitude translate into success?

If Clara Carswell remembered Theo's diary, she could point Gwen and Betty in the right direction to find it.

If the diary provided any glimmer of who might have caused the bride-to-be's death on her wedding day, Ben might be able to close Theo's cold case.

But first, he had to find it.

He began with the cabinets. The folders were supposed to be arranged in alphabetical order by the last name of the victim. Just in case Theo's had been misfiled, he checked every folder, moving half a dozen to their proper spots. Twenty minutes later, he slammed the last drawer shut and turned to the shelves.

The boxes appeared to be chronological, but Ben wouldn't risk missing Theo by making assumptions. Smaller boxes were two deep on the shelves, forcing him to shuffle them around. For the next hour, he studied the labels: type of crime, victim's name, year of event, internal department number assigned.

His neck and arms aching from his initial foray into the boxes, Ben locked the evidence room door and made his way to the station's kitchenette, hoping the coffee in the urn wasn't too stale. He took a single sip and dumped it down the sink. Maybe the short drive to Dunkin Donuts would give his body and mind a much-needed refresher before he resumed his search.

***

When Gwen and Betty entered the Plymouth retirement complex, party noises echoed down the hallway. With no receptionist at the front desk, they signed the visitors register and followed their ears until they discovered the source.

At the door of an expansive great room, an oversized poster surrounded by colorful balloons proclaimed *100th Birthday Celebration for Clara Carswell!*

Inside, senior citizens and uniformed staffers were scattered throughout the room, sipping from glasses of punch and munching on slices of cake.

Betty glanced at Gwen. "I think we've arrived a little late, but I don't see any reason why we shouldn't join the party."

Gwen nudged Betty inside and indicated a small cluster of people near the fireplace. "That could be Clara."

"Let's go see." Betty led the way through the thinning crowd until they neared a petite lady sitting erect in an overstuffed chair.

Recalling Clara's portrait at the B&B, Gwen was pleased to see that the last Carswell had aged with grace. Her clouds of blonde hair had faded to a flattering shade of silvery gray.

Clara reached for Betty's hand. "I'm so glad you came."

"Happy birthday, Clara," Betty responded.

"Thank you, dear. Are you taking good care of my home?"

"We certainly are."

"And the B&B is working well for you?"

"Just like we planned. Robert and I are proud to share the Carswell House with our guests."

"That's good to hear." Clara moved her focus to Gwen. "Who did you bring with you?"

Betty urged Gwen closer. "This is my good friend Gwen Andrews. She's helping me research an issue with Theo. We're hoping you have time to chat with us."

Clara's delicate laugh tinkled. "Betty, dear, I've got nothing but time. Why don't we see if the library is unoccupied?" She pointed across the room, which was quickly clearing of the birthday guests. Placing her hands on the arms of the chair, Clara hoisted herself to her feet. No wheelchair or walker for this Carswell matriarch. After taking a second to find her balance, Clara strode toward the library at an admirable pace.

Gwen hoped to be as spry as Clara at one hundred.

Inside the elegant shelf-lined room filled with books, Betty placed the family history binder on the round table without disturbing the jigsaw puzzle in progress.

Clara clicked the door closed. "As far as I know, no one in this facility is aware that I lived in a haunted house. I'd rather they not find out now." She waved toward the binder. "If you brought that family album to jiggle my memory, it wasn't necessary. I remember every document and photo preserved in those pages." Clara sat down and intertwined her fingers. "Tell me the issue you're having with Theo."

"First, a short review of recent events," Betty began. "Last Wednesday, I hosted the annual garden club Christmas party. During a tour of your family home, one of our members fell down the servant steps and died."

Clara unclasped her hands and placed them on her knees. "Oh, my. How tragic."

"Since then, Gwen and I were told by the woman's husband that she was a Brewster descendant. Her nephew Charlie Brewster happened to be staying in a third-floor maid's room and experienced an unusual problem of his own."

Her eyes bright, Clara said, "I suspect there's much more to your story."

"There is, Clara. Gwen and I came upon Theo's wedding invitation. Her intended bridegroom was Nehemiah Brewster."

"Oh, dear," Clara murmured. "I hope you're not thinking that Theo had anything to do with that woman's death on the off chance she was descended from Mr. Brewster."

"We considered that possibility at first," Betty revealed.

Clara's forehead wrinkled. "Unfortunately, I don't know any details of Nehemiah's family tree."

Betty flipped to the first page of the binder. "This is the first volume of the family history you left with me and Robert. The third book stops in 1924. Are we missing any books?"

Smoothing a non-existent wrinkle on her skirt, Clara said, "No, there are only those three. After Theo died, my parents stopped preserving family news. You won't find anything past December twentieth of that year."

Betty grasped Clara's hand. "That's unfortunate. So there's no record of your life celebrations past your seventh birthday?"

Clara gave a wave of her small hand. "Don't feel sorry for me, dear. After my parents ceased to analyze every little thing I did as potential content for the family scrapbooks, my life became much easier. The pressure was off to be a productive and news-worthy daughter."

Gwen wondered if the second child Winnie shared that same opinion. How had both sisters' lives progressed after Theo's tragic death? Clara still used the family surname, implying she never married. Had Winnie?

Easing back in her chair, Clara spoke. "You said you suspected Theo's involvement in that woman's death at first. Does that mean you've changed your minds?"

Betty waved at Gwen. "Why don't you answer that?"

Gwen leaned forward, keeping her volume low. "Parker was my husband for thirty-seven years until he died unexpectedly.

Two Septembers ago, his spirit appeared to me, and he's visited several times since then. I enlisted Parker's spirit to locate Theo and ask her if she witnessed unusual activity in the sitting room during the time of the incident. Also to learn more details surrounding the day she died."

Clara's eyes widened. "Oh, my, one ghost talking to another. Did Theo answer his questions?"

"She did," Betty confirmed. "Unfortunately, she'd retreated to the third floor before the incident happened."

"Oh, good." Clara switched her gaze to Gwen. "And what did she say about the day she died?"

"That she felt fingers on her lower back before she tumbled to the bottom. She's been wandering around the Carswell House all these years looking for that person."

Clara's face paled. "Oh, my. The family had always been aware of Theo's presence, but as far as I know, her ghost never spoke to anyone. I had no idea why she didn't pass over."

The three of them sat quietly until Clara broke the silence. "You implied there's another reason for visiting me today."

"There is." Betty shifted her weight. "Theo revealed a clue."

"Well, don't stop now," Clara commanded, an unexpected sharpness in her tone.

Gwen sat forward. "Theo kept a diary. Each night, she made another entry and hid it under a loose board in a maid's closet. Theo wants us to find her diary and figure out who pushed her."

Clara's eyes sparked. "And did you find the diary where she said it was?"

"Unfortunately, no," Betty answered. "Were you aware of your sister's diary? Do you know where it might have gone?"

The centenarian once again folded her hands in her lap.

227

Gwen mentally reviewed the body language tips that Ben had shared. Throughout their meeting, Clara had looked away and picked at non-existent threads. Clara – who'd lived in the Carswell house for decades beyond Theo's death – knew a lot more than she was saying, but grilling the old lady would be impolite at best.

Before Clara had a chance to respond to Betty's questions, a knock preceded the opening of the library door and a staff member poked her head inside. "There you are, Clara. It's time for your medication and afternoon nap. You need to rest after all your birthday excitement."

Without a word of protest, Clara struggled from her chair and reached for the outstretched hand of the nurse, turning at the last second. "I'm so glad you both came to celebrate with me this afternoon."

The nurse placed her palm under Clara's elbow. The centenarian instantly leaned into the offered support.

***

After settling into the driver's seat, Betty touched Gwen's sleeve. "I appreciate you coming with me today."

"I'm as curious as you are, Betty. Did you find it odd the way Clara acted when the nurse interrupted us?"

Betty inserted her key but didn't start the engine. "I did at first. Then I recalled Clara didn't want anyone to find out she used to live in a haunted house, so I chalked up her sudden frailty as a ruse to protect her secret."

"You're probably right," Gwen agreed. "We can return another day to ask her about Theo's diary."

Betty started the engine, but didn't shift into reverse. "I'd still like to know if Myrtle and Charlie are descendants of

228

Theo's bridegroom. Do you suppose the records at the Mayflower Society might be helpful?"

"It's worth a try. Let me check their hours." On her cell phone, Gwen typed the destination into Google maps and read the details. "Ten to three-thirty, Monday through Friday."

Glancing at the dashboard clock, Betty shifted into reverse. "We have time. Let's go."

***

Approaching the two women behind the front desk of the Mayflower library, Betty said, "We're looking for the descendants of Nehemiah Linus Brewster. Can you tell me where to find his family history?"

The elder woman took charge. "The society created a series called *The Mayflower Families*." She ambled to a shelf filled with silver hard covers, ran her finger along the bindings, and slid one from the collection. "Here we go. Volume 24, Elder William Brewster."

Accepting the book, Betty flipped the pages, stopping every once in a while to read the referenced dates. "There don't seem to be any listings past the 1700s."

The silver-haired woman commented, "For each of the Mayflower families, the Society long ago verified the first five or six generations."

"Do you have more recent volumes?" Betty asked.

The elderly clerk's face clouded. She led them to a nearby shelf and removed two hard-cover books, handing one each to Betty and Gwen. "These are the only other volumes about the Brewster family."

Turning her book sideways, Betty read the spine out loud. "These are dated 1908."

The younger woman strolled over from the reception desk. "Perhaps I can clarify. There are now over thirty-five million Mayflower descendants. Valid descendants usually bequeath their ancestry documents to the next generation."

Gwen looked over at Betty. "Didn't Fletcher say he was offering Myrtle's records to the Society?"

Betty nodded. "Yes, he did say that."

"If you don't mind me asking," the younger woman continued, "what's the year of your Nehemiah Brewster?"

"He was supposed to be married in 1924," Betty answered.

"In that case, we won't have any details to share with you. Why don't you try the Plymouth Public Library? They have local history books that might provide more recent information. It's located on South Street. Only a mile or so from here."

"I'm acquainted with that library," Betty said. "Thank you both for your assistance."

Belted in the van, Betty shoved her key into the ignition. "Damn, I didn't know there are that many descendants."

"Me neither," Gwen commented as she buckled her seatbelt. "But those two women adjusted my thinking. We don't need to prove Myrtle was a Mayflower descendant. We only want to know if she's descended from Theo's bridegroom. Do you have time for us to stop at the Plymouth library this afternoon?"

"I do if you do." Betty started the engine and maneuvered through the rambling one-way exit from the society's parking lot, turned left on Winslow Street, then a second sharp left. Laughing, she pointed at the sign identifying the side street. "What do you know?"

Gwen looked up. "Brewster Street? Must be an omen."

Betty slapped the steering wheel. "Hope it's a good one."

***

Minutes later, they parked at the Plymouth Public Library, hurried inside, and approached the reference desk. After Betty explained their search, the staffer made a list of a half-dozen titles. "These are in the history room and can't leave the building. I'll meet you ladies upstairs to unlock the door."

When the clerk disappeared around the corner, Betty and Gwen retraced their steps and climbed the center stairs. They circled the mezzanine, surprised to see the reference clerk standing at the door.

Inside, he guided them to the far end of the adjacent room and pointed first at a group of books and then to the matching index numbers on his list. "These are our Brewster volumes. Just return them to the same location after you're finished." Turning on his heel, he left them to their research.

Betty and Gwen scanned each book, murmuring to each other that nothing was dated more recently than the 1700s.

A voice called over. "Excuse me. Maybe I can help."

They turned to see a be-speckled man seated behind a table, unnoticed as they'd followed the library staffer into the history room. The man smiled at them. "Sorry to eavesdrop, but I overheard that you're checking into the Brewster family. I used to work at the Society of Mayflower Descendants."

Betty headed toward his table with Gwen on her heels. "How interesting. Thank you for offering your assistance."

"Don't thank me yet. Which Brewster books did the Society show you?"

"Volume 24 of the Plymouth Families series and two Brewster books dated 1908."

"And those details were no help?"

Betty shook her head as she sat in the next chair. "They don't contain information past the 1700s."

"Who are you looking for?"

"Nehemiah Linus Brewster. I'm guessing he was in his twenties in 1924."

"If you don't mind me asking, what are you searching for?"

Gwen answered, "We're looking for Nehemiah's descendants into the 1990s."

The man removed his glasses. "You might start with the city directories to confirm his address."

"Where would we find those?" Betty asked.

"Most town libraries maintain a set." He walked to the shelves along another wall, squatted to the bottom shelf and perused the skinny spines. "These are the Plymouth directories. I believe we have 1924." He selected a book and carried it to the table, flipping quickly to the 'B's'. "Your man isn't listed."

"Can I take a picture with my cell phone for reference?" Gwen asked.

"Sure." He held the book open as Gwen snapped a photo on her cell phone.

"Is it possible he lived in a different town?" the man asked.

"I suppose so," Betty answered. "His bride-to-be lived in Harbor Falls."

"Then I'd suggest you try there."

Gwen asked, "Do you know if the ancestry.com website includes census records that will show if our Brewster married and had children?"

The man shrugged his shoulders. "Maybe, but depending on the penmanship of the census taker, they can be difficult to read." He tapped his glasses. "Could just be my aging eyesight.

If you can stay for a while, this library has a subscription." He returned to his project. "Good luck with your research."

As Gwen and Betty were leaving the history room, the man's voice shouted, "It just dawned on me that some towns created their own census. Try the Harbor Falls library."

"We'll check there," Gwen called back. "Thank you for your suggestions."

Settled in Betty's van, Gwen tossed out a question. "Do you want to stop at the Harbor Falls Library today?"

Betty glanced at the dashboard clock. "Can't today. Robert and I have a few projects to tackle."

"That's okay. I'll check at the new library as soon as I get a chance."

"That's fine, Gwen. We're not desperate to find out if Myrtle and Charlie are related to Nehemiah. But it would be interesting to know."

Chapter Thirty-Five

...early evening, Monday

"Hi, Tess. Didn't expect to hear from you so soon." Gwen fought to remember how recently they'd chatted, deciding it was Friday morning when she'd shared Hal and Jenna's Saturday flight to Florida for house hunting.

"Two reasons for calling my favorite little sister."

Gwen laughed at their decades-old joke, because she was Tess's *only* sister. "What's the first?"

"Do you remember Cousin Sally?"

"The one with the blonde Shirley Temple ringlets?"

"The same, though I imagine those curls are gray by now."

"Gosh, I lost touch with Sally after her family moved west."

"She's back in New England."

"Do you know where?"

"Sally didn't specify and hung up before I had a chance to ask. Anyway, Cousin Harry told her I was hosting a reunion dinner on Christmas Day. Sally phoned to ask if there's room for one more. Of course I said yes." Tess took a breath. "And Aunt Nellie has been calling every day. If she still had a car, I think she'd have driven herself up my mountain by now."

Gwen waited for Tess to run out of steam.

"And guess what I found in the attic! A box of old photos and mom's hand-written notes identifying each person and how they're related to our family."

Gwen wasn't surprised to hear of this discovery in the attic of their childhood home. Their mom's will had bequeathed the

234

decades-owned family house to both sisters. Because Gwen was already settled in Harbor Falls with Parker, Tess and Nathan bought out her half. That jam-packed walk-up attic probably held more secrets than the sisters could begin to fathom.

"I'd be interested to see those pictures and notes, Tess. Will you have them on display next weekend?"

"You bet. After the holidays, I'm going to continue mom's project and research our family tree. Aunt Nellie and the cousins should be a good source of family history. I've asked them to bring old pictures and share what they know."

Gwen was relieved to learn of her sister's project. After Tess's husband Nathan passed away the previous spring, Gwen had worried how Tess would spend her days. Delving into ancestors would certainly fill the bill.

"Didn't you say you had two reasons for calling, Tess? What's the second?"

On the other end of the phone, Tess cleared her throat. "I've been thinking about your situation with Hal, and I'm going to share my wise sisterly advice." Tess didn't wait for Gwen to accept or reject. "Over the decades, many friends, students, and professors have come and gone. Some were more important to you than others. Of course, Parker was the most important, but then Hal came along to take his place."

Shocked to hear her sister's words, Gwen wasted no time correcting Tess's impression. "Hal was never a replacement for Parker. No one will ever replace Parker."

"Sorry, Gwen. I didn't say that quite right."

"That's okay," Gwen soothed. "Before this discussion gets out of hand, let me fill you in on the rest of Hal's plan."

"And what's that?"

Gwen could envision her sister's expression darkening. "He expected me to pack up and move to Florida with him."

Tess's silence was deafening.

"Before you get too wound up, Tess, I'm not moving."

"Oh, thank goodness, Gwen. You and I are a few hours' drive, but Florida is much further. If you lived there, I'd hardly ever see you."

"My sentiments, too, Tess. Harbor Falls holds too many precious memories of Parker for me to ever leave."

"I know what you mean. I could never abandon the mountain home I shared with Nathan."

As before, Gwen didn't mention that Parker's ghostly appearances were the real reason she'd never leave. Even though Tess had participated in last April's séance, she hadn't seen Parker's spirit, so never believed he'd manifested.

"Gwen, will you be okay without Hal in your life?"

"I'll be just fine, Tess." Gwen knew she'd miss Hal's companionship, but not his new aggressive attitude.

"Okay, I won't give the man another thought."

"Good," Gwen said, and she meant it. "You have enough to juggle getting ready for your reunion dinner."

"That's for sure. What will you do with yourself between now and then?"

Though Gwen had not mentioned Myrtle's death during their previous phone conversation, she thought it prudent for someone else to know she'd signed on as Ben's confidential informant. After all, Tess lived nearly three hours away, so she couldn't endanger Gwen's undercover status in Harbor Falls.

"I'm involved in a new project that's keeping me busy."

"Well, you can't just say that and stop. What's this project?"

"Do you remember Detective Ben Snowcrest?"

"Of course I do." Tess paused for a beat. "Oh, no. Don't tell me you've gotten yourself tangled up in another investigation?"

"Only because I'm the V.P. of the garden club." Gwen explained Myrtle's death during the Christmas party plus a general accounting of her arrangement with Ben to provide background details of the club members.

Tess said, "I don't like the sound of this."

"You don't need to worry, Tess. Before I meet with a garden club member, I text Ben, and after I walk in my door, I text him again. Plus I carry a can of pepper spray, just in case."

"Oh, like that makes me feel any better," Tess protested. "I suspect there's more."

"Well, Ben's also pursuing a parallel cold case."

"What does that mean?"

Gwen briefly outlined Theo's story.

"What is it with you and ghosts, Gwen? First the séance last spring, and now the B&B."

Although Tess couldn't see her through the phone, Gwen shrugged a shoulder. "The afterlife has always fascinated me."

"Is the detective taking Hal's place as your new buddy?"

Gwen laughed out loud. "You're impossible, Tess. Ben is simply the detective in charge." She didn't dare mention their non-date of dinner and dancing two nights before.

A ding from Gwen's email interrupted, canceling any follow-up questions Tess would have surely asked.

"Sorry, Tess, but I gotta go. I volunteered to return buffet dishes to the members who left them behind after the party, and another email just arrived. We'll talk again soon." Gwen disconnected before Tess could object.

***

Gwen had locked both doors and was turning off the downstairs lights when the doorbell rang.

Ben grinned at her from the top step. "Sorry for stopping by so late, but I saw your lights. I debated whether to stop in and tell you tonight or wait until our next meeting."

Gwen waved him inside. "Tell me what?"

His eyes brightened, his body nearly vibrating with excitement. "I found Theo's cold case."

"That's fantastic!" Gwen wanted to grab the detective and kiss him but caught herself. "What did you find in her folder?"

As she led him to the living room couch, he elaborated. "Well, Theo's cold case is more than a folder. It's a box holding the records and evidence from the 1924 investigation."

"Like what?" Gwen asked, her every nerve tingling.

Ben ticked off the contents on his fingers. "The detective's overview of the investigation, black and white photographs, hand-written interviews with the household members. The investigator's questioning of Carswell relatives in Boston to learn family dynamics. It appears none of them were aware of any friction. At least nothing they were willing to admit to that detective."

"Was there any physical evidence?"

Ben settled into the cushions. "Forensics didn't exist in 1924, so there's no blood analysis or DNA testing."

"You mentioned black and white photos."

"A few dozen. But there was one other piece of evidence."

"Are you going to tell me or make me guess?"

Ben grinned at her. "The gown Theo was wearing when she tumbled down those servant steps. I'm going to have the lab run a new test to reveal fingerprints."

"That's exciting!" Gwen nearly squealed. "Any chance I could see her evidence box in person?"

"I don't see why not, Gwen. The evidence room is usually off-limits to civilians, but there's no reason your C.I. status can't apply to this cold case. Can you meet me at the station around nine tomorrow morning?"

Gwen mentally reviewed her calendar for the next day and recalled no conflicting plans. "I'll be there."

Chapter Thirty-Six

...early morning, Tuesday

Gwen had set her alarm for seven-thirty so she wouldn't be late to meet Ben at the police station. Out of bed, showered, and dressed, she stood in the kitchen swallowing the last sip of her morning coffee when her house phone rang.

"Hi, Gwen. I didn't bother you yesterday, so I thought you wouldn't mind if I called this morning."

"I don't mind, Hal, but I'm heading out in a few minutes. Did you find any promising houses?"

"A small cottage two blocks from the beach has some features I like." He sounded upbeat and positive.

"Is Jenna still working on her tan?"

He laughed. "If she's not soaking up the sun at the hotel pool, she's shopping at the mall next door. I only see her for breakfast and dinner."

Hal sounded like his old jovial self, and not the man who'd expected Gwen to sacrifice her plans in favor of his house-hunting trip to Florida. "What's on today's schedule?"

"Three double-wides in different retirement parks. There's one at nearly every intersection." He took a breath. "Are you sure you don't want to change your mind and join me?"

Gwen kept her smart remark in check. "Nice try, Hal, but I'm driving to Tess's on Friday." She glanced at the kitchen clock. "Listen, I've got to get to an appointment."

"Okay, Gwen. I'll stop hounding you about joining me, but I'll keep you updated on my progress."

Feeling silly that she'd brought her pepper spray to the police station, she arrived at nine on the dot.

Ben led her into the evidence room and flipped a switch. The garish overhead fluorescent lights illuminated the windowless room.

At the desk just inside the door, Ben withdrew white cotton gloves from a drawer, handing two to Gwen. "These prevent contamination." After slipping on his own, he hauled a cardboard box to the worktable.

Gwen glanced around the cavernous room filled with cabinets and bulging shelves. "Where did you find Theo's file?"

"The last place I looked," he teased. "It was pretty much the last place *to* look. I'm pretty sure I've touched every file in every cabinet and most every box in here." Ben pointed to a shadowed corner that the brash overhead light avoided. "Her box was buried and out of sight." He slid the lid sideways and withdrew a large paper bag, followed by file folders and envelopes.

Moving closer, Gwen peered at the label: *Homicide, Theodosia Carswell, Dec 20, 1924.* Wooziness overtook her and she reached for the edge of the table.

Ben reached out and grabbed her arm. "Are you okay?"

"I think so. Just a touch of dizziness. Being this close to a cold case gave me a start."

"It's sobering," Ben agreed. "Why don't you sit a minute?"

"Good idea." Gwen lowered herself to the chair he dragged over from the desk. "Thanks, Ben. What's in that paper bag?"

"Theo's dressing gown." He pulled it closer and opened the top, tilting it sideways so Gwen could see inside, but he didn't remove the gown or let her touch it. "I'll be submitting this to the state lab."

"What will they be looking for?"

"Fingerprints."

Gwen sat bolt upright. Theo told Parker's spirit she'd felt fingers on her lower back an instant before she tumbled down those back steps. Gwen wouldn't risk mentioning that conversation between the two ghosts, but she was curious how Ben had concluded he should check for prints. "What made you think there could be fingerprints on Theo's gown?"

"Mrs. Mueller."

"I'm not following."

"Didn't I show you the photo Otis took during his autopsy?"

Gwen shook her head.

He reached into his briefcase and rummaged through the various documents, pulling out an 8-1/2" x 11" photo. "Any idea what this is, Gwen?"

She squinted and tilted her head. "Nope."

"This is a photo of Mrs. Mueller's left arm." Ben pointed to the oval marks. "According to our medical examiner, these were fresh bruises. He suggested they were left by the person who pushed Mrs. Mueller hard enough to send her flying."

Gwen placed her fingers atop Ben's printout, finding her span too small.

Ben did the same. His hand was much too large. "These bruises were inflicted by either a man with a small hand, or a woman with a larger-than-normal hand."

"The lab can find fingerprints on clothing?"

"That's right," Ben answered. "Scottish researchers developed a method of revealing prints on fabric. The lab techs will be using that technique on Mrs. Mueller's jacket sleeve."

"So you're thinking if Theo was also pushed, the lab will find fingerprints on her gown?"

"Exactly. The deaths are too similar to ignore the potential. Though it's unlikely we have the same suspect," he said with a wink.

Gwen was impressed that Ben had deduced the similarity without benefit of Theo's words to Parker's spirit.

"Unfortunately, we don't have photos of any bruises found on Theo's body, so the lab will have to check the entire gown."

Gwen itched to suggest they concentrate on the lower back section of the bodice but held her tongue.

"If the lab tests reveal fingerprints," Ben said, "they could be critical for solving her cold case."

"Wow." Gwen said. "This is feeling more and more like a TV forensics show."

"Oh, I don't know, Gwen. Real detecting takes a lot longer." Ben again tilted the bag for Gwen's inspection of the contents. "Do you know what kind of fabric this is? Some fibers retain fingerprints better than others."

She peeked into the shadows without touching. "If I had to guess, I'd say silk."

"That's one of the better fabrics," Ben said. "The next question is whether a record of the Carswell family fingerprints exists. The military started using fingerprints in the early1900s, but law enforcement didn't adopt the practice until a few years later. The national data base wasn't developed until the '80s. Before that, comparisons were handled manually."

Gwen's admiration for the detective inched up a notch. "You're very knowledgeable, Ben."

He shook his head. "Police academy training plus annual update classes. I was in such a rush to drive to your place and tell you I found Theo's cold case that I didn't get to the bottom of her box." One by one, he removed the other evidence, finally pulling out several cards filled with black ink fingerprints. "Here we go. Looks like they printed not only the family members, but the servants as well. These will come in handy if the lab is successful."

Gwen eyed a bulky envelope peeking out between Theo's folders. "Are those the black and white photos?"

"They are. Go ahead and have a look."

With her gloved hand, Gwen slid the photos onto the worktable. Noticing date and time hand-written in the upper right-hand corners, she positioned them in chronological order without focusing on the images themselves.

Drawing a steadying breath, she concentrated on the first photo: a young woman's body lying crooked at the bottom of the B&B's servant steps, eerily similar to Myrtle's position. The image was sobering to say the least, but Gwen controlled her physical reaction.

The next few images were the same scene taken from various angles. The contrast between Theo's flattering portrait at the top of Betty's front staircase and these pictures of a broken bride-to-be saddened Gwen more than she expected. Tears threatened to spill, but she held them in check.

The remaining pictures showed what appeared to be blood on the landing floorboards.

Gwen turned to Ben. "Are these similar to Myrtle's crime scene photos?"

Ben's cell phone dinged with an incoming email. "Timing is

everything, as they say. It's the DA's photographer. He's apologizing that he forgot to forward his photos, but they're attached."

As the photos loaded, Ben held his cell phone next to the array of Theo's pictures. The resemblance was striking.

Because none of the people in Robert's tour had seen anyone push Myrtle, the unsettling notion that maybe Theo *had* been at the top of those steps reared its disturbing head again.

Questions swarmed through Gwen's mind. Had the ghost of the bride-to-be lied to Parker's spirit? Had she *not* retreated to the third floor before the incident? Had she been invisible to everyone except Myrtle? Did Theo's ghost resent Myrtle as a possible descendant of Nehemiah? Did Theo have more strength than Gwen had assumed?

If she did, Theo could have shoved Myrtle while everyone was preoccupied with the family history. But could Theo have left those bruises on Myrtle's arm? Gwen was overwhelmed by uncertainty. She tapped Ben's arm. "Is it okay if I read through these old reports and witness statements?"

Ben's cell phone buzzed again. As he listened to the caller, his expression changed from excitement to concern. Pressing the end button, he turned to Gwen. "I'm sorry, but I have to go. One of my detectives is about to arrest the leader of a theft ring. After I'm finished there, I'll drive Theo's gown to the state lab. Cross your fingers."

As he returned the reports to Theo's cold case box, Ben said, "Sorry, but I can't let you stay here by yourself. You'll have to review this evidence another day." He secured the lid and returned the box to the shelf. Making a notation on the evidence log, he picked up the paper bag holding Theo's gown and led Gwen from the room before locking the door.

As they rode the elevator to the first floor, Ben took up a position beside her. "How was your visit with Clara Carswell? Was she any help about finding Theo's diary?"

"Unfortunately, we had just asked her about Theo's diary when a nurse poked her head in and whisked Clara away for a nap and her medications."

"So she never had a chance to tell you if she knew what happened to the diary?"

"No. Betty and I will visit again but haven't picked a date."

The elevator moved in slow motion.

Ben held the station door open for Gwen to exit into the parking lot and walked her to her car. "I'll catch up with you later. Keep texting me."

Gwen slid into her driver's seat. "I will."

Despite her frustration that she hadn't had a chance to read those reports, Gwen was nevertheless pleased that Ben had found Theo's cold case. Although it was much too late to bring Theo's murderer to justice, Ben seemed determined to identify the person who'd most likely pushed Theo to her death.

Chapter Thirty-Seven

...late morning, Tuesday

Arriving home, Gwen made a beeline to her laptop to check for emails and then her answering machine, disappointed to find no replies in either place.

Retrieving her list of party attendees, she began the task of contacting each of the remaining members for dish-retrieval plus card-signing. After they had been handled, she'd re-connect with the initial members to sign Myrtle's condolence card and be done with it.

Gwen had definitely over-volunteered herself, but this was the only way she could continue her assignment to identify those elusive whisperers. Using her house phone for caller ID purposes, she dialed last year's club president Wanda Webb and went straight to voicemail. The second call to plant-sale-guru Dolores Greensmith ended the same way. Catching up with these women was becoming increasingly frustrating. Did Ben deal with these constant roadblocks during every investigation?

As she was dialing snack-provider Loretta Baker, Gwen's cell phone buzzed and vibrated atop the granite countertop. She glanced at the caller ID. "Hello, Betty. What's up?"

"You won't believe who just walked through our door."

"I have no idea. Who?"

"Clara Carswell."

"You're kidding!"

"I kid you not. She was driven here in the van from her senior complex. Said she has something to share with both of us. While we wait for you, she requested a tour of the changes Robert and I made to her family home."

"Her sudden frailness is gone?"

"Clara's alert and talking nonstop. She's giving me no hint of why she came."

"I'll head over there in a few minutes."

Returning to the party list, Gwen called Queenie Kemp, Jessica Davenport, and Ursula Yarborough, the three who hadn't participated in the house tour. Gwen was relieved when all went to voicemail.

Before she headed over to Betty's, Gwen phoned rather than texted Ben. Of course, her call went to voicemail. After listening to Ben's recorded greeting, she waited for the beep and said, "Clara Carswell is at the B&B. If you're finished with that arrest, you might want to drop by the B&B and ask her for family history that relates to Theo's cold case. If you're not able to make it, I'll share her visit with you later."

***

Betty led Gwen into the living room where Clara sat primly on the sofa, gazing at Betty's artfully decorated Christmas tree.

As Gwen approached, Clara extended her hand. "Nice to see you again. After our meeting at my complex was cut short yesterday, I decided we deserved another chat."

Reaching into a tote bag at her feet, Clara lifted out a red-bound book and clasped it tightly. "Theo's diary was the only family record I held back from you and Robert."

Gwen noted that the diary was not the familiar lock and key version of Gwen's teenage years but a hard-cover journal.

Clara extended the diary to Betty. "After Theo died, a house maid took up the task of recording the family events because my parents had abandoned the family scrapbooks. When that maid was leaving my father's employ, she gave Theo's diary to me as a keepsake. After our talk yesterday, I decided to bring this to you personally."

Betty caressed the diary as though it were a priceless antique, not opening the cover to read Theo's thoughts and dreams. "Thank you, Clara."

Clara looked on. "I understand your hesitation, Betty. I've safe-guarded Theo's story for decades, but my sister's thoughts should be treasured as part of the Carswell family history."

***

The metal knocker met the antique brass plate with its usual bang. Seconds later, the B&B door flew inward.

Mrs. Owens did not appear happy to see Ben. "Detective Snowcrest. What brings you by?"

Stepping over the threshold before she had a chance to bar him from entry, Ben removed his cap and smiled at her. "I think you'll be glad to see me after I tell you why I'm here."

"In that case, please come in." Mrs. Owens waved him into the entrance hall. "I have unexpected company. This way."

Ben followed her into the living room, pretending to be surprised to see Gwen and a little lady with a halo of silver hair who could only be Clara Carswell.

Mrs. Owens made the introductions before sitting between Clara and Gwen. "So tell me why you dropped by, Detective."

Ben eased into a chair opposite the three women. "As I've been investigating Mrs. Mueller's death, an unsolved case involving a Carswell family member came to my attention, so I did some digging."

Mrs. Owens sat forward. "And what did you find?"

"In the police station evidence room, I located the 1924 case file for Theodosia Carswell. Apparently there wasn't enough evidence to arrest anyone back then, but the detective wrote that the young woman had fallen with a little help. The similarity to Mrs. Mueller's accident is eerie to say the least."

He didn't expect Gwen to comment but thought Mrs. Owens might. Instead, both she and Clara only stared at him. Ben floundered for only a second. "There was no picture of Theodosia in the file. Do you have a portrait of her?"

Mrs. Owens turned to Clara. "Would you like to introduce your family to Detective Snowcrest?"

"I'd be delighted," Clara answered. As the four of them climbed the staircase, she identified the portraits of her Carswell great-grandparents, grandparents, and parents. Reaching the three upper portraits of three young women, Clara stopped before the middle painting and indicated one on her left. "This is me at twenty."

Ben glanced from the portrait of a fresh-faced young woman with a mound of blonde hair to the silver-haired lady standing beside him. "I have to say, Miss Carswell, you look as beautiful now as then."

Clara blushed. "Thank you, Detective."

Pointing to the center portrait directly in front of her, Clara continued the introductions. "And here is my sister Winnie. She passed years ago, so I don't mind telling you she wasn't a very nice person."

The black-haired beauty staring out at Ben possessed a witchy gleam in her eye. Was that her true personality or something the artist had added?

Ben pulled his eyes away from Winnie's magnetic gaze as

Clara touched the cheek on the uppermost portrait. "And this is my precious Theo. I was shattered when she died."

Ben was pulled-in by Theo's delicate features and her gentle aspect. How could anyone have wanted her dead?

Reaching out toward the wall, Clara broke the spell. "Excuse me, but I need to get off my feet. If I stand for too long, I get light-headed."

Ben supported Clara on her left and Betty on her right as they descended the staircase and eased the elderly Carswell onto the living room sofa.

Settling against the cushions, Clara gazed into Ben's face. "If you don't mind me asking, Detective, what are your plans to resolve Theo's cold case?"

He assumed the word *murder* was much too traumatic for the centenarian so proceeded in as delicate a manner as he could summon. "There's a relatively new technology that reveals fingerprints on fabric. This technique wasn't available in 1924. I've submitted Theo's gown to our lab. I won't go into the details of the process, but the technicians should be able to photograph any fingerprints that may have been left."

Clara's hand flew to her throat before she slumped sideways in a dead faint.

Mrs. Owens flew into action and turned to Ben. "Detective, go into the kitchen and wet a hand towel with cold water. Gwen and I will stay here with Clara."

Ben rushed around the dining room table and through the swinging door. As he wet the towel at the kitchen sink, he felt a touch on his shoulder. He made a quarter-turn and stared into a translucent face identical to the portrait he'd just viewed. A white-gowned young woman wavered before him. Theo brushed her fingers across his cheek, her touch light, but a touch he could not deny.

Ben didn't question his sanity as he struggled to remain standing, grasping the edge of the sink for support.

When he dared to glance her way a second time, Theo was pointing at his hands, as if to remind him of his mission. Trying to control his shaking, he wrung out the excess water and grabbed another cloth to catch any errant drips.

Turning to leave, he fully expected to see Theo's ghost.

She wasn't there.

***

Ben didn't hear Mrs. Owens calling him until Gwen wrestled the cloth from his grip and applied it to Clara's forehead.

When Clara stirred, Betty assisted the elderly woman to a sitting position and plumped a pillow behind her. "Are you feeling all right, Clara?"

"I'm fine now, Betty. Thank you."

Mrs. Owens glanced up at Ben. "I know that expression, Detective. Similar to the old *deer in the headlights* look. Did you encounter Theo in the kitchen?"

For some reason, Ben couldn't speak. Had the shock of Theo's apparition frozen his vocal cords? He glanced at Gwen, recalling his declaration that he didn't believe in ghosts. She starred back at him, her eyes wide.

"You'd better have a seat, Detective." Mrs. Owens guided him to the chair where he'd sat earlier. "I remember my first glimpse of Theo. My grandmother convinced me long ago that ghosts existed, but I hadn't yet seen one for myself. The day we began our conversion project, Theo appeared by my side in the kitchen. After that first time, she manifested once a week or so. I began to watch for her."

As Ben listened to Betty's soothing voice, he lowered his head into his hands and waited for the light-headedness to go away. His plan to question Clara Carswell about the day Theo died would have to wait.

**

"Boy, did I miss a lot!"

Minutes before, Robert had returned to the B&B and was immediately inundated with a replay of events. He offered to drive Ben to the station.

"No need, Mr. Owens." Ben walked to the front door on unsteady legs, then turned back. "I'll be sure to let you all know what the lab finds on Theo's gown."

"Thank you, Detective," Betty responded. "As you can imagine, we're very curious."

**

Ben arrived at his desk without remembering the drive from the B&B, parking his SUV in the lot, entering the station, or riding the elevator to the second floor. If any of his detectives or the chief had approached him, he wouldn't have found the words to explain his odd behavior.

Theo's unexpected appearance had more than thrown Ben for a loop. She'd totally side-swiped him, blowing his doubt out the window. Gwen had never questioned Mrs. Owens' revelation that the Carswell House was haunted. Now he had no choice but to believe in Theo's ghostly existence.

In nearly slow motion, he retrieved the key to the evidence room, unlocked the door, and walked directly to the cold case box. Theo deserved to know who had pushed her to her death.

Until the lab processed Theo's gown for fingerprints, there was little Ben could do. He re-read all the reports, spotting no clues that he'd missed. The 1924 detective had followed procedure, but lacking modern tools of evidence gathering, had taken the case as far as he could. Ben studied the fingerprint cards, though he had nothing for comparison...yet.

Only Clara Carswell remained as a potential source of information into her eldest sister's tragic end. But Clara had been only seven years old. How possible was it that she knew some small detail that she'd never shared with anyone?

Not knowing if it was appropriate or not, Ben made a mental note to visit the elderly lady at his first opportunity. He'd ask Gwen for the name of the senior complex.

A voice called out, "There you are, Detective."

Ben swiveled to see Chief Brown at the door. "Hey, Mike."

"I noticed your car keys on your desk but didn't see you in here until a second ago. This cold case got you puzzled?"

Ben nodded, relieved that his ability to speak had returned. "The state lab is using that new test to raise fingerprints on Miss Carswell's gown."

Mike stepped closer. "Same technique as the Mueller jacket? Spooky that this cold case parallels the Mueller death. You might be breaking our budget, but if you can clear both cases, I'll deal with the town treasurer. Catch up with me after you hear from the lab."

Chapter Thirty-Eight

...late afternoon, Tuesday

After Ben left, Gwen remained beside Clara Carswell on the couch. The woman's lovely features were transformed with concern when she asked, "Do you think your detective's lab will find fingerprints on Theo's gown?"

Gwen was at a loss for an answer. "There's no way any of us can predict what they'll find."

Robert leaned against the archway, his arms crossed. "I'd never heard of that process, but it must be useful to the police in solving cases."

"You know," Betty added, patting Clara's hand, "just when I think nothing else can be invented, along comes another discovery."

Clara reached into her pocket, pulled out a business card, and passed it to Betty. "Would you be a dear and call the van driver? He shouldn't be far away."

"You're leaving so soon?" Robert asked.

She gifted him with a gentle smile. "Unfortunately, I need my afternoon medication and a nap."

Robert strolled over and extended his hand to Betty. "Let me have that card. I'll make the call." Less than a minute later, he disconnected his cell phone. "The driver's leaving the Sugar 'n Spice Café now. Let's make sure Clara is bundled up."

They helped Clara maneuver her arms into the sleeves of her fur-collared coat. She turned grateful eyes to Betty and Robert. "I so enjoyed my visit with you this afternoon. You've done a wonderful job converting my family home into your B&B. And I feel better now that Theo's diary is returned to the Carswell House where it belongs."

Betty hugged the sweet woman. "Thanks for bringing it to us. We'll preserve her diary alongside the family history binders. And you know you're welcome here any time, Clara."

When the front knocker clanged against the brass plate, Robert opened the door and waved the uniformed driver inside.

The man smiled at Clara, his eyes bright with tenderness. "I hope you had a nice visit, Miss Clara. I have a cup of hot chocolate waiting for you in the van."

"How sweet of you, Charles. May I have your arm, please?"

Gwen marveled that by-gone manners still existed.

***

For the next hour or so, Gwen, Betty, and Robert took turns reading Theo's diary out loud.

The eldest Carswell daughter had begun recording her daily life during her early teens, her postings redolent with teenage angst throughout the years.

Beginning in January 1924, Theo repeatedly recorded her aggravation with her younger sister. Winnie consistently pestered Mr. Brewster when he came to call on Theo. Month after month, the complaints persisted.

On December 21, the day after Theo died, the distinctly different penmanship indicated the maid's recording of the goings on inside the Carswell House. She detailed her mistress's mysterious fall, the family's devastation, and the cancellation of all Christmas celebrations.

Betty murmured, "That's the day Clara's parents stopped preserving family events. Let's keep reading."

Within a month after Theo's death, Mr. Brewster asked Winnie's father for her hand in marriage. Though the family was not pleased with Brewster's actions so soon after Theo's death, the father relented to Winnie's pleas for his blessing. The maid wrote that she'd suspected Brewster had dallied with Winnie for months before Theo's untimely demise. And there the diary entries stopped.

"Oh, my," Betty commented. "That must be when the maid left. You never know what happens within the best of families."

Gwen sat forward, her tone sober. "Do you think Winnie pushed Theo?"

"I'd say it's very likely," Robert agreed. "She was obviously interested in Theo's gentleman caller. Who else would have wanted Theo out of the way?"

***

That evening Gwen opened her door to admit Queenie and Jennifer, enveloped by the sensation that weeks, rather than days, had passed since she'd reunited club members with their food containers. Delving into Theo's life and death had stretched the concept of time beyond its normal passage.

Gwen dragged her attention to her visitors. "Come in."

Both women stomped the snow from their boots before stepping across the threshold.

Gwen closed the door, noting that the sun was attempting to break through the grey clouds. "Would either of you like a cup of tea or coffee or perhaps hot cider?"

Queenie answered, "We don't want to make any extra work for you. Gwen."

"Oh, it's no trouble. Follow me to the kitchen and let me warm you up."

Jennifer glanced around the open floor plan and swooping staircase to the second level mezzanine. "Your library home is lovely, Gwen. I missed your garden and house tour last year."

"Thanks. My husband designed the conversion ten years ago. His clever spaces are extra special now that he's gone."

"Very unique," Queenie quipped. "You must love it here."

While the coffee brewed, Gwen kept their chit-chat on the light side, asking her guests to share their holiday plans, finally placing mugs in front of each woman. "I admit I have another reason for asking you to pick up your party dishes in person."

As Gwen reached behind her to grasp the condolence card, Jennifer said, "Oh, does it have anything to do with the threat you overheard in Betty's front parlor?"

More interested in what they might know, Gwen dropped the card back onto the counter. "You know about that?"

Queenie stirred sugar into her coffee. "I bumped into the Hobart twins yesterday and they told me. I told Jennifer during our drive over. Have you figured out who they were?"

Gwen shook her head. "I haven't. Are you aware of a member with money problems or having an affair?"

"What makes you think they were club members?" Queenie challenged.

Gwen had to think fast. "I'm not sure. I guess it's because there were so many more of us than any others at the B&B. And most of the guests didn't seem to know one another."

Queenie appeared to accept Gwen's reasoning. Both women answered the same way as all the others. Other than Myrtle's complaint about her grandson's tuition, they knew of no member in financial straits or cheating on her husband.

Draining her cup, Queenie slid off her stool. "Thanks for

your hospitality, Gwen, but Jennifer and I planned to do some shopping while we're in town. If you can show us the dishes you're holding, we'll grab ours and be on our way. Ursula is my sister-in law, so I'll take her bowl as well."

Gwen was only slightly disappointed that she'd have no face-to-face chat with Ursula, but based on the disappointing answers so far, the likelihood that the woman would provide any earth-shattering details was doubtful.

Gwen slid the condolence card and pen across the counter. "I'll get the boxes while you two sign this."

Queenie murmured the wording from the cover before opening to the inside sentiment. "How lovely. Where did you get this card?"

"It's from Holly's shop. She dropped it off and asked me to collect everyone's signature."

Nodding her approval, Queenie signed with theatrical flair. "Is it okay if I sign Ursula's name? I don't think Myrtle's family would know it's not genuine."

"That shouldn't be a problem," Jessica chimed in. "I'll never tell."

Having the signatures applied by the actual person didn't seem all that important, so Gwen let it go as she lifted the last cardboard box of dishes to the island counter.

Chapter Thirty-Nine

...early-morning, Wednesday

The next morning, luck was on Gwen's side when she stopped a second time at the homes of club members.

Alicia Reed advised her that Travis and the kids were feeling much better, but she didn't budge from her doorway. She signed the card and sent Gwen on her way.

The Hobart twins were busy with housecleaning, which delayed their answering of the doorbell. Zelda apologized that she hadn't remembered anything beyond the church kitchen conversation she'd shared during Gwen's last visit.

Evelyn Woodley signed the card, saying she was on her way out. Gwen didn't bother repeating her request for guesses about the whisperers, knowing Evelyn would consider it gossip.

As usual, Gwen learned nothing new.

Would Ben regret he'd asked for her help? So far, she hadn't contributed much of anything.

Continuing her rounds, Gwen's luck held. She found Eunice, Frankie, and Nadine all busy in their respective houses. Gwen obtained a signature from each and nothing else.

Concerned she was running out of time to collect the last two signatures, Gwen drove to the final two addresses. No success in either location, as neither Wanda Webb nor Loretta Baker responded to Gwen's knock. If she wasn't able to connect with them before Friday morning, Gwen would simply forge their names and drop off the condolence card at the Mueller house on her way to Tess's.

***

"Good morning, Gwen."

Hal's voice on the phone brought her up short. She hadn't thought of him even once since his last call.

She regained her composure. "If you'd called a few minutes earlier, Hal, I wouldn't have gotten home yet."

Without asking where she'd been so early in the day, Hal launched into his house-hunting news. "Well, I did it. I made an offer on that cottage a few blocks from the beach. Got a call from the real estate lady last night that the owners accepted."

Gwen heard the triumph in his voice. "Congratulations."

"I've already spoken to my banker. We're trying to close by the end of January."

Gwen's emotions were mixed. Within the month, Hal would leave Harbor Falls. He'd no longer be nearby for an impromptu walk in the woods or a quick bite to eat. "What's the latest on selling your nursery?"

Hal chuckled. "I suggested to my foreman that he manage the place until I find a seller. Oscar and his brother are thinking about buying the nursery outright."

"That must be a load off your mind," Gwen commented. "Oscar knows your fields and greenhouses as well as you do."

"You've got that right." Hal hesitated. "Hang on a second. Someone wants to talk to you."

Gwen waited as the phone was handed over.

"Mrs. Andrews, this is Jenna."

"Hi, there, sweetie. Are you enjoying Florida?"

"You bet. You should see my tan." The girl laughed.

"Lucky for you your grandfather didn't force you to tour all the properties."

"That's for sure. The cottage he bought is so cute. I've got some other news to tell you, Mrs. Andrews."

"You know, Jenna, I haven't been your music tutor for more than a year. I'd like you to call me Gwen."

"Really? I've always thought of you as Gwen, but I didn't want to be disrespectful."

It was Gwen's turn to laugh. "What's your news?"

"I think you'll be pleased. I've decided a career as a performer is too unreliable, so I've switched my spring courses to music history. I want to be a professor, just like you were."

A lump formed in Gwen's throat. "That's wonderful, Jenna. Have you approached the dean about your change of career?"

"I did and he said my timing is perfect. Baylies is initiating an accelerated Masters program next fall, and he suggested I apply now."

"You've maintained excellent grades. I see no reason why they won't accept you into the program."

"I'm really excited, Mrs...uh, Gwen. I'm hoping I can land a summer job in the music department. Granddad offered to pay a portion of the tuition, and I'll apply for scholarships and grants and student loans. It should only add another year on to my schooling."

Gwen warmed as Jenna's news sunk in. "So you won't be traveling around the world wowing the crowds with your flute?"

"Nope. Granddad might be moving to Florida, but I'm staying put in Harbor Falls."

"You know what, Jenna? With your grandfather selling his nursery, you'll have nowhere to live after you graduate in May. You're welcome to settle in my guest room for the summer and commute to Baylies. You can walk to the campus from here.

And if you'd like, you can stay even longer."

On the other end of the line, Jenna drew in a deep breath. "Really? That's so generous of you! I'd love to live with you in the old library, and I promise I'll be the best guest ever. Besides, you'll be a built-in study-buddy."

Gwen chuckled at the girl's upbeat attitude, chatting until Jenna mentioned another tanning session at the pool.

After ending the call, Gwen was struck by the similarity between Jenna and Herbert Mueller, both under the care of their grandparents. Hal had raised Jenna since she was four after her parents were killed in a car accident. What was the reason Myrtle and Fletcher had shared custody of Herbert?

Unable to quell her curiosity, Gwen dialed *The Gazette*.

The young woman who answered explained the saving of archived newspapers. "The older ones were transcribed onto microfilm and are stored at the library. I believe they have an index. Do you know where the new library is located?

"I know it well. Thank you." Gwen disconnected and gazed out the bay window toward her winter-weary rear gardens. If the weather hadn't been so consistently bleak of late, she would've taken the shortcut from her backyard and through her wooded lot to the new library out the other side.

But Parker's trails were most likely blocked by fallen branches from the winter winds. His footbridge spanning the gorge probably slippery with snow and ice. Traipsing through the woods might not be the smartest option. She decided to drive to the new library.

***

"Hello, Maggie," Gwen called as she approached the reference desk. "You ready for the holidays?"

"I am. My turn to host the family dinner this year. What are your plans, Gwen?"

"Driving to my sister's home in the Berkshires."

"That's cool. I'll pray for no snowstorms. What can I do for you today?"

"I need to search through old issues of the Harbor Falls Gazette. How do I access the microfilm?"

"I'll show you. Follow me."

After climbing several sets of stairs, Margie led Gwen into a room at the front of the building and pulled open a drawer in a tall wooden case. "These are the rolls of microfilm." She waved to a monstrous machine on the next table. "That's our old reader, but now we can connect to a computer."

"Do you have an index?"

"We sure do. We're one of the few libraries that contracted an outside indexer. Let's log on and I'll walk you through it."

A minute later, Gwen scanned the index file that grouped the newspaper editions into five-year clusters.

"What year are you looking for?"

Gwen stopped to calculate. In his early twenties now, Herbert was born in the mid-nineties. At some point between his birth and the present, Myrtle and Fletcher Mueller had become the boy's legal guardians, but Gwen could only guess what year that had happened. She glanced at Maggie. "I need to search the last twenty years."

Maggie reached for the mouse, clicked into the index for 1996-2000 and pointed. "What's the last name?"

Gwen spelled out Mueller while Maggie typed. Nothing came up.

"Don't panic yet, Gwen. Let's try the next index."

264

No results in 2001-2005 either. And nothing in 2006-2010. The Muellers had apparently lived a very quiet life and never rated newspaper coverage.

Not giving up, Maggie pulled up the index for 2011-2015 and typed in the name. Up popped an article dated September 2015. "Here we go, Gwen. There are several articles concerning the Mueller family. Are any of these first names the ones you're looking for?"

Gwen scanned the list, seeing Fletcher, Myrtle, Herbert, and a few other first names she didn't recognize. "Some of these names are familiar."

"Good," Maggie said. "The index provides only a one-sentence description of the article. The date and page number are referenced at the end of the line."

From the drawer, Maggie removed the roll of microfilmed newspapers for September 2015. She showed Gwen how to thread it onto the reader, and manipulate the contents.

"Sorry, Gwen, but the reference desk needs my attention. Just scroll forward to the date and then the page to find the article. If you want copies, hit this button. Ten cents each. After you pay at the front desk, they'll print the pages for you. I'll be at the reference desk if you need me."

Gwen followed Maggie's instructions and was soon reading an interview Fletcher gave to Gazette reporter Shirley Knapp after a court hearing. Fletcher and Myrtle had accused their son and his wife of neglect based on alcohol and drug abuse.

The judge ordered shared custody while Herbert's parents served their sentences in a rehab facility, with a review every six months. Fletcher ended the interview by stating he wanted to serve as an example to other families if their kids were caught up in the rampant drug problem. Grandparents needed to step up and take charge to protect their grandchildren.

Gwen requested a copy to show Ben, removed the microfilm from the reader and returned it to the drawer. She pulled up the index for the next group of years, thinking there might be a follow-up article.

Sure enough, when she searched 2016-present, a different article popped up, revealing a follow-up interview with Fletcher. At six-month intervals, the judge had reviewed the case as promised. He'd ruled that although both parents had made positive strides in their rehabilitation, they were not yet ready to take on the responsibility of their son.

Because Herbert had entered Baylies College, and remained a dependent on his grandparents' tax return, the shared custody would prevail until Herbert graduated and became an independent adult. Fletcher stated to the reporter that he was proud to provide moral and financial support to his grandson.

After requesting a second printout, Gwen took a moment to absorb this unsettling situation. Couples could never guess if the child born to them would bring joy or heartache.

Chapter Forty

...mid-morning, Wednesday

As Gwen stored away the final roll of microfilm, she remembered her promise to Betty that she'd research the offspring of Winnie Carswell and Nehemiah Brewster and their possible relationship to Myrtle and Charlie.

Navigating the two flights of stairs, Gwen reached the reference desk to find Maggie nowhere in sight. A tap on Gwen's shoulder made her jump.

"Sorry I gave you a fright," Maggie apologized. "Do you need my help with the microfilm reader?"

Gwen shook her head. "I'm all set with *The Gazette.* Returned the canisters to the drawer and everything."

Maggie chuckled. "That'll save me another trek up those stairs. Do you need me for another project?"

Gwen hefted her purse strap higher on her shoulder. "I was told that some towns created their own census. Is Harbor Falls one of those towns?"

"We sure are. Every ten years, beginning in the late 1800s. Which one do you need?"

"I'll start with 1930."

Maggie crooked a finger at Gwen. "Follow me."

This time, Maggie led Gwen to the opposite end of the library and unlocked a room. In the center of a huge oak table lay several volumes of *The Mayflower Families,* open as though someone was in the middle of browsing the pages.

"I didn't know you had a set of those," Gwen commented.

"Normally we wouldn't," Maggie explained. "The series was donated by a member who'd been a patron for decades."

From the next row, Maggie selected a black hard-bound book and opened to the introductory pages. "This 1930 census was taken in April of that year. The individual details are a bit different from the federal census. The residents are listed alphabetically by name of their street."

"Oh," Gwen said. "I don't know where my subject lived."

"In that case, let's check the city directory first." Maggie placed the census record on the table and walked to another section, plucking a book from an extensive collection taking up three shelves. "Here you go. This shows who lived in Harbor Falls by last name in 1930. If you need more recent years, they're filed numerically. Have fun!"

As Maggie exited the room, Gwen opened the city directory, flipped to the 'B' section, and immediately located Nehemiah Brewster at 19 Sturdy Way. She wasn't familiar with this particular street.

Pushing the town directory aside, she pulled the 1930 census closer, shivering with anticipation. Relieved that the handwriting was legible, Gwen turned the pages until she reached the 'S' section. Sliding her finger down the listings, a little noise escaped her when she came to 19 Sturdy Way. Residents were listed as follows:

Nehemiah Linus Brewster, 28, b 12/30/1902, M, bank clerk
Winifred C. Brewster, 26, b 4/29/1904, F, housewife
William Carswell Brewster, 5, M, b 6/14/1925, son
Sophia Clara Brewster, 3, b 5/5/1927, F, daughter
Florence Theodosia Brewster, 6 mo, b 10/11/29, F, daughter

Gwen found it charming that Winnie had retained her Carswell heritage by assigning family names to her children. And then William's age caught Gwen's eye. According to the maid's entry in Theo's diary, Winnie married Nehemiah in early 1925. If William was born in June of that same year, Winnie obviously became pregnant months before Theo's death, which explained why Brewster proposed marriage so quickly after Theo died.

For the purpose of sharing these details with Betty, Gwen snapped a picture of the page with her cell phone and returned the book to the shelf. Next, she located the 1950 Harbor Falls census and brought it to the table. Because Myrtle's maiden name was Brewster, her descent – if she was indeed related – had to come from Winnie's son and not the daughters.

Maggie's voice called over from the open door. "There's another set of books called *Births and Deaths in Harbor Falls* that might be useful. You'll find them on the top shelf to the left of the census records."

"Thanks, Maggie."

Maggie waved and again disappeared.

Gwen perused the 1950 city directory to see if son William remained in Harbor Falls twenty years later.

Not only had he stayed in the town of his birth, but had moved from his parents' home. His address was registered as 20 Mooring Lane. Again, Gwen was unfamiliar with that street. Perhaps Mooring Lane and 19 Sturdy Way had been gobbled up over the years as Harbor Falls grew and changed.

Finding William's address in the 1950 census report required little effort. Living in his household were wife Felicity; first child Isaac, six years old; second child Myrtle, four .

Gwen nearly fell off the chair. Could this child be the same Myrtle? How common was that name in the '40s and '50s? The coincidence was too close to ignore, and like Ben, Gwen didn't believe in coincidences.

Assuming that the older brother Isaac could be Charlie's grandfather, Gwen soon confirmed that Isaac begat Henry, who bore a son named Charles. Bingo!

Overwhelmed with satisfaction, Gwen let her discoveries sink in. But what did these details prove beyond the fact that Myrtle and Charlie were descended from Nehemiah? Like Betty, Gwen couldn't bring herself to believe Theo would harm the granddaughter and great grandson of her cheating fiancé. That assumed Theo realized they were descendents.

Again Gwen took a photo on her cell phone for Betty before re-shelving the volumes. Not willing to leave any stone unturned, she located *Births and Deaths in Harbor Falls.*

After confirming the births she'd already uncovered, Gwen searched through the deaths, and came upon Winnie's 1939 obituary. Cause of death: tuberculosis. That was enough for Gwen. Without taking a cell phone picture, she returned the book to the shelf and made her way to the reference desk.

Maggie's gaze shifted from the computer screen to Gwen's face. "Did you find what you were looking for?"

"I did, Maggie. Thanks for your help."

"That's why I'm here. Come and see me any time."

Chapter Forty-One

…mid-afternoon, Wednesday

Gwen planned to update Betty after running her vacuum, a never-ending chore with a cat in residence. The roar of the Eureka upright nearly drowned out the ringing of the house phone. When the insistent noise reached Gwen, she stepped on the power button and rushed to pick up the kitchen receiver.

"Gwen," Betty said, "I was afraid for a second that you weren't home."

"I'm here. Just doing housework. What's up?"

"The nurse called to tell me Clara's in the infirmary and wants to see us. She asked if you and I can drive over there."

"Did the nurse say what's wrong?" Gwen asked.

"Not specifically. Can you come with me?"

"Of course. How soon?"

"I'm waiting for a batch of muffins to come out of the oven. I'll pick you up in about half an hour."

"I'll be watching for you."

***

During the drive to Plymouth, Gwen shared the history of Nehemiah's family history that she'd unearthed at the Harbor Falls library.

"Well, don't that beat all," Betty commented as she pulled into the complex's parking lot. "Who would have thought you could prove Myrtle and Charlie are related to Nehemiah?"

Inside the main building, they approached the reception desk and Betty took charge. "We're here to see Clara Carswell."

The woman behind the desk checked her clipboard. "You must be Betty Owens and Gwen Andrews?"

At Betty's nod, the woman leaned over the wooden counter and pointed. "The infirmary is the second door on the right."

In the sick room, Clara sat upright, an oversized bandage swathing the right side of her head. Seeing Betty and Gwen, Clara's face brightened. She rolled her eyes at the nurse taking her pulse. "Oh, I'm so glad you two were able to come."

The nurse turned and nodded in greeting. "I'm the one who called. Like I told you on the phone, Clara's been asking for you ever since she was brought in here earlier today."

"What happened?" Betty asked.

"She fainted in the community room and hit her head on a glass coffee table."

"I can hear every word you're saying," Clara called over, her voice energized. "If you want my opinion, Nurse Nancy here is being overly cautious."

Gwen hid a grin at Clara's reference to a childhood story character until she noticed that the nurse's nametag actually read *Nancy*.

"Now, now, Clara," the nurse chided. "We don't take any chances with head injuries. You couldn't even tell me the last names of your friends or their phone numbers."

"That has nothing to do with the bump on my head. That's simply old age forgetfulness."

The nurse focused on Gwen and Betty "It took us a while to figure out who you were from the visitors' sign-in sheet. Thank you for coming on such short notice."

Again, Clara spoke. "If you don't mind, please leave us to have a private chat."

The nurse took a hesitant step toward the door.

Betty said, "We'll call you if Clara needs attention," and held the door open.

Nurse Nancy acquiesced. "All right. I won't be far away."

After the door closed, Clara waved Betty and Gwen to either side of the bed. "I'm afraid I'm not a very good patient."

Betty placed her hand on Clara's arm. "Did you want to see us because of your injury?"

When Clara wagged her head in a negative response, she winced. "No. There's something I should have shared with you yesterday." Clara toggled her focus between them as though she were watching a tennis match. "You need to remember that I was only seven when Theo died. My parents kept everything hush, hush, so I didn't discover or understand what I'm going to tell you until years later."

Smoothing the blanket, Clara began. "Mr. Brewster married Winnie because she was pregnant. Our father was furious. He wanted to toss the newlyweds out on their ears, but our mother insisted the couple live in the Carswell House during Winnie's pregnancy. Their son William was born the following June."

Betty and Gwen glanced at each other. They already knew this chain of events from the Harbor Falls census records.

Clara continued. "After Winnie recovered from a difficult delivery, our father made it clear that Brewster needed to provide a home for his wife and child, so they moved to a house at the waterfront. Back then, houses near the harbor weren't as charming as they are today. My father forbade my mother from visiting Winnie or the new baby. When I came of age, I sought out Winnie and grew to love her children. By then, she'd given birth to two girls Amelia and Florence. If my father had ever discovered I was seeing my sister in secret, he probably would have tossed me out as well. I hope those names help you discover if your garden club member and her nephew were Nehemiah's descendants."

Betty patted Clara's hand. "Thanks for those details. Is there anything else you want to share with me and Gwen?"

Clara glanced at Betty. "As a matter of fact, there is. If I don't get this off my chest, I might go into cardiac arrest. Gwen, it has to do with your friend Detective Snowcrest."

Gwen instantly decided not to deny Ben's friendship, knowing that her protest would only strengthen Clara's assumption. "Can you be more specific, Clara?"

"I can and I will. I need to bolster my courage." Clara reached for a glass of water and took a healthy gulp.

Gwen and Betty both waited for Clara to compose herself.

Clara finally spoke, her voice quivery. "It won't be long until your detective receives news from his lab that their special process revealed fingerprints on Theo's gown."

"And that alarms you?" Betty wanted to know.

Clara took another swallow, her glance moving between them. "I know whose fingerprints they are."

Betty inched closer. "Are you about to tell us that Winnie pushed Theo?"

Clara burst into tears, her hand moving to the bandaged side of her head. "No, no, you've got it all wrong. Winnie didn't do it. But she convinced me that Theo would think it was funny if I did." Clara continued to sob, huge tears dropping onto her hospital gown. "I'm the one who shoved Theo down those steps. Detective Snowcrest will find *my* fingerprints on Theo's gown! You need to bring him here so I can confess."

Shocked by Clara's unexpected revelation, Gwen stared at Betty before saying, "Clara, the blame is not all yours."

Clara closed her eyes and collapsed against the pillows.

Betty rushed to the door and flung it open. "Come quick! Clara has passed out."

Within seconds, Nurse Nancy entered the room and rushed to Clara's side. "You two wait in the hallway," she commanded.

Finding themselves outside the infirmary, Betty leaned against the wall and fanned her face with her hand. "I can't believe it was little Clara who pushed Theo."

"Beyond that, Betty, she's been guarding this secret since she was seven. What a heavy weight for her to carry."

"Should we do as she asked and call Detective Snowcrest?"

"I don't think we have any choice. Let me see if I still have his card in my shoulder bag." Although Ben was listed in Gwen's contacts, she needed to pretend they weren't that close.

Seconds after she dialed, Gwen said, "Detective Snowcrest, this is Gwen Andrews. I'm with Betty Owens at Clara Carswell's retirement complex in Plymouth. You need to get here as soon as you can. Clara wants you to hear her confession about Theo Carswell's death." Before hanging up, she added the name and address of the complex.

"What did he say?" Betty asked.

"Nothing. I left that message on his voice mail. I don't know when he'll listen to it or how soon he'll arrive. You realize that Clara's confession will close Theo's cold case?"

Betty's eyes grew wide as the implication settled. "Oh, I hadn't thought that far ahead."

Nurse Nancy stuck her head out the infirmary door. "I've called an ambulance. Clara's awake and asking for you both."

***

The decline of Clara's appearance startled Gwen. The elderly lady appeared even tinier as she lay beneath the blanket, her face an ashen gray. Her eyes were closed. Only the nearly indiscernible movement of her chest indicated she was alive.

Approaching the bed, Betty leaned over and whispered, "We're here, Clara."

The last Carswell fluttered her eyelids. A long moment passed before she focused on Betty and Gwen. When Clara spoke, she slurred her words. "Thank you for staying. You need to tell Theo that I'm the guilty person she's searched for all these years. It doesn't matter that Winnie talked me into it. My poor dear Theo has suffered long enough."

Clara's eyes fluttered and she went limp against the pillow.

An older man in a doctor's tunic banged the door against the wall and rushed to Clara's side his fingers taking her pulse. "What's the status of the ambulance?"

Nurse Nancy swallowed a sob. "On its way."

***

After Ben listened to Gwen's voicemail, he broke the speed limit all the way to Plymouth, his siren blaring.

In the parking lot, the lights of an ambulance flashed as two uniformed men removed a gurney. Ben beat them through the entrance, held up his detective badge, asked for Clara Carswell, and was directed to the infirmary.

As Ben raced along the hallway, he spotted Gwen and Betty sitting on a bench. "We'll talk later."

They nodded and waved him inside.

An older man in a white coat was pressing a stethoscope against Clara's chest. He turned at the sound of the door opening. "I'm sorry, sir, you can't come in here. We're rushing this woman to the hospital as soon as the ambulance arrives."

"The EMTs are in the parking lot. I'm Detective Benjamin Snowcrest from Harbor Falls. Miss Carswell asked for me."

Clara stirred on the bed, her trembling hand coming out from under the blanket and reaching toward Ben. "Please come closer, Detective. I have something to tell you."

The doctor shook his head and took one step back.

Ben flipped on his cell phone's recorder and held it close to Clara's mouth as she whispered her confession.

***

Out in the hallway, Betty shoved her hands between her knees. "I'm not sure what to do, Gwen. Should I repeat Clara's confession out loud to Robert so Theo will overhear us?"

"That's one option," Gwen agreed, having no idea of the best way to deliver this sad news to Theo's ghost. "I can also try to contact Parker's spirit for another conversation between them. He might be able to soften the blow."

"I guess either way will grant Clara's wish that Theo is told what really happened that morning. But do we tell Theo that Nehemiah impregnated Winnie long before her wedding day?"

"I just don't know, Betty. Theo must have seen Nehemiah and Winnie living together in the Carswell House, and then the difficult birth of their first child. But maybe spirits have no sense of time passing."

Betty stood up from the bench and began to pace. "Do you think Theo's ghost will disappear from our B&B?"

"I have no idea, Betty, but it's a distinct possibility."

Chapter Forty-Two

…late afternoon, Wednesday

Clara Carswell had barely finished her confession when the door flew open and two EMTs entered with their gurney. She reached out and touched Ben's arm. "Thank you. I feel so much better now." She sighed and closed her eyes.

"Move aside," the doctor instructed.

Ben extended a business card. "Please keep me updated."

The doctor murmured under his breath and tucked the card in his jacket pocket.

The EMTs loaded Clara onto their stretcher and rushed her from the infirmary. Glancing at his cell phone, Ben speculated that Clara's confession might be her last spoken words.

***

As the EMTs wheeled Clara toward the exit, Gwen leaned toward Betty. "I hope she'll be all right."

"Hard to know," Betty said. "Do you think Clara held on this long so she could confess and clear her conscience?"

Ben emerged from the infirmary and headed toward them. They scooted closer on the bench and made room for him.

Gwen said, "You look beat, Detective."

"Thank you, Mrs. Andrews."

Gwen wondered how long they could maintain their charade before one of them slipped up and revealed their connection as detective and confidential informant.

Betty leaned around Gwen and spoke to Ben. "Did Clara give you her confession?"

He nodded and held up his cell phone. "I recorded her story. I've heard lots of criminals admit their guilt, but none of their stories were as sad as Clara's."

"What will happen to her?" Gwen asked.

"That's not for me to decide, but she was only seven when it happened." Ben replied. "I've got to update the police chief. If I need a statement from either of you, I'll be in touch."

***

Wishing the station elevator could move a little quicker, Ben shifted from one foot to the other until the doors opened on the second floor. He headed for Mike Brown's office and knocked on the door frame. "Got a minute, chief?"

Mike looked up from his stack of documents. "Come in, Ben. You have an update?"

Ben held up his phone as he collapsed into the side chair. "Only a recorded confession that closes our oldest cold case."

The chief leaned across his desk. "Play it for me."

After Clara's tiny voice stopped speaking, Ben clicked off the recorder. "The lab results should confirm the fingerprints on the gown belonged to Clara."

"No doubt," Mike agreed. "Why would she confess if it wasn't true? I need to call the district attorney."

Ben squirmed. "Would a seven-year-old be held criminally liable for the death of a sibling given the circumstances?"

"I just don't know, Ben. That'll be up to the D.A." Mike placed the call and spoke to the assistant D.A., switching on the speaker while he detailed Clara Carswell's confession.

When Ben's cell phone vibrated, he walked into the hallway to take the call. A deep voice came through the line. "We were never introduced, Detective, but I'm the doctor who attended

Clara Carswell at the retirement complex. I'm sorry to tell you that she passed away a few minutes ago without waking up. I suspect a traumatic head injury from her contact with the glass coffee table was the reason. I won't know for sure until the M.E. completes the autopsy." The doctor hesitated. "It was the strangest thing. She was smiling like an angel when she took her last breath."

Thanking the doctor, Ben disconnected and stepped into the chief's office, holding up a finger to signal an urgent update.

"Hold on," Mike said into the phone. "What is it, Ben?"

"Clara Carswell just died."

Visibly shaken, Mike resumed his phone call with the assistant DA, cancelling their discussion of potential criminal charges against the last Carswell.

***

Rather than call, Ben wanted to soften Clara's passing by delivering the news in person. First Gwen, then the Owens couple.

Gwen led him to her warm kitchen where he settled on his usual island stool. Gwen sat on the next stool, releasing a whiff of her vanilla scent. For a second, Ben forgot why he was there. "Unfortunately, I'm here with upsetting news."

"Is it Clara?" Gwen asked. "Did you get the lab results on the fingerprints? Are you going to arrest her?"

Ben reached over and enclosed Gwen's hands. "Clara passed away at the hospital a little while ago."

When Gwen squeezed, Ben sensed her reaction would have been the same no matter whose hands were holding hers. Was her grasp simply her reaction to death and loss or was Gwen developing feelings for him?

Her downcast eyes found his. "Did she wake up?"

"No. But the doctor said she was smiling when she took her last breath."

"That's somewhat comforting." Gwen glanced at their entwined fingers, but made no effort to untangle them. "What was Clara's cause of death?"

"The doctor suggested complications from her head injury."

"The same as Theo and Myrtle," Gwen murmured.

Ben hadn't yet arrived at that parallel, appreciating Gwen's innate talent for making connections.

"Have you told Betty and Robert?" she asked.

"Not yet. You were my first stop. Do you want to go to the B&B with me?"

Gwen's head shook ever so slightly. "If I show up with you again, Betty is bound to guess we're working together. That would expose my informant status and prevent me from working with you again. At least in Harbor Falls."

Her statement brought Ben up short. After her frustration during the Myrtle Mueller case, he figured Gwen would never agree to work with him again. Knowing she wouldn't turn him down next time – if there was a next time – improved Ben's somber mood. "I'll ask Mrs. Owens to call you with the news about Clara. You'll have to act surprised."

"I'm getting good at that."

Ben released her hands and slid off the stool. "Are you all right, Gwen? I can delay my drive to the B&B."

"This isn't my first loss of someone dear. I'll be fine."

He helped her down from the stool and Gwen walked him to the foyer.

***

Ben shivered as he waited on the front porch of the B&B.

Betty Owens appeared and stared at him. "Didn't expect to see you twice in one day. Come in out of the cold."

Robert Owens joined his wife. "What brings you by again, Detective?"

As the three of them stood in the entrance hall, Ben delivered the news of Clara's death.

Mrs. Owens reached behind her and grasped the arm of a nearby chair before sitting down. "Clara was such a sweet lady. Was her confession too much for her heart?"

Ben couldn't let Mrs. Owens make a possibly incorrect assumption, "We won't know the cause of death until the autopsy, but I'm guessing she died from her head injury."

Robert Owens said, "You think if she hadn't bumped her head, she might not have died?"

"We can't know that for sure, but it's a possibility."

Mrs. Owens pushed herself from the chair. "The most I can hope for is that Clara is reunited with Theo. When I told Robert about Clara's confession, we don't know if Theo overheard us."

Unsettled by the ghost's possible anguish, Ben remained silent, unsure if he should admit his encounter with Theo.

"You don't have to pretend, Detective," Betty said. "I know you met Theo yesterday. No need to deny it."

Chapter Forty-Three

...early morning, Thursday

The next day, still rattled by Clara's death, Gwen dialed Wanda Webb's home phone and waited until she was greeted with a cheerful hello.

"Wanda, this is Gwen. If you're going to be home this morning, I'll drop off your cheese board."

"Oh, Gwen, I'm so sorry to make you go to all that trouble. I would've picked it up at your house a few days ago, but my car's still in the shop."

"No need to apologize. I'll see you soon."

Gwen's next call to Loretta Baker went again to the answering machine. Hoping the woman was not already gone for the day, Gwen left a message that she'd stop by with the truffle bowl within the hour.

Pausing at the foyer table, Gwen threw a kiss at Parker's photograph and tucked the can of pepper spray in her pocket. As her Sonata warmed up in the driveway, she texted Ben and then registered Wanda's address into the GPS.

The snow-covered road conditions slowed travel, but Gwen considered it practice for the three-hour drive to Tess's the next day. She took care not to turn the wheel too quickly or floor the gas pedal. The last thing she needed was to slide into a ditch.

She pulled up to the Webb house and spotted Wanda in the open doorway, her arms crossed against the chill. "Come in, Gwen. Thanks for returning my cheese board. I can't believe I left the party without it."

"Everyone did after Myrtle died," Gwen offered.

"I'm so glad I chose Betty's group. I heard the members in the other tour are still being questioned by the police."

"That's my understanding, too," Gwen agreed. Reaching into her shoulder bag, she extended the condolence card and a pen. "I also need you to sign this for Myrtle's family."

As Wanda affixed her signature, she posed a question. "Have you learned the identity of those whisperers?"

"No, I haven't," Gwen answered, discouraged by the truth of her answer.

Wanda held out the signed card and pen. "Myrtle's the only one I know of who needs money. I don't know any of the women having an affair. I wish I could be more help."

"Don't apologize. I guess I'll never know who they were." Gwen hoisted her bag to her shoulder and stepped toward the door. "I'd love to stay and chat, but I have one last delivery."

***

Despite the snow and ice cleaving to the paved surfaces, Gwen's careful drive to Loretta's house several miles outside Harbor Falls was thankfully uneventful. There were no vehicles in the driveway and no answer to Gwen's knock.

Resettled in her driver's seat, Gwen again dialed Loretta's phone and left a second message. "Loretta...sorry I missed you. I don't want to leave your glass truffle bowl on your doorstep because it might crack in the cold. I'm leaving town for a few days, so I'll keep it at my house until I return. We'll get together after the holidays."

As Gwen buckled up, she grudgingly admitted she was a failure as Ben's confidential informant. How soon would he realize he should have never requested her assistance?

***

Driving into Harbor Falls, Gwen stopped at the local grocery store and wandered the aisles, plucking the ingredients for her date nut bread from the shelves. She kept adding other necessaries to her basket, resulting in two full bags. As she exited the store, Gwen nearly collided with Veronica.

Righting herself, Veronica said, "Oh, Gwen, I'm glad we bumped into each other...literally. After I finish my shopping, can I stop over for a chat?"

Because Veronica had grabbed a shopping cart and was already halfway to the first aisle, Gwen didn't bother asking why they couldn't talk right then. "Of course," she called after Veronica's retreating figure. "See you later."

"Great," Veronica shouted over her shoulder. "I'll be there in less than an hour."

After Gwen's non-stop inquires since Myrtle's death, she'd looked forward to a quiet afternoon of baking and packing. But given Veronica's impending visit, an uninterrupted afternoon of preparation was not on Gwen's schedule.

Chapter Forty-Four

...early afternoon, Thursday

Gwen schlepped her reusable fabric bags from the driveway to her front walk, concerned that the ice melt she'd sprinkled earlier hadn't begun to penetrate the thick frozen coating.

In the foyer, with no extra hand, she didn't remove the pepper spray and place it on the table next to Parker's photograph. No big deal. She'd do it later. The small can was barely a blip in her jeans pocket.

Carrying the groceries to the kitchen, she transferred the ingredients for date nut bread to the counter and stored the other items. After texting Ben that she was home for the rest of the day, she mixed enough batter for three loaf pans and slipped them into her oven. From the first loaf, she'd serve warm slices during Veronica's mysterious stop-over. The second loaf she'd donate to Tess's dessert table, and the third she'd freeze for another day.

After placing a pot of spiced apple cider on the stove to warm, Gwen stacked wood in the fireplace and struck a match to the crumbled newspaper beneath the kindling. The chill of the gray afternoon dissipated as the flames licked the wood, the sap snapping against the heat.

She carried the bin of ribbons and bows, plus rolls of paper to the second floor and glanced out the bank of windows into her rear gardens. Even in the dull afternoon light, the snow covering every surface painted an idyllic scene. Pretty unless a person had to drive in it.

Should she have accepted Ben's offer to drive her to Tess's? Unwilling to risk possible embarrassment, she filed his offer in the back of her mind.

Transferring the warmed cider to a crock pot, she carried it to the living room coffee table and plugged it in, then added two snowmen mugs, a ladle, and cinnamon sticks for stirring.

As Gwen moved from one task to the next, she wondered why Veronica wanted to have a chat. The club treasurer had been out of town on party night, so hadn't witnessed Myrtle's accident. The receipt for the club donation was handled the other day. Was it wishful thinking that Veronica might know the identity of the whisperers?

Were Gwen and Ben on the right track to assume Myrtle was the blackmailer? Every other club member had thought so.

The adulterer would then have to be one of the six women in Robert's tour. But which one? As Frankie had said, if the cheater was a member of the garden club, she sure knew how to keep a secret. Gwen had no solid evidence to lay blame on any of the five who were still in town.

That left the sixth club member…Ruby Cox. Had she flown to Denver to avoid arrest?

The dinging of the stove timer drew Gwen to the oven. She transferred her date nut breads to wire racks. The instant she removed her oven mitts, the front doorbell chimed.

***

"Come in, Veronica. I see it's snowing again."

Veronica flipped her hat from her head and dusted off her coat. "I'm wondering if it will ever end."

Entering the living room, Veronica wandered toward the fireplace where the blaze crackled in earnest. "Oh, Gwen, this is lovely. I'm glad I invited myself over." Veronica laughed. "And what are you baking? It smells delicious."

"Date nut bread." Gwen waved at the crock pot. "We'll have a slice with this hot spiced cider."

Gwen's cell phone chirped and she let it go to voicemail. From a side table, she picked up the condolence card and pen, holding them out. "First I need you to sign Holly's card from the club to Myrtle's family. You're next to last."

Veronica applied her signature. "Who's the hold-out?"

"Loretta Baker," Gwen answered. "I've left her several voice messages. If I don't hear from her by the end of the day, I'll sign her name so I can drop this card at the Mueller home on my way out of town tomorrow."

Veronica handed back the card and pen. "Going somewhere for the holiday?"

Before Gwen had a chance to share her plans, the doorbell again chimed and someone turned the knob. Seconds later, Holly emerged from the foyer. "Gwen, your door was unlocked, so I let myself in." Removing her gloves and jacket, she said, "Veronica? I thought I recognized your car. Can't miss that Tesla. What are you doing here?"

Gwen sensed rather than saw Veronica tense, the air suddenly charged with foreboding.

Tossing Gwen a subtle shake of her head, Veronica answered, "Nothing special. I bumped into Gwen at the grocery store, and she invited me over for a cup of cheer."

Not yet ready to panic, Gwen wondered what was going on between the club president and the treasurer. Not only had Veronica invited herself, but she hadn't yet revealed her reason for the visit. So why was she fibbing to Holly?

Veronica stiffened. "I'll ask you the same question, Holly. Why are you here?"

Holly took a step forward. "I knocked my purse off Gwen's dining room table the other day and spilled everything. I can't find my favorite lipstick."

Drawn into the conversation, Gwen had no choice but to respond. "I didn't notice a tube, but you can look for it."

Backtracking to the dining room, Holly dropped onto all fours and disappeared beneath the table. A few seconds later, she called out, "Here it is," and crawled out from under.

Had Holly really lost her lipstick or was her claim only an excuse to discover why Veronica had dropped by? After all, when anyone's car came to a stop at the crest of Harbor Hill on the other side of the village green, any vehicle parked in front of Gwen's home was easily visible.

Gwen's house phone rang.

"Don't you want to answer that?" Veronica asked.

"No, no. Probably a scammer or a telemarketer. Whoever it is can leave a message."

Holly spoke as if the phone hadn't rung. "Have you delivered Myrtle's condolence card?"

"Not yet. I finally caught up with Wanda this morning, but Loretta wasn't home, so I might be signing her name myself. I'll drop the card at the Mueller house in the morning."

Holly's attitude flipped without warning. "You're going to forge Loretta's signature? Fine VP you turned out to be, Gwen."

Veronica turned from the fireplace. "Hold on, Holly. Don't attack Gwen just because you're messing up your own life."

Rushing past Gwen, Holly stopped inches from Veronica. "I knew you were lying. You're planning to tell her, aren't you?"

Gwen wasn't following their conversation. "Wait, wait. What are you talking about?"

Holly whirled to face Gwen. "I'm not stupid. You've been talking to all the garden club members."

The wide-eyed gleam in Holly's eyes worried Gwen. She needed to defuse Holly's anger. "But you asked me to have everyone sign your condolence card. That's why I've been visiting everyone."

"Oh, no, little Miss Gwen. You've taken it far beyond signing the damn card. I know. The garden club ladies have been in and out of my shop almost daily since the party. You've been asking all of them about those whisperers. You're getting close to figuring out who was in Betty's front parlor that night, and I just can't allow that to happen."

Chapter Forty-Five

...mid-afternoon, Thursday

Sitting at his desk in the police station, Ben had called Gwen twice to wish her safe travels to her sister's house and a wonderful holiday. If he was honest, he longed to go with her and enjoy her family celebration. He'd missed his own family gatherings since his mother's death.

But Ben's calls to Gwen's cell phone and then her house phone had both gone unanswered. His detective gut began to churn. Gwen was a stickler for answering a ringing phone. He checked his texts. She'd returned home more than an hour ago.

Ben decided to wait a few more minutes before dialing again. Pulling out his notebook, he flipped to his first interviews and reviewed each statement.

After re-reading Holly Nichols words, Ben swore under his breath. Why hadn't he noticed this detail before? During her witness statement on party night, Holly reported she was studying a Carswell photograph when she heard Myrtle scream. Everyone else had said, *When I heard someone scream.* Why had Holly specified Myrtle?

Ben grabbed his coat, flew out of the station, and hopped into his SUV, speeding toward the village green and Gwen.

***

Veronica, Holly's equal in height, shoved Holly's shoulder, forcing her to spin away from Gwen. "I haven't told her anything, Holly. Why don't you stop talking and go home?"

"Too late now, dear friend." Holly's tone dripped with

291

cynicism. "I've been so busy with Christmas shoppers that my brain hadn't given much thought to our little Gwen here."

Taking advantage of Holly's distraction, Gwen backed away.

Holly broke free of Veronica's grip and pivoted in Gwen's direction. "So convenient that the detective came into my shop while you happened to be there. And then Kristen saw you eating lunch with the white-haired detective. I'm almost positive you're working with him to frame someone for Myrtle's death."

Gwen, being so much shorter, had to look up. "There is no framing going on here, Holly."

Holly kept talking as if Gwen hadn't spoken. "I read an article in *The Gazette* this past spring about the attack on that nasty man who set up a cigar bar across the street from my shop. When the criminal was arrested, the police chief thanked our Gwen here for her assistance. Fast forward to now, and I have no doubt she's working with the detective."

Veronica stepped around Holly, again blocking her access to Gwen. "You're not doing yourself any favors, Holly. You need to stop talking and leave."

"And let you expose me to Gwen? No way."

Though Gwen should have stopped talking herself, she blurted, "Were you one of the whisperers, Holly?"

The club president's laughter bounced off the bricks of the chimney. "Bingo, Gwen. You're not as dumb as you seem. Yes, I was the adulterer in Myrtle's little drama. I've been having an affair with Alicia's husband for months. She's so busy with those brats of hers that she pays Travis no attention. And my husband is equally busy with his company. Not that I object to his generous donations to keep my shop open."

"But we talked about the whisperers in your shop a few days ago. You pointed your finger at everyone but yourself."

"I was lying," Holly sneered. "You're so naïve."

Unable to keep her curiosity in check, Gwen touched Veronica's sleeve. "Is this why you invited yourself over? To tell me Holly was the adulterer?"

Before Veronica could answer, Holly tossed her head back and cackled. "Oh, it goes way beyond that."

Gwen stared, the unbelievable truth sinking in. "You're the one who shoved Myrtle?"

Again, Holly laughed way too loud. "I had to get rid of the old bat before she ruined my marriage. Asking Betty for a tour of the Carswell House was a stroke of genius on my part. I must have sensed I'd find a way to get rid of that bitch Myrtle."

Holly's lips curved in the rictus of a smile, a prideful look transforming her features as she bragged about her actions on party night. "While the others were staring at the photographs and reading about the family, I noticed Myrtle standing on the other end of a scatter rug at the top of those steps. At first, I thought I could yank it out from under her, then came to my senses and realized that would be too obvious and I might get caught. So I simply stretched my nice long arm behind Ruby Cox and gave the old biddy a hard shove."

Staring at Holly's hands, Gwen calculated they were larger than her own, but smaller than Ben's. Just the right size to match those bruises on Myrtle's arm.

Veronica again placed herself between Gwen and Holly. "I can't believe you told us how you did it. The most I could have shared with Gwen was that you were the adulterer. Now what are you going to do?"

"I was just wondering that myself, no friend of mine." Holly's demeanor transformed to that of a caged animal. With each passing second, her volume increased. "You and little Gwen here can't tell anyone what I did. I'm not going to jail just because I wanted to save my marriage."

Holly stretched her arm and seized the fireplace poker, sending the cast iron tool stand crashing to the hearth and cracking two of Parker's embossed tiles.

Gwen grabbed Veronica's arm and pulled them both to a safer distance, screaming, "Don't, Holly. If you kill us, you'll only make it worse for yourself."

Swinging the poker above her head, Holly sneered, "Oh, I don't know, Gwen. I can mess up your sweet little home like the intruder I am. No one will ever know I was here."

Desperate to give Holly something to slow her down, Gwen shouted, "Detective Snowcrest will catch you."

Again, Holly laughed. "Seems to me he wouldn't get far without you working behind the scenes. Why would he suspect I had anything to do with your death?"

Knowing her next words were based on TV forensic programs, Gwen forged ahead anyway, tilting her chin toward the poker. "Your fingerprints and DNA are all over that handle. You can wash it, but you won't remove every trace."

Beside Holly, a wavering image formed as Parker's spirit materialized. "You in trouble, Gwen?"

Relief flooding her, Gwen focused to the right of Holly's shoulder. "It appears so, Parker. What do you suggest?"

Holly lowered the poker. "Who are you talking to, Gwen?"

Like Robert Owens, Holly couldn't hear Parker's voice.

"It's my husband's ghost. He's standing behind you."

Holly whirled and raised the poker, ready to pounce. "Where? I don't see anyone."

Like Betty Owens, Holly couldn't *see* Parker either.

Holly swung with all her might. Parker didn't flinch as the tool sliced through his corporeal body leaving no damage.

Gwen slipped her hand into her pocket and pulled out the pepper spray, raised it toward Holly's face, and hit the button.

Screaming, Holly dropped the poker and collapsed to the hearth rug, her hands covering her face. "What did you do? My eyes are stinging! I can't see!"

Gwen spun to see Veronica frozen in place, her mouth open, her eyes wide. Gwen tossed the can of pepper spray aside and grasped Veronica by both shoulders, shaking as hard as she could. "Veronica! Help me fold Holly in this rug."

Veronica blinked. "Uh, what?"

Gwen repeated her instructions, nudging Veronica to move. They kneeled and pushed Holly to the edge of the rug, forced her arms to her side, and rolled her into a tidy bundle.

Holly's anger exploded, her volume rising as she screamed, "Let me out of here this instant!" With tears staining her cheeks, she quieted as she looked into Veronica's face. "Please let me out. I promise I won't hurt you."

Veronica glanced over at Gwen, who shook her head. "Don't believe her. The minute she's free, she'll attack us both. Straddle her, Veronica. I need to call the police."

Holly resumed her screams, filling the old library with desperation.

Chapter Forty-Six

...late afternoon, Thursday

As Ben approached Gwen's home, screeching from inside assaulted his ears. He pulled his gun and burst through the door, only afterwards realizing it had been unlocked. He rushed toward the sound, skidded to a stop, and assessed the scene.

Encased like a cocoon, Holly Nichols' head protruded from one end of a rolled-up rug, screaming at a long-haired young woman sitting astride her like a horse. "Get off me. Get off me. I can't breathe!" Out the other end, Holly's booted feet banged the hardwood floor.

Holstering his gun, Ben hustled forward.

"She was going to kill us!" the long-haired sitter squealed, rocking as Holly bucked like a Brahma bull.

"I was not," Holly screamed. "She's lying."

"I am not. You were going to clobber Gwen and me with that poker."

Gwen held up her cell phone and shouted, "I was just about to call you, Detective."

Ben roared, "Everyone, quiet!" He pointed his chin at the sitter. "Who are you?"

"Veronica Waite, garden club treasurer."

He motioned her off before he squatted beside Holly. "Lady, if you want me to get you out of this thing, shut the hell up. Believe me; you'll have a chance to tell your side of the story."

Before doing as he promised, Ben glanced over at Gwen. "I can guess what happened here, Mrs. Andrews, but I need you to tell me. I'm sure it's a damn good story."

As Ben unrolled Holly, careful that her head didn't touch the sharp corners of the brick hearth, he listened as Gwen ticked off the events of the past half hour. "Holly was the whispering adulterer, Detective. She's the one who sent Myrtle flying down the servant steps."

After one last roll, he freed Holly from her carpet prison. Cautioning her that resistance was futile, he hauled Holly to her feet and cuffed her wrists behind her back. "Holly Nichols, you're under arrest for the murder of Myrtle Mueller." He recited the Miranda warning from memory and then called dispatch, requesting a police van for prisoner transport.

With the police station only a short distance to the north, the wailing blare of sirens grew louder as vehicles circled the village green and parked at Gwen's curb. Officer Ed Bells surged into the old library, followed by Chief Mike Brown. They walked directly to Ben who gripped the cuffed Holly.

"Ed, transport her to the station lock up," the chief instructed. "I'll be along soon."

***

As the now docile Holly was led out, she glanced at Veronica and Gwen. Water droplets streamed down her cheeks.

Relieved that Holly had been caught and was no longer a threat, Gwen didn't care whether her tears were anguish at being captured or the aftereffects of the pepper spray.

As Chief Brown headed toward Gwen, she met him halfway. With his short stature, he was one of the few people in Harbor Falls that Gwen could look in the eye.

He extended his hand. "Hello, Mrs. Andrews. Good to see you again, though I wish the circumstances weren't so gloomy."

"My thoughts exactly, Chief."

"Who is this?" he asked.

Gwen turned to Veronica. "This is garden club treasurer Veronica Waite."

"Nice to meet you. Stay here." The police chief switched his gaze back to Gwen. "I need to have a chat with Detective Snowcrest. May we use your kitchen?"

"Be my guest."

As the two men circumvented the staircase, Gwen waved Veronica to the leather sofa and ladled the hot spiced cider. "May as well drink this while we wait."

Her face downcast, Veronica accepted the snowman mug. "I had no idea Holly had become so desperate. I've been pleading with her for weeks to end her affair with Alicia's husband."

"Is that what you were doing in front of her shop?"

"Yes," Veronica confirmed. "That wasn't the first time."

Zelda's story popped into Gwen's mind. "So it was you and Holly arguing in the kitchen during the November club meeting?"

"I'm afraid so. Holly was out of control. I didn't want her to ruin her marriage and Alicia's, too, if I could prevent it."

"Can I ask you another question, Veronica?"

"Of course."

"Myrtle overheard Holly discussing her affair in a public place, which provided ammunition for her blackmail scheme. Were you Holly's confidante?"

Again Veronica nodded. "That was the day I met her for lunch at the Bayside Café. I thought we were keeping our voices low, but apparently not low enough. I didn't think anyone was close enough to hear." Veronica sipped the cider. "Now I have a question for you, Gwen."

"Go ahead."

"You told Holly that your husband's spirit was standing beside her. Was that true or just a distraction?"

Without knowing if Veronica had seen or heard Parker, Gwen debated how much to share. "I wasn't fibbing. Parker has appeared several times over the past year or so."

Releasing a breath, Veronica sighed. "Oh, good. I thought for a minute I was hallucinating."

Gwen needed to confirm. "You saw him?"

"And heard him as well. I have to tell you, Gwen, his appearance resolves my personal debate about the afterlife. You must find comfort in his visits."

Relieved to find yet another person in Harbor Falls who believed in ghosts and spirits, Gwen said, "That's an understatement. Parker was taken from me so suddenly that I never had a chance to say good-bye. His spirit assures me that he's just fine."

Veronica's eyes glistened. "I'm happy for you, Gwen."

Footsteps announced the return of the men. Chief Brown was the first to round the corner. "Detective Snowcrest explained you were both very resourceful to contain Mrs. Nichols in such a clever way."

"We didn't have a choice," Veronica said. "It was either Holly or us. Gwen's pepper spray saved us."

The chief clapped Ben on the shoulder. "I'm thinking the solving of this case plus the cold case deserves a press conference. Check with me later about the timing. You stay here and take statements from these two ladies."

After the door closed behind the chief, Ben pulled out his trusty notebook. "Have a seat, Ms. Waite."

Ten minutes later, her statement duly noted, Veronica reached for her coat and hat. "I need to go. My groceries are still in the car. Let's get together soon, Gwen, and continue our earlier discussion."

"I'd love to. I'll call you after the holidays to pick a date."

Ben held Veronica's coat as she slipped her arms into the sleeves. "Thanks for your assistance."

"Like I said before, it was either Holly or us." Veronica shoved her hands into her leather gloves. "I'll see myself out."

***

Spotting the can of pepper spray near the leg of the sofa, Ben picked it up and drifted to Gwen's side, holding it out. "I believe this is yours."

She opened her palm. "Thank you."

"Any of that cider left?"

"Sure. Why don't you add another log to the fire while I grab another mug?"

Ben watched Gwen ease around the fireplace wall, envisioning her passing through her music studio before entering the kitchen. The circular pathway was Ben's favorite feature of her unusual home.

When she returned, he'd not only added the requested log, but had stoked the fire and was straightening the hearth rug.

She ladled cider into his mug and refilled hers.

"Cute snowmen," he commented.

"I spotted them at Holly's shop a few days ago." Gwen paused. "What's going to happen to her, Ben?"

"Hard to say. Her punishment for Myrtle Mueller's death depends on the defense her lawyer chooses and how the jury sees her crime. No idea what will happen to her marriage or her craft shop." He heaved a sigh. "Do you want to discuss this afternoon's events or simply provide your witness statement?"

"A little of both, I guess." After Gwen finished dictating a more detailed account of events, Ben stored his cellphone recorder. "I'm glad you bought that can of pepper spray."

"Me, too. I've been taking it out of my pocket and placing it on the foyer table, but today my arms were full of grocery bags, so I never did get around to it."

"Fortunate for you. I don't think you could have tangled Holly in that hearth rug if she hadn't been rubbing her eyes."

"After the pepper spray, that was the only way to keep Holly contained until you got here." Gwen plated two slices of the date nut bread and handed one to Ben. "I didn't know how long the effects of the pepper spray would last."

"Well, that was quick thinking. I don't want to imagine what would have happened if you hadn't overpowered her."

"Wait a minute, Ben. You haven't told me why you showed up before I'd even called you."

Ben set his mug and plate on the coffee table and stepped to the mantel. "I'm a little embarrassed to admit I overlooked something Holly said during her first interview."

"What was that?"

"She was the only witness who mentioned Myrtle's name when she heard the scream."

"Did you think that was a slip of the tongue because by then Holly knew it had been Myrtle?"

"That would have been a valid explanation if you'd answered your cell or house phone. Your back-home text was an hour old. I knew something was off, so I rushed over. By the time I got here, you had everything under control."

Gwen grinned at him. "It could have gone very wrong."

"But it didn't, Gwen. That only goes to show that you were the perfect C.I. for this case."

"Thanks, Ben. I thought I was wasting my time and yours. Do you mind if we don't talk about the case anymore?"

"Fine with me." He switched his focus to the front windows and noticed a thin veil of white falling from the sky. "It's snowing again, Gwen."

She got off the couch and turned to look. "Like Veronica said, I'm not sure it will ever stop."

Ben hesitated, resurrecting his concern about the road conditions. If he repeated his offer to drive Gwen to the Berkshires the next day, would she accept? No way to know unless he took the chance. "Gwen?"

Her olive-green eyes looked into his. "What is it?"

"I'm not sure you believed me the other day, but I was serious about driving you to Tess's home tomorrow. I wish you'd reconsider and say yes."

Her skin turned a flattering shade of pink and she glanced away for a brief second. "To be honest with you, I almost accepted your offer. I wasn't sure you meant it. And I'd hate to take you away from your plans."

"I wouldn't have offered if I didn't mean it. So you'll let me drive you? We can take my SUV, which handles better in the snow than your Sonata."

Gwen stepped closer. "You don't mind backing out of your dinner plans with the guys from the station?"

"Not at all. They're big boys, and they'll have each other."

"In that case, yes, yes, I accept. I'll call Tess and let her know you're coming with me."

"Your sister won't mind?"

"I doubt it. She likes you."

Though he might be over-stepping, Ben tossed caution up the chimney and grabbed Gwen in a bear hug.

When he released her, she said, "Well, I guess this means you like me."

"Like you? If you hadn't been tangled up with that Jenkins fellow last April, I would have asked you out on a proper date. I'm not unhappy that he's leaving town."

Gwen laughed again. "That's almost exactly what Tess said when she found out."

The tension in Ben's shoulders dissipated "Sorry, but I need to get back to the station and finish the paperwork. I'll put in for a few days of vacation. Considering we've solved two cases, I don't think Mike will refuse me."

"I'll walk you to the door, Ben. We still need to firm up our travel plans for tomorrow."

"We'll have to work around the chief's press conference. I'll call you with the timing and pick you up in the morning."

Ben kissed Gwen on the cheek and strode triumphantly toward his SUV.

Chapter Forty-Seven

...early evening, Thursday

Amber appeared from nowhere and meowed at Gwen's feet. Picking up her pet, Gwen squeezed the critter. "The drama is over, sweetie. You don't need to hide anymore."

When the events surrounding Holly's arrest resurfaced, Gwen shivered. Without Parker and the pepper spray, Holly might have gotten away with another murder or two.

Lowering Amber to the floor, Gwen lifted the house phone from its cradle and dialed Tess's number.

"Hi, Gwen. Don't tell me you're not coming."

"I'll be there," Gwen assured her sister, "but there was an incident here." Beginning with Holly's adultery and Myrtle's blackmail, Gwen moved to the house tour and Holly shoving Myrtle down the servant steps, finishing with Holly's confession and attack and Gwen using her pepper spray before rolling Holly in a rug until she was arrested by Ben.

"Not again, Gwen," Tess moaned. "I hope you won't ever involve yourself in another police investigation."

"I don't do it on purpose, Tess. I don't look for trouble."

"Well, then I guess trouble finds you. I'm just glad you're okay." Tess released a breath. "Change of subject. What time are you planning to arrive tomorrow?"

"That's the other reason I called. The police chief is holding a press conference in the morning and Ben asked me to attend."

"If the good detective thinks you should be there, then you'd better show up."

"I'll have no choice because Ben is picking me up. But there's something else, Tess. He convinced me to let him drive tomorrow because of the road conditions. I hope you don't mind him joining your Christmas dinner."

On the other end of the call, Tess burst out laughing. "I asked you days ago if Ben was going to take Hal's place. You should always listen to your big sister." Tess said nothing for a beat, until, "Give me a sec to think out loud about the overnight arrangements. I'll switch Aunt Nellie to the guest room with you and Ben can take the daybed in my office."

"Perfect," Gwen said. "I'll text you with our timing."

The details settled, Gwen hung up the portable handset and pulled on a sweater. She wandered out to her deck and lifted her face to the softly falling snow, sticking out her tongue like a child, letting the flakes land where they pleased. The crisp winter air refreshed her mind and spirit.

She was saddened by Myrtle's death and blackmail scheme. If Holly hadn't admitted her guilt, would Ben have ever gotten to the bottom of what happened? Even if Veronica had told the police that Holly was the adulterer, there was little evidence that Holly had shoved Myrtle. Would the lab have found Holly's fingerprints on Myrtle's sleeve? Would Ben have thought to match Holly's finger span to those bruises? After all, not all cases were solved.

But Ben's chasing of Theo's cold case had impressed Gwen. Without his announcement that the lab was checking for fingerprints on Theo's gown, Clara might have never confessed.

"Gwen, Sweetheart?"

"Parker?" Gwen felt her smile widen as she whirled around to see him taking shape at the railing. "Where have you been?"

"Oh, around." His pale green eyes sparkled with their usual mischief. "You handled that tall woman like a pro."

"And I haven't thanked you for distracting Holly."

He waved his see-thru hand in a dismissive motion. "I'm aware that you appreciated my interference."

As he stood beside her, the snowflakes tumbled through his transparent body and landed on the deck boards. "I heard your conversation with the detective. I like the man, and I'm glad you're letting him drive you to Tess's."

"Do you have any idea, Parker, how strange it is to have you approve of a new man entering my life?"

"Can't say that I do, Gwen, but if my opinion makes you happy, that's all that matters."

He floated over and wrapped his feather-weight arms around her body.

She imagined – more than felt – the pressure of his embrace. "No man will ever replace you in my heart, Parker."

Chapter Forty-Eight

...early-morning, Friday

The next day, the sun tried to peek through the clouds, but was having a difficult time.

In the conference room of the police station, Gwen recognized Shirley Knapp from the Harbor Falls Gazette, several reporters from the surrounding towns, and two cameramen from Boston TV stations. A few members of the Harbor Falls town council lingered along the far wall.

Betty and Robert Owens came through the door, spotted Gwen, and hurried over to stand beside her.

Robert said, "Chief Brown is right to hold this press conference. He'll provide closure so we can enjoy our guests."

Betty pointed. "There's Fletcher Mueller."

Grateful that Fletcher's appearance would save her a stop at his house, Gwen said, "I'll go give him our card." As she closed the distance, she rummaged in her shoulder bag.

"Mr. Mueller?" Gwen extended the envelope. "This is a condolence card from the garden club members."

Fletcher accepted the envelope. "Thank you, Mrs. Andrews." He sauntered away without saying more.

The chief approached the microphone and the room quieted. "Good morning, everyone. Thank you for coming. I'm Chief Michael Brown of the Harbor Falls Police Department. I have two announcements this morning."

Mike cleared his throat. "Yesterday afternoon, Mrs. Holly Nichols was arrested the murder of Mrs. Myrtle Mueller that occurred recently at the Harbor Falls Bed & Breakfast, previously known as the Carswell House." He proceeded to detail Myrtle's fall down the servant steps and the confrontation that ended with Holly's confession.

Glad the chief had omitted her involvement in the capture, Gwen glanced over at Fletcher Mueller. His stiff stance and determined expression confirmed his ability to keep his emotions under control.

Mike Brown continued. "I'd like to acknowledge the dogged persistence of Detective Ben Snowcrest in getting to the bottom of this case." Mike waved Ben to the podium.

Ben's white hair gave him an air of authority. "Fortunately, the Harbor Falls Police Department doesn't have to untangle the details of a murder very often, but when we do, it takes many professionals to capture the perp. I'd like to thank our medical examiner, the detectives in my unit, the forensics techs, and others for their assistance in solving this case. You know who you are." Ben gave a subtle nod in Gwen's direction, then stepped from the podium and stood to the side.

The chief again commanded the microphone "My second announcement involves the solving of our oldest cold case. Detective Snowcrest will provide the details."

Ben spoke of Theo Carswell's death on her wedding day in 1924 and how the lack of modern forensic tools thwarted an arrest based on the thin evidence collected. He moved to the present day and explained a recently-developed process that reveals fingerprints on fabric.

"Clara Carswell, the last member of the family, recently sold her childhood home and moved to a retirement community. A few days ago, she celebrated her 100th birthday."

A murmur swept through the audience, quieting when Ben raised his hand and continued to speak.

"Our discussion of the fingerprint technique alerted Clara that her part in her elder sister's death might be exposed. Clara was only seven in 1924, encouraged to pull the prank by the middle sister Winnie Brewster. We believe Clara did not intend to harm her sister. Though she was not alone in the deed, Miss Carswell asked me to record her confession."

Shirley Knapp raised her hand. "Will she be charged?"

"Yesterday afternoon, Chief Brown and the assistant DA were discussing their options when the news arrived that Clara Carswell had passed away at the hospital."

A collective gasp filled the conference room.

Shirley again raised her hand. "Did the stress of her confession cause her heart to give out?"

Ben shrugged. "The medical examiner will provide his findings after the autopsy is completed."

Chief Brown returned to the podium. "Thank you, Detective. That's all we have at the moment. Updates will be provided as they become available. Thank you for coming."

As the men and women filed from the room, Shirley made her way to Gwen's side. "Hello, there. Why do I think you had your hand in solving both of these cases?"

"Hi, Shirley. What makes you think that?"

"Oh, I don't know. Perhaps it's my keen reporter instincts. Why else would you attend a police press conference?"

Aware that she should admit nothing to the feisty Shirley, Gwen swiftly created an explanation she hoped the reporter would buy. "This isn't my first press conference, and probably not my last."

"All right, Gwen. If you're not going to tell me, I can't force you." Shirley whirled around and worked her way through the crowd toward the exit.

Minutes later, as Ben held his passenger door for Gwen, a movement caught her eye. Shirley was waving from the next row of parked cars. The reporter saluted Gwen and winked.

***

During the short drive from the police station to Gwen's home, she shared her research on Myrtle's grandson Herbert. The drug and alcohol abuse by the Mueller son and his wife that drove Myrtle and Fletcher to seek shared custody and assume the burden of his education.

When she finished, Ben shook his head. "Unfortunately, that's not an unusual situation these days." He cleared his throat. "There's something I need to tell you, Gwen."

"You're sounding mysterious, Ben. What is it?

He took a right onto Library Lane, parked at Gwen's curb, and faced her. "Theo's ghost appeared to me in the B&B's kitchen the day Clara fainted."

Gwen swiveled in her seat so she could gauge his reaction. "I suspected you had, though you didn't admit it that day. Does this mean you now believe in ghosts?"

"I believe in Theo's ghost because I saw her."

"So you won't believe a ghost exists unless you witness it with your own eyes?"

"That about sums it up."

During Gwen's time with Hal, she'd never told him of her encounters with Parker's spirit. But she wanted to be up front with Ben. After all, Parker would be the reason she'd keep her friendship with Ben just that…friendship.

Should she wait until they returned from the Berkshires? Nope, she'd tell Ben now. If he thought her loony and reneged on his offer to chauffer, she'd drive herself to Tess's. Gwen figuratively donned her big girl panties and took the chance.

"Ben, I have something to tell you as well."

"Am I going to like it?"

"I can't possibly guess, but it's only fair that you're aware of this detail in my life before our friendship goes any further."

Ben squinted. "Go ahead."

Gwen began her story on the day her husband Parker was struck by lightning on the golf course. She told Ben about her extended grieving, moving forward in time to preparing Hal's granddaughter for the music competition and the house guest who disappeared. One evening during her quest to prove herself innocent of any wrongdoing, she heard the sound of Parker's voice and collapsed. When she awoke, she found his spirit in the living room.

Ben's eyes could get no bigger. "Hold on. You saw your husband's ghost?"

"As clear as day. He was sitting in his recliner. I believe in Parker's spirit because I've seen him."

Staring out the windshield, Ben didn't speak. Gwen waited patiently to let him absorb her tale.

He finally turned and looked at her. "Have you seen him again since that first appearance?"

"Several times. And he speaks with me as well. The most recent was yesterday. When Holly threatened me and Veronica with the poker, Parker appeared and distracted Holly. That's when I used my pepper spray. And, before you ask, Veronica also saw Parker's form and heard him."

"I don't recall that detail in either of your witness statements," Ben commented, his eyebrow lifting.

In that instant, Gwen knew Ben believed her.

"Do you have anything else I should know, Gwen?"

"No, that's it, Ben. But I truly hope that one day you'll meet Parker's spirit. Until then, you won't believe he found a way to visit me from the afterlife."

Without comment, Ben slid from the driver's seat, walked around and opened Gwen's door.

Letting the topic drop, she said, "We should hit the road as soon as possible."

"I agree. My weekend bag is in the back. Is everything you're bringing ready for me to carry out?"

***

Sliding the last box of gifts into the rear section of Ben's SUV, Gwen's thoughts turned to Alicia and Travis, Holly and Kyle. Would their marriages survive? Would Travis apologize and beg Alicia to forgive him for the affair with Holly? Would Alicia keep the marriage alive for the sake of the children?

Would Kyle stick around during Holly's trial and possible jail time?

Too soon to know. Let the dust settle, Gwen decided. She'd check on both couples after she returned from the Berkshires.

While Ben rearranged her gifts and suitcase for a better fit, Gwen hurried inside and circled the first floor to make sure she hadn't left anything behind.

Scooping Amber into her arms for a farewell hug, Gwen gave the cat an extra squeeze. "Goodbye for now, sweetie. Mrs. Miller from next door will stop by to make sure your food and water bowl are full. I'll only be gone a few days"

Amber squirmed to be released and bounded halfway up the staircase, stopping at the midway split to toss a glance over her furry shoulder. What was going through the feline's mind? *You're leaving me again?* Or more likely, *Get out of here so I can have the place to myself.* With cats, it was impossible to know what they were thinking, if anything.

***

As Ben steered his SUV around the village green and onto North Street, Gwen's cell phone buzzed. "Hello, Hal. What's the latest on your seaside cottage?"

She glanced over at Ben, aware he'd hear her side of the conversation.

"Finances are moving faster than I thought," Hal answered. "The owners are anxious to sell, so the lawyers are putting the closing on a fast track."

"You must be excited."

"I am. Even Jenna is getting into the spirit. We spent yesterday afternoon deciding what needs to be painted, fixed, or replaced. She picked her bedroom for vacations and decided what colors she wants to paint the walls."

"That's a positive step."

"Listen, Gwen, I'm sorry my decision to avoid the New England winters has ruined our friendship. I honestly thought you'd move with me." Without waiting for her response, he jumped to another topic. "When are you driving to Tess's?"

Despite the fact that she and Ben were on their way, Gwen answered, "In a little while."

"Well, you be careful. I'll call after Jenna and I get back and let you know how the sale is progressing."

"Talk to you then." Gwen ended the call. "Sorry, Ben."

He turned onto Rt. 3 north. "Don't apologize. Every new relationship drags along baggage from the past."

"Is that what we have here, Ben? A relationship?"

"That's my plan." He slid his right hand across the console and squeezed her gloved fingers before re-gripping the steering wheel. "I don't expect I'll ever replace your husband, Gwen, and I may never be more than a friend, but I'm hoping this drive to your sister's is just the first in a long line of adventures."

Astonished that she could move toward another man so soon after the shock of Hal's impending fade from her life, Gwen found herself almost giddy to learn more about Ben during this trip to the Berkshires. Not to mention the weekend at Tess's house surrounded by Aunt Nellie and the cousins.

Gwen had felt very comfortable with Ben the detective. During dinner and dancing on Saturday night, Ben the man had given her no reason for concern. How many more layers of his personality would she uncover in the coming days? And was Ben thinking the same about her?

"I like your plan." Gwen pointed out the windshield and laughed. "Look, Ben. It's snowing...again!"

THE END

Made in the
USA
Middletown, DE